TIGERLILY'S ORCHIDS

OMNIBUSES: COLLECTED SHORT STORIES | COLLECTED STORIES 2 | WEXFORD: AN OMNIBUS | THE SECOND WEXFORD OMNIBUS | THE THIRD WEXFORD OMNIBUS | THE FOURTH WEXFORD OMNIBUS | THE FIFTH WEXFORD OMNIBUS | THREE CASES FOR CHIEF INSPECTOR WEXFORD | THE RUTH RENDELL OMNIBUS | THE SECOND RUTH RENDELL OMNIBUS | THE THIRD RUTH RENDELL OMNIBUS | **CHIEF INSPECTOR WEXFORD NOVELS:** FROM DOON WITH DEATH | A NEW LEASE OF DEATH | WOLF TO THE SLAUGHTER | THE BEST MAN TO DIE | A GUILTY THING SURPRISED | NO MORE DYING THEN | MURDER BEING ONCE DONE

ALSO BY RUTH RENDELL

| SOME LIE AND SOME DIE | SHAKE HANDS FOR EVER | A SLEEPING LIFE | PUT ON BY CUNNING | THE SPEAKER OF MANDARIN | AN UNKINDNESS OF RAVENS | THE VEILED ONE | KISSING THE GUNNER'S DAUGHTER | SIMISOLA | ROAD RAGE | HARM DONE | THE BABES IN THE WOOD | END IN TEARS | NOT IN THE FLESH | THE MONSTER IN THE BOX | **SHORT STORIES:** THE FALLEN CURTAIN | MEANS OF EVIL | THE FEVER TREE | THE NEW GIRL FRIEND | THE COPPER PEACOCK | BLOOD LINES | PIRANHA TO SCURFY | **NOVELLAS:** HEARTSTONES | THE THIEF | **NON-FICTION:** RUTH RENDELL'S SUFFOLK | RUTH RENDELL'S ANTHOLOGY OF THE MURDEROUS MIND | **NOVELS:** TO FEAR A PAINTED DEVIL | VANITY DIES HARD | THE SECRET HOUSE OF DEATH | ONE ACROSS, TWO DOWN | THE FACE OF TRESPASS | A DEMON IN MY VIEW | A JUDGEMENT IN STONE | MAKE DEATH LOVE ME | THE LAKE OF DARKNESS | MASTER OF THE MOOR | THE KILLING DOLL | THE TREE OF HANDS | LIVE FLESH | TALKING TO STRANGE MEN | THE BRIDESMAID | GOING WRONG | THE CROCODILE BIRD | THE KEYS TO THE STREET | A SIGHT FOR SORE EYES | ADAM AND EVE AND PINCH ME | THE ROTTWEILER | THIRTEEN STEPS DOWN | THE WATER'S LOVELY | PORTOBELLO

ruth
rendell

TIGERLILY'S
ORCHIDS

HUTCHINSON

LONDON

Published by Hutchinson 2010

2 4 6 8 10 9 7 5 3 1

First published in Great Britain in 2010 by
Hutchinson
Random House, 20 Vauxhall Bridge Road,
London SW1V 2SA

www.rbooks.co.uk

Addresses for companies within The Random
House Group Limited can be found at:
www.randomhouse.co.uk/offices.htm

The Random House Group Limited Reg. No. 954009

A CIP catalogue record for this book
is available from the British Library

ISBN 9780091936860 (Hardback)
ISBN 9780091936877 (Trade paperback)

The Random House Group Limited supports
The Forest Stewardship Council (FSC), the leading
international forest certification organisation. All our titles that
are printed on Greenpeace approved FSC certified paper
carry the FSC logo. Our paper procurement policy
can be found at www.rbooks.co.uk/environment

Mixed Sources
Product group from well-managed
forests and other controlled sources
www.fsc.org Cert no. TT-COC-2139
© 1996 Forest Stewardship Council

FSC

Typeset in Fairfield LH Light by Palimpsest Book Production Ltd,
Falkirk, Stirlingshire

Printed and bound in Great Britain by
Clays Ltd, St Ives plc

To Valerie Amos

CHAPTER ONE

Olwen was in Wicked Wine, buying gin. She understood from Rupert whose shop it was that these days 'wicked' meant smart or cool, not evil, just as 'gay' in some circles was starting to signify bad or nasty. She didn't much care, though she wondered why a shop which sold beer and spirits and Coca-Cola and orange juice advertised itself as purveying only wine. Rupert said, 'That's the way it is,' as if this explained everything.

She bought three bottles of the cheap kind. Bombay Sapphire came expensive if you consumed as much of it as she did. Gin was her favourite, though she had no objection to vodka. Purely for variety's sake, she had tried rum but rum was vile if you drank it neat and she couldn't stomach orange juice or, God forbid, blackcurrant.

'Can you manage,' said Rupert, 'or do you want me to do you a double bag?'

'Not really.'

'Your neighbour, Stuart, is it, don't-know-his-other-name was in here this morning stocking up on champers. Having a party? I said, and he said it was a house-warming, though he's been here for months, and he was inviting all the other folk in Lichfield House.'

Olwen nodded but said nothing. Outside it was snowing

and not the kind of snow that becomes a raindrop when it touches the ground. This snow settled and gradually built up. Olwen, in rubber boots, trudged through it along Kenilworth Parade. The council had cleared a passage in the roadway for cars – a passage that was rapidly whitening – but done nothing for pedestrians apart from scattering the ice-coated slippery pavement with mustard-coloured sand. She passed the furniture shop, the pizza place, the post office and Mr Ali's on the corner and turned up into Kenilworth Avenue. Most of the time the place was as dreary as only a London outer suburb can be, but the veiling of snow transformed it into a pretty Christmas card. Small conifers in the front garden of the block poked their dark green spires through the snow blanket and the melting icicles dripped water.

Olwen staggered up the steps with her bag of bottles. The automatic doors parted to receive her. In the hallway she encountered Rose Preston-Jones with her dog McPhee. On the whole Olwen was indifferent to other people or else she disliked them, but Rose she distrusted, much as she distrusted Michael Constantine. If not herself a doctor, Rose, with her acupuncture and dabbling in herbalism, her detoxing and her aromatherapy, was the next best (or worst) thing. Such people were capable of interfering with her habit.

'Is it still snowing?' Rose asked.

'Not really.'

Olwen had long ago discovered that this is a response which may be made with impunity to almost any enquiry, including, 'Are you well?' and 'Are you free on Saturday?' Not that people often asked her anything. She made it plain that she was mostly inaccessible. Rose looked at the carrier bag, or Olwen thought she did, maybe she just looked down at the dog, looked up again and said she must get on with McPhee's walk.

The lift was waiting, its sliding door open. Olwen had just stepped in when Michael Constantine came running through the automatic doors. He had the sort of legs which, when possessed by models, are described as so lengthy as to reach up to their necks, and was six and a half feet tall, so his stride was very long. He was the politest of the residents and asked Olwen if she was well.

'Not really.' Olwen forbore to ask him how he was and, though she knew his flat was on the first floor, pressed the button for the second. It was a peculiarity of the lift that once this floor had been signalled, the intermediate could not be, so Michael had to go up to the top with her. He remembered to be a doctor, though it was only recently that he had become one.

'Keep warm,' he said. 'Look after yourself.'

Olwen shrugged, her alternative response. She got out of the lift without a word just as one of the girls came out of the flat she shared with two girls of similar age. None of them had ever been seen dressed otherwise than in jeans with a T-shirt, sweater or flouncy dress on her top half. One was rather overweight, one thin and one in between. As well as jeans, this one had a red quilted coat over what seemed like several jumpers. Olwen had been told their names over and over but she had contrived to forget them. She let herself into Flat 6 and put the bag down on the kitchen counter.

The flat was furnished for comfort, not for beauty. There were no books, no plants, no ornaments, no curtains and no clocks. A deep, soft, shabby sofa occupied one wall of the living room and faced, along with a deep, soft and comfortable armchair with a detachable footrest, the large flat-screen television set. A window blind was seldom raised or lowered from its present position of halfway up and beneath it could

3

be seen the solid cupola-topped tower of Sir Robert Smirke's church and the tops of trees at Kenilworth Green. And of course the snow, now falling in large feathery flakes. The bedroom was even more sparsely furnished, containing only a king-size bed and, facing it, a row of hooks on the wall.

All but one of the kitchen cupboards were empty. Food, such as there was of it, lived in the fridge. The full cupboard was rather less full than it had been at the beginning of the week, but Olwen replenished her stock by putting her three new bottles on the shelf alongside a full bottle and one that was half empty. This one she removed and poured from it about three inches of gin into a tumbler. There was no point in waiting until she was sitting down to start on it – there was no point in Olwen's present life of ever doing anything she didn't want to do – so she drank about half of it, refilled the glass and took glass and bottle to the sofa. It was low down near the floor, so no need for a table. Glass and bottle joined the phone on the woodblock floor.

Reclining, her feet up on a cushion, she reflected, as she often did, on having, at the age of sixty, attained her lifelong aim. Through two marriages, both unsatisfactory, seemingly endless full-time work, houses she had disliked, uncongenial stepchildren and dour relations, she was at last doing what she had always wanted to do but had rigidly for various reasons stringently controlled. She was drinking the unlimited amount of alcohol she had longed for. She was, she supposed, but without rancour or regret, drinking herself to death.

The list Stuart Font had made read: Ms Olwen Curtis, Flat 6; girls – don't know names, Flat 5; Dr and Mrs Constantine, Flat 4; Marius something, don't know other name, Flat 3; Ms Rose Preston-Jones, Flat 2; me, Flat 1. This last entry he crossed

4

out as it was unnecessary to invite himself to his own house-warming party. The flat he had moved into in October was still unfurnished but for three mirrors, a king-size bed in the bedroom and a three-seater sofa in the living room. The place looked a bit desolate but Stuart had noticed a furniture store in Kenilworth Parade, its prices much reduced due to the credit crunch. Remembering to take his key with him – he had twice forgotten his key and had to hunt for and eventually find the porter or caretaker or whatever he called himself – he went out into the hallway to check on names and flat numbers on residents' pigeonholes.

The girls at Flat 5 appeared to be called Noor Lateef, Molly Flint and Sophie Longwich, and the man on his own at Flat 3 Marius Potter. That was everyone documented. Stuart, who hadn't yet been outdoors that day, ventured on to the front step. The snow was still falling and had settled on pavements, patches of grass, rooftops and parked cars. Stuart noticed that if he stood on the step the front doors remained open, letting in a bitter draught. He hurriedly went indoors and back into his own flat where he sat down once more, added names to his list and wondered whether he should ask the porter (Mr Scurlock), the Chinese (Vietnamese, Cambodian?) people opposite, the elderly chap next door to them, Rupert at Wicked Wine, his best friends, Jack and Martin – and Claudia. If he invited Claudia wouldn't he also have to invite her husband Freddy, incongruous though this seemed in the circumstances?

Stuart added the names to his list, went into the kitchen and made himself a mug of hot chocolate, a drink of which he was particularly fond. He was realising, not for the first time, that though he was twenty-five, he had serious gaps in his knowledge of social usage, a deficiency due to his having lived at home with his parents all his life. Even his three years of business studies had taken place at a university easily reached by Tube. The company where he had worked since taking that degree until he resigned on coming into his inheritance, was also accessible by the same means, being no more than a hundred yards from Liverpool Street Station. The only breaks from home life had been holidays and the occasional nights he had stayed away in various girlfriends' flats.

All this had meant that inviting people round, stocking up on drink, buying food, gaining some understanding of domestic organisation, remembering to carry his keys with him, arranging with people his mother called tradesmen and paying services bills, were closed books to him. He couldn't say he was learning fast but he knew he had to. Since coming here he hadn't done much but run around with Claudia. Making that hot chocolate without scalding himself was a small triumph. He was thinking how pleasant it would be if he could have his mother living here, but his mother changed, different, tailored as it were to his requirements: as admirable a housekeeper and cook and laundress as she was but silenced so that she spoke only in the occasional monosyllable; able to remove herself without a word or a look when Claudia came round; deaf to his music, invisible to his friends, never, ever criticising or even appearing to notice the areas of his behaviour of which she might disapprove. But if she became this person she wouldn't be his mother.

He was thinking of this, finishing his drink, when she phoned.

'How are you, darling? Have a nice weekend?'

Stuart said it was all right. In fact, it had been spectacularly good, since he had spent most of Saturday and part of Sunday afternoon in bed with Claudia, but he couldn't even hint at that.

'I've been thinking.'

6

He hated it when his mother said that. It was a new departure for her, dating from since his own departure, and invariably led to something unpleasant. 'I've been thinking that don't you think you ought to get a job? I mean, I know you said when you came into Auntie Helen's money that you'd take a gap year but a gap year's what people take between school and university. I wonder if you didn't know that.' She spoke as if she had made some earth-shaking discovery. 'Daddy is getting very anxious,' she said.

'Has he been thinking too?'

'Please don't use that nasty sarcastic tone, Stuart. It's your welfare we're worried about.'

'I haven't time to get a job,' he said. 'I've got to buy some furniture and I only spent half what she left me on this place. I've got plenty of money.'

His mother laughed. The noise she made was more like a series of short gasps than laughter. 'No one has plenty of money any more, dear. Not with this economic downturn or whatever they call it, no one. Of course you would go ahead and buy yourself a flat the minute you came into your inheritance. Daddy always thought it a mistake. I don't know how many times he's said to me, why didn't he wait a while. With house prices falling so fast he'd soon get that place for half what he paid. It only calls for a little patience.'

Stuart was beginning to think that there could be no circumstances in which he would want his mother here, no matter how much washing, cooking and cleaning she might do, for he could imagine no radical change taking place in her character. He held the phone a long way from his ear but when she had said 'Are you there, Stuart?' three times he brought it back again, said untruthfully that his front doorbell was ringing and he had to go. She had barely rung off when his mobile on the floor on the other side of the room began to play 'Nessun dorma'. Claudia. She always used his mobile. It was more intimate than the landline, she said.

'Shall I come over this afternoon?'

'Yes, please,' said Stuart.

'I thought you'd say that. You're going to give me a key. Aren't you? I've told Freddy I'll be at my Russian class. Russian's a very difficult language and it'll take years to learn.'

'What shall we do when you get here?' Stuart asked, knowing this would provoke a long description in exciting detail. It did. He sat down on the sofa, put his feet up and listened, enraptured. Outside it continued to snow, coming down in big flakes like swans' feathers.

The Constantines had lunched late, the only customers at that hour in the Sun Yu Tsen Chinese restaurant which was on the other side of Wicked Wine in the parade and next door to the hairdresser.

'I must get some pictures before the light goes,' Katie said, producing her camera from her bag. 'We could have a little walk. We never get any exercise.'

She was enchanted by the snow and skipped along, picking up handfuls of it. Michael wondered if he could write something about it for his column, something about the crystals all being of a different pattern, or maybe he should disabuse readers' minds of the fallacy that it could get too cold for snow to fall at all. But by the time his piece appeared the wretched stuff would no doubt have *dis*appeared.

'Can we make a snowman, Michael? When we get back, can we make a snowman in the front garden? They won't mind, will they?'

'Who's to mind?'

'I've seen pictures of snowmen. I want one of my own.'

'It will melt, you know. It will all be gone tomorrow.'

'Then I'd better get taking my photos.'

The extent of their exercise was walking round the block, up the roundabout, down Chester Grove, along the parade and home, Katie pausing now and then to get a shot of children throwing snowballs, a dog rolling in the snow, a child with a toboggan. Back at Lichfield House she pointed out to Michael the houses opposite, their roofs all covered with snow but for the central pair.

'Isn't that funny? I'll just take a picture of it and then we'll go in, shall we? It will soon start getting dark.'

In the hallway they encountered the three girls from Flat 5, plump Molly Flint and skinny Noor Lateef shivering in see-through tops and torn jeans, Sophie Longwich comfortable in a padded jacket and woolly hat.

'I'm frozen,' Molly was saying. 'I think I've got pneumonia.'

'No, you haven't,' said Michael, the medical man. 'You don't get pneumonia through going out dressed like it was July. That's an old wives' tale.' Maybe he should write something about that too . . .

Noor had gone back to the doors, looking out through the glass panel. 'It's started to snow again.'

'That roof will get covered up now,' said Michael to Katie, pressing the button for the lift. While they waited Noor and Sophie told Molly that if she put on any more weight she would have to travel in the lift on her own. Its doors had just closed on the five of them when Claudia Livorno came through the swing doors, carrying a bottle of Verdicchio and walking gingerly because the step outside was icy and her heels were high. She rang the bell of Flat 1.

*

Olwen had nothing in Flat 6 to eat except bread and jam, so she ate that and when she woke up from her long afternoon sleep, started on a newly opened bottle of gin. She never went near a doctor but Michael Constantine said it was his opinion she had the beginnings of scurvy. He had noticed her teeth were getting loose. They shifted about, catching on her lips when she spoke. In the flat below hers, Marius Potter was sitting in an armchair that had belonged to his grandmother reading *The Decline and Fall of the Roman Empire* for the second time. He would finish the bit about the murder of Commodus and then go downstairs to have supper with Rose Preston-Jones. This would be his third visit, the fifth time they had met, and he was looking forward to seeing her. He had already once cast the *sortes* for her and would do so again if she asked him.

The first day he moved in they had recognised each other as kindred spirits, though they had nothing much in common but their vegetarianism. Marius smiled to himself (but only to himself) at her New Age occupation and lifestyle. Rose was no intellectual, yet in his estimation she had a clear and beautiful mind, was innocent, sweet and kindly. But something about her teased and slightly troubled him. Taking *Paradise Lost* from his great-uncle's bookcase, Marius once again thought how he was almost sure he recognised her from further back, a long way back, maybe three decades. It wasn't her name, not even her face, but some indefinable quality of personality or movement or manner that brought back to him a past encounter. He called that quality her soul and an inner conviction told him she would call it that too. He could have asked her, of course he could, but something stopped him, some feeling of awkwardness or embarrassment he couldn't identify. What he hoped was that total recall would come to him.

Carrying the heavy volume of Milton, he went down the stairs to the ground floor. Rose, admitting him to Flat 2, seemed to be standing in his past, down misty aeons back to his youth, when all the world was young and all the leaves were green. But still he couldn't place her.

CHAPTER TWO

Thanks to the recession, the solicitors Crabtree, Livorno, Thwaite had less than usual to do, so Freddy Livorno had taken the afternoon off and gone home. Now he was in the living room of his pretty little house in Islington, dismantling a basket of dried flowers which stood in the centre of an occasional table. Carefully he removed the plumes of pampas grass, the prickly stems of teasels with their spiked crowns and the slender brittle stalks of honesty (honesty!) bearing their transparent oval seedheads. Into the now empty basket he put the high-tech bug he had bought from a shop in Regent Street and replaced the plants, carefully concealing the deceitful little gizmo.

Now for Claudia's computer, the machine she exclusively used for her journalism as the deputy fashion editor of a national newspaper. A small widget, minute, almost invisible, went in between the keyboard lead and the socket. That should do it, Freddy said to himself. Technology was a wonderful thing, what an improvement on private detectives! As a solicitor, he knew all about that variety of gumshoe, though now he thought their days were numbered. His gizmos were costly and for the two of them he hadn't had much change out of eight hundred pounds, but that was nothing compared to a private eye's charges.

Freddy wasn't the sort of man to speculate about the

character or even the identity of the man who was his wife's lover. Those details would be revealed in time. As to how she had met him, he supposed she had interviewed him for some aspect of her work. She could well have taken up with a male model. But it was of little interest to him. He couldn't even have said if he loved her any longer. If there was one thing of which he was certain it was that he didn't want to lose her, had no intention of losing her. On the practical side, he had a mortgage to pay on this small but extremely expensive house, the repayments of which were considerably helped by her contribution. In these hard times you could never be quite sure what steps building societies might take to recover their money if householders defaulted. No, he couldn't lose the thirty-three and a third per cent she put into it. Also, though no more than two years younger than he, she was a trophy wife whom he was proud to show off, good-looking, lovely figure, well dressed and clever.

Today, apparently, she had gone to her Russian class. Freddy didn't believe in the Russian class but he couldn't be bothered to check on it. No need for that now he had his handy gadgets. He looked in the wine rack and saw that a bottle of Verdicchio was missing, a bottle he was sure he had noticed there this morning. No doubt she and Mr Mystery were enjoying it now, relaxing between bouts. Tomorrow, she had told him, she'd be at home all day, working on this piece she was writing on how to dress well during an economic downturn. Everything she typed on that computer, every email she sent, would be accessible to him when he put in a simple code after she'd gone to bed; everything she said in this room he'd be able to hear when he dialled the mobile number of the gizmo in the dried-flower basket. And then what?

He would take steps.

*

Pieces you wrote for the newspapers these days had to be full of references, or at least make allusion, to television programmes, celebrities and pop music. Claudia was too young ever to have known anything else so she had no difficulty in comparing something to Coldplay, pointing out the resemblance of an up-and-coming model to Cheryl Cole and referring in a scathing yet amused way to Jonathan Ross's latest escapade on air. These were the kind of things her readers understood. Most of them were under forty. Claudia had no patience with those writers who quoted Shakespeare or made reference to *Rigoletto* as if anyone likely to read their articles had ever been inside the Globe theatre or an opera house.

Claudia began by writing about shopping. Could it cease to be the principal leisure activity of the British female both under and over forty? Her research into the subject had furnished her with a lot of shopping anecdotes, lists of excessive amounts spent by individual women, the most allegedly spent by any one woman in three hours in Knightsbridge, the stampedes occasioned by the 7 a.m. openings of new West End stores and, to show her compassionate side, a rundown on the suffering statistics of small children operating sewing machines in Chinese sweatshops. Now on to the difference the credit crunch might make to curtailing women's shopping sprees, but first to pour herself a cup of coffee from the pot she had made before she began.

Two more sentences must be typed before she took her break. Claudia followed a principle of *getting into the next bit* before stopping either for coffee or lunch. Once *getting into the next bit* had been done there would be less of a problem in *getting on with it* when she returned to work after half an hour. The coffee was black and strong, its surface made frothy by the artificial sweetener she had put into it, an additive she roundly condemned when writing about healthy diets.

She shifted the coaster along the table surface before putting the mug down, slightly pushing aside the bowl of dried flowers. It seemed to her that they were less attractively arranged than usual but she must be imagining it. After all, who but she would touch them? Maria was far too lazy and to associate Freddy with any household task, however minor, was a joke.

Her mobile told her the time was 10.31. She dialled Stuart Font's number. He answered sleepily but livened up after she had told him in some detail how much she had enjoyed the previous afternoon. No, she couldn't come today. Some badinage ensued on the alternative meaning of the verb she had used, after which she suggested he take her out to lunch the day after, not in his neighbourhood, absolutely not. Why not Hampstead which wasn't too far away to get back, somewhat the worse for wear, to his place in the afternoon? The suggestions he made for ways to spend the following hours evoked from her a 'Stuart, you are sweet', and a 'I can't wait to try *that*'.

She'd call for him – 'Don't forget I've got a key now!' – but would leave her car in Kenilworth Avenue and they'd take a taxi. 'And now I must *get on*. Some of us have to work for our livings, you know.'

He said something about emailing her with the name of the restaurant to see if it was all right and she said that was a good idea, having some doubts about his standards when he was paying. Their conversation stimulated her to continue with her piece about fashion in a time of downturn and she moved on to high-street shopping for men.

It was in a men's boutique, though not the high-street kind, that she had first met Stuart. At first she thought he was gay. The man in the Jermyn Street shop who was contemplating and delicately caressing a vicuña coat was too slender and too beautiful to be straight – and too interested in this garment which had been reduced in price to a still hefty thousand pounds. Claudia advanced on him, introduced herself as a journalist, and started questioning him about buying clothes. Which designers did he prefer? Would he ever buy from M&S? Had he ever had a suit made? The admiration in his eyes and what she called his 'edgy' comments soon told her she had been mistaken in his sexual orientation. No, he wasn't going to buy the coat, he'd just bought a flat, but he'd like to take her somewhere and buy her a drink. Their ideas of where this drink should come from differed but Claudia quickly made it clear that she favoured a select bar in St James's over the Caffè Nero. Next day they met at the fashionable champagne bar at St Pancras Station, watched the Eurostar come in from Paris and after Stuart had spent fifty pounds on a bottle of champagne, took a taxi to Lichfield House.

Claudia had long since incorporated Stuart's fashion comments in an article (naming no names) but managed to recycle some of them for this one. A thousand words and she was done. She made herself more coffee and had a look at her emails. The top one in her inbox was from Stuart to tell her that he had booked a table at Bacchanalia in Heath Street. Would that do? Claudia googled Bacchanalia, found it satisfactory and far from cheap. She emailed back to say she would let herself into his place at twelve noon next day. That way they could be back from the restaurant by three *as we shall have plenty to do in the afternoon.* She was pleased he hadn't suggested texting her as the necessary abbreviations of such messages would have militated against the sexy tone of their correspondence.

It was hard for Stuart to pass a mirror without looking into it. His own reflection brought him a lot of pleasure. He usually turned away from it satisfied that he had rarely seen a man better-looking than himself. Aware that men are not supposed to feel this way, are expected to take no interest in their appearance apart from being clean and adequately clothed, must be deprecatory and indeed embarrassed should anyone make a favourable remark about their looks, he was careful to dress with discreet casualness or, in the days when he was at work in the City, in sober suits and plain ties. But one of his indulgences was to drop into boutiques of the Jermyn Street kind or wander through the men's department of Harrods, imagining how superb he would look in this Armani tweed jacket or that Dolce and Gabbana sweatshirt.

This morning he was dressed in jeans, a black shirt and a blue sweater. As he eyed himself in the living-room mirror – there was another in his bedroom and a third in the passage – he saw that the sweater was the exact colour of his eyes. No doubt Claudia had already noticed. If she remarked on it he would put on his embarrassed look; unfortunately, he had never mastered the art of blushing. Though nearly sixty, his father so far showed no sign of going bald and Stuart, who had heard that baldness occurs on a gene carried by the male progenitor, thought comfortably that he stood a good chance of keeping his hair into old age. His was thick and a beautiful shade of rich dark brown, almost but not quite black.

He had completed his invitation cards the night before, excluding Freddy Livorno, put them in envelopes, and was going out to buy stamps and post them. The idea of simply placing them in residents' pigeonholes had occurred to him and been dismissed as looking mean. There must be some sort of etiquette about this but he didn't know what it was. Best be on the safe side.

It was very cold outside, one of those English midwinter days when the sky is bluish-grey with pale clouds, no snow has fallen and no frost is to be seen but every small puddle of water has become a slab of ice. A light yet sharp east wind was blowing. Stuart possessed a winter coat but seldom wore it. Young people don't wear coats. Young people wear T-shirts in below-freezing weather. Maybe he wasn't quite young enough for that and he ventured out in the blue sweater that matched his eyes.

The post office was a counter in the newsagent's in Kenilworth Parade next door but one to Mr Ali's. Further along was the furniture shop. Everything in its window had become a sale item, chairs, tables, beds, lamps, some labelled 'Unbelievable Reductions!'. Stuart went to the post office, bought his stamps and posted his invitations, then to Design for Living where he weighed up the advantages of buying furniture at knock-down prices but which he didn't much like, against going down to the West End and buying furniture he liked a lot at twice the cost. His mother's words on the subject of money and getting a job came back to him. Auntie Helen's legacy had seemed a fortune when it first came to him but now half of it had gone on the flat, plenty more on the sofa, the king-size bed and the mirrors, and he was spending a great deal on Claudia. A lot more drink would have to be bought for the party. He began to regret posting those invitations but it was too late now. He had to have the party and he couldn't have it in a semi-unfurnished flat.

The assistant who came up to him in Design for Living could hardly believe his luck when Stuart picked out a dining table and six chairs, two armchairs, a coffee table and a standard lamp like a half-open sunflower on a gilt metal stalk. If all went well this would be the first sale he had made that week. Mirrors were Stuart's weakness and they had a couple they had no chance of ever selling, one in a gilt frame with curlicues, the other framed in matt black. The assistant said he would throw that one in for nothing. Stuart didn't much like any of the stuff he had bought so he had to keep telling himself what a bargain it was. Delivery next day, said the assistant as Stuart handed over his credit card.

The automatic doors at Lichfield House came open as he approached. He stood outside on the doorstep studying Design for Living's receipt, all the items he'd bought listed. Waves of heat from the hallway bathed him as he informed himself anew that the armchairs had cost four hundred pounds apiece and the standard lamp two hundred and fifty. Were those really knock-down prices? His reverie was interrupted by Wally Scurlock the caretaker tapping him on the shoulder and telling him he was letting all the heat out.

'If you stand there, sir, the doors stay open and when the doors are open all the bloody heat goes out. Right, sir? Savvy?'

Wally seemed to think that reiterating sirs and madams to the residents compensated for the gruffness of his tone and the harshness of his words. Stuart went inside, feeling thankful that he hadn't sent the caretaker an invitation. He let himself into his flat and contemplated his reflection in the mirror, three feet long by eighteen inches wide and framed in stainless steel, on the living-room wall. Cold as it was outside, his face remained its normal pale olive, neither pinched nor reddened. He smiled to show himself his white even teeth, went into his bedroom and put on a tie, in case Bacchanalia demanded it. Surely they wouldn't, not for *lunch*. Stuart reasoned that if a restaurant required men to wear ties and a jacket at *lunchtime* it was likely to be more expensive than one which did not.

He went into the kitchen and made himself a big mugful of hot chocolate, spooning into it quite a lot of long-life cream. The nearest place to buy fresh cream, as far as Stuart knew, was Tesco up beyond the roundabout. You never really knew, when you bought a place, how convenient it was for things like that.

Only living in it for a few weeks told you. When you hadn't a car and the only bus to come anywhere near you was the 113 which went nowhere he wanted to go, when the nearest Tube station was on the universally loathed Northern Line, the nearest cinema probably miles away at Swiss Cottage and no decent restaurants were to be found within a file-mile radius, you began to wonder if you wouldn't have been better off keeping your job and spending *all* Auntie Helen's money on a flat in central London.

Helen Morrison had been his godmother. The first annoying thing she did was to assert her rights in this particular role and name her godson. Stuart's parents had intended to call him Simon George but Annabel Font was very aware of the advantages of having her aunt as his godmother and soon persuaded her husband to give in. As well as being unmarried, apparently childless and rich, Helen was a Jacobite. She still adhered to the view that the present royal family were German usurpers, though their tenure of the throne went back three hundred years, and believed that its present incumbent should be an obscure prince no one had ever heard of living some-where in central Europe. To her, Stuart was an almost sacred name and Windsor (or Saxe-Coburg-Gotha or Hanover or whatever you liked to call them) a laughable misnomer. So Stuart was christened and wasn't even permitted to have George for a second name as that had been the name of several Hanoverian kings.

The Fonts, though they had agreed to this condition, weren't really the kind of people to suck up to a relative in the hope of getting her money for themselves or their only child. Helen sometimes came to them for Christmas, she sent them postcards from the distant places she went to on her solitary holidays and on his birthdays Stuart regularly received a cheque from her, quite a small cheque. Annabel and she wrote to each other two or three times a year. They occasionally spoke on the phone. When Stuart got two Bs for his A levels a rather larger cheque arrived, and when he graduated from the east London university no one had ever heard of, the sum he received was a hundred pounds. His mother forced him to write polite thank-you letters, actually standing over him while he did so, but she did this for his letters to the donors of such presents as a paperback book or a CD of music he never listened to.

Helen was eighty-four when she died and Stuart twenty-four. She left four hundred thousand pounds to Stuart but her Edinburgh house in elegant Morningside and two million pounds to the fifty-year-old child no one knew she had ever had and who had been adopted by a butcher and his wife forty-nine years before. Annabel commented on the will, saying that Helen had been a dark horse but conceded that in the circumstances Stuart was lucky to get anything at all. He agreed, handing in his notice next day to his immediate boss who, accepting it, remarked that anyway, what with this imminent recession, Stuart would shortly have been asked to consider his position.

He walked round the flat, deciding where to put the new furniture. Where should the two new mirrors go? One in the spare bedroom and the other in here? His sofa was dark red with a hint of purple and now, with a slight sinking of the heart, he realised that the chairs he had bought were a shade of orangey coral. Would it look dreadful? He would have to brazen it out, insist that this was the latest colour scheme. He was back in his bedroom, wondering if this might be the best place to put the sunflower lamp and wondering too if he'd be *hiding* it in here from the critical eyes of his guests, when he heard the front door open and someone come into the flat. A split second of shock-horror

21

and then he realised. Claudia. Claudia had a key. He went out to meet her.

They kissed, lasciviously rather than with affection. She wore a tight black suit with a very short skirt and a jacket cut away in a U-shape to show a lot of cleavage. Her heels made her taller than him which he didn't much like.

'The taxi I came in is waiting,' she said. 'No need to hurry.'

There was every need since he would be paying.

'We'll ask him to pick us up after lunch, shall we?'

The taxi passed Wicked Wine and Stuart saw Olwen emerging with her few days' supplies in two carrier bags. The pavements were dry today so she wore her bedroom slippers. These were mules with pink fluffy tops and their wedge heels flapped up and down, clattering as she walked. Standing at the gate of his house next door to where the Cambodians lived, Duncan Yeardon watched her make her slow way up the path to Lichfield House. He liked to speculate about the lives of strangers. He was a people-watcher and he had an active imagination. This woman carried heavy bags from the shops several times a week. She seemed too old to have children to feed but she might have an invalid husband or even two people – sisters, say? – who needed supplies. Of course, there was nothing to say one of the bags didn't contain washing from the launderette. Not everyone had a washing machine. Duncan watched her climb the steps up to the double doors and saw those doors open for her.

His own house was too large for him, Victorian, semi-detached, on three floors. He had bought it because never in his life before had he owned a house like this, though he had always wanted to. Now he had it, he didn't know what to do with it. Keep it clean, of course, and that he did. Keep it immaculately tidy. Rearrange the furniture. Often, during the day, he wandered from room to room, looking out of the windows. All his working life he had worked so hard and for such long hours that he had never cultivated any occupations for his leisure hours. He watched people and made up romances for them while drinking a lot of weak watery coffee.

I nside Lichfield House, in the hallway, Michael and Katie Constantine were talking to Rose Preston-Jones. It was rather less cold today so McPhee had discarded his pink woolly coat and wore only his natural fur as a newspaper article had told Rose dogs in coats could overheat and be ill.

'If you believe one newspaper article,' said Michael, 'why don't you believe others? I mean, you believe that about dog fur but you don't believe detoxing is rubbish. Both stories come from expert sources, both are the result of serious research.'

'Oh, Michael dear, I *know* detoxing works,' Rose said, growing pink. 'I can prove it. My clients who go on my course show an amazing improvement in their health once all those impurities that clog their systems are out.'

'Their livers do that for them. Their livers detox them every day.' Michael turned to say hello to Olwen. 'Are you well?'

'Not really,' said Olwen, lumbering up to the lift.

'You can't say her liver has done anything for her,' Rose said with quiet triumph.

'Only because there won't be much of it left.'

'She told Marius she's drinking herself to death. She says she's been wanting to drink unlimited amounts all her life and now she can.'

Katie spoke for the first time. 'But she never says anything except "Not really".'

'People talk to Marius,' Rose said fondly.

'The trouble,' said Michael, 'with drinking yourself to death or smoking yourself to death is that you don't just die. It would be OK if you carried on with these excesses and felt fine till one day you lay down peacefully and died. But you don't. You get diabetes or have a stroke or a heart attack and then the long slow painful route to death begins.'

Rose picked up McPhee and hugged him as if he were in imminent danger of one or other of the fates Michael had mentioned. Laughing in rather a grim way, Michael took Katie's arm and the two of them went out to the pizza place. Instead of going back to her own flat, Rose got into the lift with McPhee and went up to ask Marius Potter for a *sortes* reading. She hadn't liked 'the long slow painful route to death' at all.

CHAPTER THREE

B y night, the place was very quiet. Aurelia Grove was far enough away from Upper Street for no more than a soft sighing from its traffic to reach these houses, embowered as they were in hedges and leafy bushes and conifers. Each was detached or semi-detached. If neighbours were noisy, their music or laughter or slamming doors affected no one but themselves. The silence was even deeper when the weather was cold. Those street marauders who wandered mysteriously, occasionally giving vent to meaningless yells or animal whoops, stayed at home or remained inside pubs and clubs when the temperature dropped.

Just before midnight, Freddy Livorno went outside, though no further than the front step. He often did this to see what the night was like and to look at the sky. Tonight it was very clear, a bright dark blue, and the air had that sharp feel about it as of a crystallisation taking place so that it seemed his breath might freeze into chips of ice. He went inside again and bolted the front door. Claudia had gone to bed early. She had gone up at ten fifteen and Freddy guessed this was so that she could be asleep or feign sleep before he entered their bedroom. Well, let her sleep or pretend sleep, as she chose. Earlier in the day, he dialled the mobile number on the device set among the dried flowers and been startled by the lascivious content of her conversations with a nameless man she called darling. Now was his chance to read what she typed during the past two days and discover part or all of that man's name. He started up her computer, put in the code which would work the gizmo – and lo and behold, it did.

His wife had sent several emails to the newspaper for whom she worked and an article about the recession affecting shopping as an email attachment. Freddy wasn't concerned with that. Those sent to Stuart.Font@Lichfieldhouse.com were what interested him. One began 'Hi, darling S' and ended 'Can't wait to do you-know-what again, it was awesome. Do I have to wait till Thursday? Your lustful C.' The rest started and finished in much the same way. The middle part was hair-raising. Freddy was amazed by his wife's knowledge and experience. She had certainly demonstrated none of it to him. And that email address contained not only the guy's name but an important clue to his address as well. Claudia also mentioned a key that had been given her. Did this key open Lichfield House or a door in Lichfield House? And was Lichfield House a private house or block of flats or the offices of a company?

He decided to leave the two little gizmos in place for a few days longer. She wasn't planning on going there tomorrow, so she would very likely send more emails and almost certainly have another conversation with this Stuart. More details must be discovered before he acted.

No sound came from upstairs. She was sleeping the sleep of the unjust, he thought. She was in the habit of leaving her handbag overnight on a small table in the hall. The one she was currently using was of black leather, absurdly (in Freddy's view) studded and barred with silver-coloured metal, as was the fashion, fitted with half a dozen useless zip fasteners which opened and closed pointless pockets, and ornamented by an unnecessary two-inch-wide belt with a large chased silver buckle. Her house keys were in one such pocket and another beside it on its own. By the time she needed a key to that fellow's place he would have had another cut and have replaced the Brasso-cleaned one with the original.

He turned off the lights and went upstairs. Light from the half-open door of their bathroom showed him the sleeping Claudia, her lips slightly parted, one white long-fingered hand resting between the powder-blue pillowcase and her pink cheek. She always slept elegantly. Freddy was not so sophisticated and hard-headed as he had thought. The words and expressions she had used, vocally and in print, had shocked him more than he would have thought possible, not because of what they were – all were of course familiar to him – but because it was his wife who had spoken and written them. He even wondered, as he stood there looking at her, if he wanted her after that. Was her contribution to the household expenses all that important to him? Did her status as trophy wife count with him that much? Perhaps not. Was it revenge that he wanted, then? On Stuart Font at Lichfield House, certainly, and that he would get. But on her? He went back into the bathroom, closed the door and said aloud, 'I want her to know that I know. I want her to be afraid of me.'

The assistant in the electrics shop at Brent Cross told Duncan that they had sold out of room heaters a week ago. Duncan didn't want a room heater, his house was warm enough even in this cold; he had been buying a toaster to replace his which had given up the ghost (as he put it) that morning.

'We've got plenty of those,' the assistant said. 'Not that we would have if you could heat a room with them. There's been an incredible run on heaters.'

'It's what you'd expect, isn't it, in this weather?' Duncan said.

'Of course it is. And it's not as if you can buy these things in the summer in case it gets cold. It's incredible but we don't stock them in the summer.'

Duncan bought his toaster and took a bus back to Kenilworth Avenue. All the cars parked along the kerb were still white with frost. Though without a garage, he had a short driveway and every time he passed it he regretted getting rid of his own car. Yet how often would he have used it? Inside the house it was beautifully warm, thanks to the efficient heating system. Never, in all the places he had lived with his parents, alone or later on with Eva, had he known such interior warmth. This was some of the coldest weather for years yet he had been able to turn off several radiators. How different it must be for those poor people trying in vain to buy fan heaters and electric radiators.

A freezing fog was closing in on Kenilworth Avenue. With gardening impossible, a good brisk walk a poor prospect and his shopping done, Duncan stood inside his front window deriving entertainment from the people who passed. Television and his new library book were for later. Since Eva's death and his simultaneous enforced retirement, the hours had passed slowly, but he regularly told himself how lucky he was to have his health, enough to live on and this comfortable warm house. Meanwhile, he looked out of windows.

On the other side of the street a van with 'Design for Living' printed on its side had drawn up outside Lichfield House. The driver and another man got out of the cab and came round to open the back. Duncan wondered why a van was needed to cover this short distance when a trolley of some sort would have done, but stopped wondering when he saw the men unload armchairs and tables, mirrors and a very ugly lamp. The young man who needed a shave and looked like one of those models advertising cars came out to supervise the transporting indoors of the furniture. Ah, the problem of why the occupant of Flat 1 had arrived with so little furniture had been solved. Men who looked like him were always homosexual. 'Gay' was a term he disliked. He saw it as misusing and spoiling a term which used to mean lovely and joyous. That young man would have a friend he called a partner, older than himself, probably the owner and principal furnisher of the flat.

Duncan lost interest and turned his attention to next door, the other half of the semi-detached pair. The occupants had only been there for a few weeks and he had barely seen them. A young woman had come out, carrying a large plastic bag in each hand, and headed to the right through the white mist where, at the top of Kenilworth Avenue past the roundabout, was a Tesco superstore. She looked very young, a girl of no more than fourteen or fifteen, though she was probably older than that, and wore a thin jacket over a T-shirt and jeans. Just to look at her made Duncan shiver in that warm room. A few seconds later a much older man came out of next door's front door and followed the girl. He made no attempt to catch up with her but maintained a distance of about twenty yards between them. I bet they'll come back together, Duncan said to himself, those bags will be loaded with shopping and that man won't even offer to carry one of them. He speculated about them and their lives. Not father and daughter, as he had at first thought, for they didn't look in the least alike. Husband and wife was more likely. Yes, that was what it would be, that man advertising and then buying (for that was what it amounted to) a young girl from some South-East Asian place. He pitied her but consoled himself by deciding that however hard her life might be here, it would be a lot better than what she had had in Laos or Cambodia or wherever it was.

The Design for Living van moved off and a woman came along the street from the Kenilworth Parade end in a fur coat that looked as if made out of a variety of a furrier's cut-offs. Duncan knew her by sight and watched her go into the house on the other side of the Asians. She didn't look English either. Nobody was any more, he thought despondently. Because he didn't know her name he called her Esmeralda. You could walk from one end of north London to the other, passing hundreds of people, without hearing a word of your own language spoken. He didn't feel like waiting to see if his prediction about the people next door, the girl carrying the shopping for that lazy man, had come true. A way of profitably spending the rest of the day had occurred to him and he went upstairs to begin tidying and reorganising every drawer and cupboard in the house.

He liked order and method and routine. His ambition when in his teens and training as a motor mechanic had been to become a detective, largely because he enjoyed finding solutions to puzzles. Tinkering with vehicles was eventually given up and he joined the police. Pacing the beat wasn't part of his life plan but he had to do it and he bowed to the inevitable. Whether it was a stroke of luck or a blow of fate, he could never quite make up his mind, but when he had been a police constable for a year he found himself and his companion outside a jeweller's at the precise moment that a couple of men had broken in. One of them had the owner at gunpoint while the other ransacked the safe. Duncan didn't know where he got the courage from, he had no memory of what happened immediately before the gun was fired, but he had flung himself at the gunman while his companion pulled the jeweller to the ground. Of course the gun went off, one bullet passing through Duncan's shoulder and another shattering the glass-topped counter. Reinforcements arrived and an ambulance, and the two men were arrested.

Duncan got a special commendation and a bravery award. But something strange had happened to him. He had lost his nerve. Whatever had impelled him to risk death saving that jeweller and his goods was gone now. The thought of even having to reprimand a couple of misbehaving teenagers filled him with fear. He left the police and returned to his other love, motor vehicles. He set about looking for a job which would combine his fondness for cars, his expertise with their engines and the pleasure he took in solving puzzles. The one he was offered and took was exactly what he wanted. It was with a breakdown rescue service and he worked for it for thirty-five years, driving his blue-and-yellow-chequered van to track down cars in difficulties or completely broken down on motorways, arterial roads, suburban streets and country lanes. One of the things he liked about it was that the rescue service's clients were always so pleased to see him. It was like being a guardian angel. Another was that nineteen times out of twenty he was able to solve the problem and the one time he wasn't, to arrange for a tow-away service and to transport the unfortunate motorist home. The advent of the mobile phone and later of satellite navigation improved things further. He had even met his wife through his job.

Eva was a young woman whose Mini broke down on the A12. She filled in the form he had to ask clients to complete but added to all the boxes she had ticked as excellent, that he was 'a lovely man who was so kind and nice'. It turned out that she lived with her parents quite near where he lived. Standing there on the muddy grass verge five miles from

Chelmsford, he asked her out and six months later they were married. It was a successful marriage and they were happy, though without children, perhaps (he sometimes thought) *because* they were without children. An only child, Eva had inherited her parents' house and their modest savings which had enabled him to buy number 3 Kenilworth Avenue when he retired two years after her death from cancer.

Duncan thought of some of these events in his past life as he moved from his own bedroom and the spare bedroom next to it to tidy one of the cupboards in the room at the back. He had brought a large carrier bag upstairs with him and into it he began putting the last of Eva's clothes. Most that she left behind her had long gone to Oxfam. He hardly knew why he had kept these, there was nothing special about them, they had no smell of her scent, none of them was a favourite of hers. Perhaps they had been left because when he got rid of the others he wasn't able to carry any more. He tied up the handles of the bag, looked out of the window. It was a funny thing, he thought, but when you went into a room you seldom entered you almost always did look out of its window.

During the hours he had worked the fog had lifted. A little snow was still lying. Patches of it lay in the shady places of next door's untended garden and on the peaked roof of the little summer house which stood up against its rear fence. Duncan called it a summer house because it wasn't a garage but next door to the garage and it was too big and – well – nice, to be a shed with its pink-painted fretwork eaves, its arched windows and its glass-panelled front door. As he watched, someone came out from the back of the house and was walking down the path towards the back fence. It was a young man this time and Duncan hadn't seen him before. The young wife's brother who was staying with them? He too was wearing only jeans and a T-shirt and Duncan wondered what beautiful country of green mountains, dense forests and perpetually blue skies he had left behind to come to this cold cloud-covered suburb. He watched the boy open the door of the summer house and go inside.

Business being practically non-existent, Freddy sat in his office at Crabtree, Livorno, Thwaite and opened the London street guide he had bought while he was waiting for a key to be cut from the one he had taken from Claudia's handbag. The chances of a block of flats – surely what the name Lichfield House designated – being listed in this guide seemed to him practically nil but he would give it a go. The index was vast and lo and behold (a favourite phrase with Freddy) here was not Lichfield House but Lichfield Road, turning out of Kenilworth Avenue, with a north London postal address. There was not necessarily a connection but after he had seen his one client of the afternoon, he would go and look.

The client's reason for this interview was rather too close to home for Freddy's liking. He wanted a divorce on the grounds of his wife's adultery. Having spent an uncomfortable half-hour in which he had resisted telling the client about useful little eavesdropping gizmos, Freddy drove up to what he thought of as beyond the bleak reaches of northern suburbs and found Lichfield Road. He parked the car in the one remaining empty space outside the Kenilworth Parade shops and went into Wicked Wine. A woman in a long coat with the hem coming down and a hat shaped like a coal scuttle was buying gin. The man behind the counter wrapped the bottles, put them into her carrier and took her cash.

'And how can I help you, sir?'

'I don't suppose,' said Freddy, 'there's a place round here called Lichfield House.'

'You don't suppose, do you? Well, you're in luck,' said Rupert. 'It's just round the corner. Olwen lives there and you can go with her. He can go with you, can't he, Olwen?'

'Not really,' said Olwen.

This greatly amused Rupert who roared with laughter and said, 'Will you listen to her!'

Freddy followed the woman in the coal-scuttle hat, now struggling along with the bag of bottles. 'Can I carry that for you?'

'Not really,' said Olwen in a considerably colder voice than she had used to the wine-shop man. She hobbled along the path, nearly slipping over on a sheet of ice, and lumbered into the block as the automatic doors opened for her.

Avoiding the ice, Freddy stood on the step, thinking about having an immediate confrontation with Stuart Font. The difficulty was that he hadn't brought a weapon with him, the walking stick he had in mind. Instead, he too went through the entrance and had a look at the pigeonholes on the right-hand wall. Olwen had disappeared. As Freddy was reading the name S. Font on the lowest pigeonhole a man he supposed to be a porter came up from a staircase beside the lift.

'Might you be visiting one of our residents, sir?'

'Mind your own business,' said Freddy.

'If this isn't my bloody business, sir, I don't know what is.'

'Piss off,' said Freddy.

Any steps he took would have to wait till after Christmas, less than a week away. On his way out he met a tall, extremely thin man with longish, sparse grey hair who, making for the pigeonholes, stopped unwillingly to listen to the porter's torrent of complaints. Freddy went to find his car. It had received a parking ticket in his absence.

*

34

Carrying his post, Marius Potter went up the flight of stairs to Flat 3, constrained to this means of ascending by a fear of lifts. Long ago he had tried to construct a name for this phobia of his, as it might be treskaidecaphobia, a fear of the number thirteen, or ailurophobia, a fear of cats, but the difficulty was that the Greeks had no lifts. He still had quite a good command of classical Greek, so he tried the verb to lift but there was no noun. The same applied to the verb to elevate. In the end he had decided on the verb to rise. Or the noun as in sunrise which seemed to be 'epidosis'. Epidosephobia was the best he could do but that didn't really satisfy him. Before he came to Lichfield House he had lived in a block on the eighth floor, so this was a breeze. Generally speaking, Marius was a bit of an anachronism or Luddite. He disliked innovations, though he possessed a fridge and a TV set which was seldom switched on.

His flat was full of furniture inherited from dead relatives, threadbare armchairs and scuffed tables and curiosities such as stuffed animals and peculiarly shaped china vessels with arms and branches protruding from them reminiscent of hugely magnified photographs of bacteria. There were also a lot of books, new books, hundreds of them, and old books, dusty, all of them non-fiction. One, thick, red with gold lettering on its spine, lay open on an iron table that looked as if it had once belonged in a pub.

Marius sat down at the pub table and looked at his post. Most of it was junk mail but there was also a letter from his sister Meriel in Aylesbury. Meriel was one of the few people he knew who didn't reproach him for his lack of a computer and therefore of email. Like him, she disliked modernity but, he had to confess, went one better than he in that she and her husband lived in a dilapidated thatched cottage, heated only by coal fires. Both he and she had a phone, however, and he had a mobile. Perhaps he would phone her and ask for her help in solving a problem.

'Rose Preston-Jones?' said Meriel, not sounding at all puzzled. 'You think you recognise her? Well, of course you do. Don't you remember when we were all living in that commune in Hackney?'

'You mean she was there?'

'Only for a few days. She moved on but she was there.'

'I don't remember the name.'

'We all knew her as Rosie.'

And then Marius did remember. No wonder he had felt awkward when he thought of asking Rose herself. Now he began to remember and he was back in that commune, that squat really in a Hackney slum, a big old house that he and his sister and a bunch of like-minded hippies had taken over. He was even thinner then than he was now and his hair was longer, bright brown and reaching to the middle of his back. They all dressed in tie-dyed clothes except Rosie who wore cheesecloth. Meriel was right when she said Rosie had only been there for a couple of days before moving on. In fact, it was a day and a night, and that night, without the aid of cannabis or wine, he and Rosie had shared a bed.

They had all been sitting in a circle, passing round joints, only Rosie wouldn't. That made him stop and just sit there with his arm around her. She didn't know where she was supposed to sleep and when he started taking her to Harriet's room she clung to him and said not to leave her . . . He remembered what happened as delightful, entirely satisfactory, and he remembered falling asleep and wanting it to go on in the morning and the next day and the next night. But when he woke at some hour he would now find an incredible time to be still in bed, midday probably, she was gone. Not just from his bed but from the house, gone no one knew where. He didn't attempt to find her. It had just been a one-night stand, nicer and somehow sweeter than most, but never intended to be the start of a permanency.

And for more than thirty years he had forgotten her.

What to do? Consult the *sortes,* of course. Where others might have used the Bible or Virgil's *Aeneid,* Marius had for many years now, sought advice from *Paradise Lost.* Not for a moment did he believe in this or any other means of divination and he was always surprised to find how many others did. But it amused him and he continued to do it for those who asked, though resisting the suggestions of those who wanted him to set up as a fortune-teller and charge for his forecasts.

Now he picked up the book and opened it as he always did at random. The rules were where his eye first alighted, and though he didn't believe, he adhered to the rule that there was no point in doing it at all if you cheated. He read, 'Her long with ardent look his eye pursued / Delighted, but desiring more her stay . . .' It could plainly be taken as a reference to the way he had felt about Rosie that night and the day after but it gave him no counsel. Milton, he had found, sometimes simply commented on the seeker's situation.

Above his head he heard a familiar sound. Olwen, though having had nothing to eat, had drifted into her after-lunch sleep, the empty bottle sliding off her lap and rolling across the floorboards.

Those of the residents whose parents were still alive went home for Christmas – they still called it home – Rose up to Edinburgh, Stuart to Loughton, the Constantines to Katie's mother in Wales. Marius's parents were dead as, necessarily, were all those relatives who had left him their furniture.

Noor left for the parental mansion in Surrey, Molly to Torquay and Sophie to join her mother, father, three brothers and a sister in Purley.

Marius was invited to his sister's vegan Christmas in Aylesbury and had to stay two nights because no trains were running. Duncan Yeardon watched them all go. He made a sort of game for himself, noting who had gone and who stayed. They all went but for Olwen and he saw her hobbling round to Wicked Wine on Christmas Eve in her old black coat and coal-scuttle hat, returning with rather more than usual supplies. Mrs Gamp, he called her. She would be having a party, he decided. A widow, no doubt, with grown-up children and possibly grand-children. She would have fetched all the requisite food in days before.

As for him, he would be alone. But he had plenty of food and the house was beautifully warm, a real treat. In time he would get to know more people now he had been invited to that gay man's house-warming party.

CHAPTER FOUR

C oming so soon after his return from Loughton, his mother's call had thoroughly unsettled him. Stuart now wished he hadn't answered the phone when it rang. He had told her repeatedly he didn't want a job. Not yet he didn't. Wasn't he taking a gap year?

'Oh, darling, something exciting,' she had said. 'Daddy's friend Bertram Dixon says he may have something for you if you'd like to phone his secretary and arrange a time for an interview. Daddy says it's a marvellous opportunity for you.'

'I don't want a job with Bertram Dixon or anyone else,' Stuart had said, but now he was in a dilemma of doubt. Should he have dismissed the offer just like that? Could he afford to? He had only been at Lichfield House since October and all the time his money was gushing away. 'Haemorrhaging' was the word he had read somewhere. When he had come into his legacy, putting half of it into this flat and investing the rest so that he had the interest to live on had looked an ideal lifestyle. Since then, the bank rate had fallen and fallen, much of his stock attracted no more than one and a half per cent. He was drawing on his capital at an alarming rate and Claudia didn't help. Walking down Heath Street after their lunch, she had pulled him after her into a jeweller's where she had expected him to buy her a necklace, reduced in their pre-Christmas sale, to 'no more than a thousand pounds, darling'. Of course he had bought it. Was it wise to have said such an adamant no to Bertram Dixon's offer? Perhaps he should call his mother back. But, no. He remembered how much he disliked Bertram Dixon, an arrogant pompous man he wouldn't want to work for in any circumstances.

Forget it. Think of something else. He made himself a mug of hot chocolate and sat down to contemplate the three replies he had had to his invitations. All, from the Constantines, the old man opposite and Rose Preston-Jones who also replied for Marius Potter, were acceptances. If they all accepted, how much was it going to cost? What had made him think that the dozen bottles of champagne Rupert had delivered to him the day before would be adequate? He would need wine as well and sparkling water and orange juice and *food*. He put his head in his hands, took it out again at the sound of a key in his front-door lock. He got to his feet. It could only be Claudia – at ten in the morning?

A man he had never seen before walked into the room, snow on his boots and an encrusting of snow on his hair.

Stuart might have asked him who he was but he didn't. 'How did you get in?' he said. An awful feeling of impending doom was starting to well up inside him.

'I have a key,' said the man.

He was in his thirties and tall but not as tall as Stuart, his hair receding a little, his features nondescript, apart from his eyes which were the kind that seem to have more white around the irises than most people's. His left hand he was holding behind his back. If asked to describe him, Stuart would have said that he looked clever, though he couldn't have said how he knew this.

'My name is Frederick Livorno, commonly called Freddy.'

Stuart said before he could help himself, 'Oh my God.'

'You may well say so,' said Freddy Livorno. 'You may well call upon your god. You're going to need him. The key with which I opened your front door I found in my wife's handbag. A highly elaborate handbag, much decorated with metal nonsense. Frivolous, no doubt, but you know what women are. As a practised adulterer, you do know what women are, don't you?'

'Look,' said Stuart, who was starting to feel frightened, 'we can talk about this. Why don't we sit down?'

'The reason I don't,' said Freddy Livorno, 'is that I prefer to stand in your company. This is not a social visit.' He had the kind of upper-class accent which is more than the result of a public school and a top-of-the-league university, it is learned at one's mother's knee, one's mother possibly being an earl's daughter. 'I knew where you lived because I read my wife's emails and deduced the rest. Now, would you like to know why I've come?'

Stuart said nothing. He could think of no answer to that.

'I've come to beat you up. No one has seen me come. Your porter is not at his post. The street was empty of pedestrians due, no doubt, to the snow.' He took a step towards Stuart and brought his left hand from behind his back. It was grasping a stick. Not a walking stick or a cane or the kind of thing you might use to tie a languid plant to, but a short stout stick about an inch and a half in diameter and made, apparently, from some tropical hardwood. 'Have you anything to say, as they used to put it in court, before the thrashing I intend to administer is carried out?'

Stuart found his voice. 'You're mad,' he said. 'Claudia told me you were mad. All right, I'm her lover. She needs me, married to a brute like you.' His mobile was lying on the new coffee table next to his mug of chocolate. He picked it up, said, 'I'm calling the police.'

For answer Livorno raised his stick and struck Stuart a glancing blow on the side of his head. Stuart dropped the phone and with a yell, for the blow had hurt, punched at Livorno with his fists, ineffectually hitting him in the face and neck. Livorno struck him again, this time on the side of his head and his shoulder, which made Stuart stagger and, like they said in the comics he used to read, see stars. Stuart took a step backwards and another, feeling around him for a weapon. He had no thoughts, his mind suddenly empty but for the need for self-preservation, the need to defend himself. A heavy glass vase, once a gift to his mother from Auntie Helen, its sides nearly an inch thick, stood on a shelf. It was too heavy to be held in one hand, so he took it in both just as Livorno lashed out at him again. It would have been a harder blow than the others, a potentially disabling thrust, but Stuart sidestepped it. He had the vase, his hands hooked over its thick smooth sides, and his mind quite empty, all morality, all fear, all caution – especially all caution – gone, and as a savage poke from the stick plunged into his lower abdomen, he tried a strike at Livorno's head, but the other man ducked. The vase struck him on the left shoulder.

Livorno fell, knocking over the mug of chocolate. He lay on his back in the middle of Stuart's oatmeal-coloured carpet, in a spreading pool of brown liquid. Stuart slumped down beside him, aching all over but particularly conscious of a sharp pain in his head and a crippling pain in the region of his lower abdomen. He was still holding the vase. He put it down, remembering incongruously that its purpose had originally been as a container for sticks of celery. Its surface, he noticed, perhaps for the first time, was chased with a pattern of flowers on one of which a butterfly alighted. Livorno had dropped the stick when he fell and the two weapons lay side by side as did the two men, Stuart's mobile phone about a foot away from them. It began to play 'Nessun dorma'.

Stuart picked it up, saw that his caller was Claudia. He let it ring. He turned his head as Livorno turned his and their eyes met. At some point he must have punched Livorno in the eye for the socket of his left one was turning purple and swelling. If this were in a film, he thought, fighting would put things right. He'd get up and I'd get up and we'd shake hands and go out and have a drink together. But we won't do that because it's not as if we fell out over one of us saying something rude to the other or impugned the other's honour or any of that shit. We fell out or he decided to fall out with me because I've been sleeping with his wife. And that makes it different. Oh *God*.

Livorno raised himself on his left elbow. He looked at Stuart, saying nothing. By this time Stuart's head was aching so badly that he knew he'd have to go to hospital, to some A & E department. He closed his eyes. When he opened them again Livorno was standing up, holding his left arm just below the shoulder and pressing it against his body. He gave Stuart a kick on the thigh, a kick of contempt rather than malice. Stuart got on to his knees, then to his feet, conscious of a sharp stabbing pain in what he thought might be his bladder. The phone made the noise it made when a text was coming. Claudia again.

He said to Livorno, 'Are you all right?'

'You've damaged my shoulder,' Livorno said. 'I hope I've done worse to you. If you come near my wife again, if you so much as speak to her, I'll do worse. Is that OK with you, Mr Stuart Fucking Font?'

Stuart sat in A & E, waiting to be seen by a doctor. It was the first time he had ever visited such a place, though he had heard tales from his friends of the long hours you could wait before being attended to and the unsavoury types who might sit next to you. ('Unbelievable, darling, the smell!') The conversation around him was all about the cold and the snow, how unusual it was in London, must be global warming or something. Some of them had fallen over on icy pavements and broken their ankles, their wrists, or slipped and strained their backs. Stuart had been told not to use his mobile in there and when he asked if there was somewhere he could get coffee, was directed to a machine. It was as well he was currently job-free – he liked that term better than 'jobless' – as he had already been there three hours with no sign of reprieve.

After four hours less ten minutes a nurse called him and said the doctor would see him now. Rather triumphantly, as she led him to a cubicle, she said that she had told him his wait would be a maximum of four hours and she had been spot on, hadn't she?

The doctor, a very pretty young woman like an actress in one of those hospital sitcoms, asked him how he'd come to bash his head like that and get what she called an abrasion to his lower abdomen both at the same time. Stuart said he had fallen over in the snow.

'Standing on your head on the pavement, were you,' said the doctor, 'and then you got up and kicked yourself in the prostate?'

She laughed knowingly. She asked no more questions but sent him off to have an X-ray. They wouldn't tell him what was wrong, he would have to wait a few days for the results, but they assured him nothing was broken.

Fifteen missed calls, said his mobile screen the minute he switched it on in the taxi. Then it rang and showed Claudia's name.

'I've been calling and calling you. I've texted you twice. Where have you been?'

It sounded as if she didn't know. But she must by now. He spoke cagily.

'I went out to buy things for the party and I fell over in the snow. I'd forgotten to take my phone with me.'

'Oh, sweetheart, were you hurt?'

She obviously didn't know. Freddy hadn't told her. Stuart said he'd been at A & E for seven hours, a gross exaggeration.

'There's no point in having a mobile if you don't carry it with you,' she said, and then, 'You're going to kill me, darling, but I think I've lost your key. I mean the key to your flat. I know I took it out of yesterday's handbag last night and put it into today's handbag, I *know* I did but it's not there. It must have fallen out on the Tube. I was digging stuff out of it on the Tube and it must have fallen out. You'll have to have the lock changed.'

Stuart didn't feel up to telling her that no one on the Tube would know whose door it opened. Besides, she hadn't lost it on the Tube, she hadn't lost it at all. Freddy had taken it and let himself in with it . . .

'So if I come round after work you'll have to let me in, OK?'

'I'm all over bruises,' he said.

'Oh, but that's quite sexy. I'll imagine you're a wounded warrior. It'll be about seven.'

He had started to ache all over. Distantly, he heard St Ebba's Church clock strike four. There was nothing to eat in the flat, he had eaten nothing since nine in the morning and he was very hungry. It was still snowing but he would have to go out and get something, being very careful not to fall over and make his lies into truth. Marius Potter was in the hallway, retrieving his post from the Flat 3 pigeonhole. Marius was in Stuart's eyes a throwback to the distant past of the sixties, an ancient hippie, and he found such people irritating in an

45

indefinable way. Perhaps not so indefinable, though. It had something to do with the way Marius Potter greeted him with 'Good afternoon', an old-fashioned salutation Stuart thought was meant sarcastically.

The snow had stopped but, as Maria in the pizza place said, the sky was full of it. She spoke as if the heavy dark clouds which massed above Kenilworth Parade were bags of snow, liable to drop their loads at the slightest pinprick. Stuart, who was conservative in most things, asked for a cheese and tomato pizza. The more outré kind with pineapple and crab horrified him.

'You want to look after that arm,' said Maria. 'That could turn nasty.'

As if his shoulder was a bad-tempered dog, thought Stuart. He really ought to get his camera and take photographs of Kenilworth Avenue and the parade under snow. He ought to go up past the roundabout and take pictures of Kenilworth Green and St Ebba's and the cemetery under snow. In future years no one would believe it unless records were kept. But he wouldn't be able to hold a camera. He could barely hold his mobile and he had always been useless with his left hand. Like a fairy tale it was, he thought without much originality, something from the Brothers Grimm, all those houses with little Christmas trees in their front gardens, poking out of blankets of snow.

He ate his pizza and drank a glass of orange juice. He had never been much good with alcohol – it didn't agree with him and he got drunk remarkably fast, experiencing a hangover after only two glasses of wine. Very different from Claudia who could put away an amazing amount without showing the least sign she hadn't been drinking water. It had been puzzling him that she didn't seem to know about Freddy's injuries but of course she easily might not. She had been out doing some sort of research for an article all day, was still at it, and if those two weren't often in contact he wouldn't have told her. The fact was that if you didn't work yourself, as he didn't at the moment, you got a bit out of touch with people who did. She would be here in three hours. Should he tell her? Considering his injuries had been sustained in a fight with her husband he couldn't not tell her, could he?

Normally, at this time of day when he was expecting Claudia, he would be very excited, anticipating her arrival by putting a bottle of wine – for her, not him – in the fridge, making sure the bathroom basin was clean, checking the bed, where he usually ate his breakfast of toast and his mother's home-made marmalade, for crumbs and coffee stains, if necessary changing the bottom sheet. Today his usual elation was missing. His head ached, his shoulder throbbed, his various bruises were sore and the ache in the pit of his stomach – or wherever – was getting worse. He wouldn't be able to change a sheet even if he wanted to. The prospect of making love to Claudia usually enhanced his afternoon, giving rise to all sorts of delicious fantasies. But this afternoon, even when he thought of her undressing, an icy chill took hold of him. He couldn't do it, not with that pain *down there*, not after fighting with her husband. Freddy Livorno's parting remark came back to him. If you come near my wife again, if you so much as speak to her, I'll do worse. What would worse be? More than anything Stuart feared facial disfigurement. Was that what Freddy meant?

Bending down to pick up the tray on which were the pizza plate and the orange-juice glass, he saw a dull gleam of something up against the base of the sofa. It was the key Freddy had let himself in with. Stuart put it in his pocket, sat down and got Claudia on his mobile. Not her voicemail but her own true voice.

'Claudia, I've got to put you off. I'm not well. Actually I feel pretty awful.'

'Because you fell over in the snow? What's happened to you?'

'It was a bad fall,' he said. 'I think I've ruptured something.'

'Darling, you can't have. You're such a wimp, Stuart. But that's what I love about you. Look, I'll be with you in an hour at the most. If only you didn't live out in the sticks.'

He didn't have to let her in, he thought. But he knew he hadn't the strength to keep her on the doorstep, he would have to let her in. It was true he was a bit of a wimp, he couldn't deny it.

Rose Preston-Jones was preparing a meal for herself and Marius Potter: salt-free carrot and cumin soup, to be followed by a salad of roquette and artichoke hearts with spelt and pumpkin-seed bread. Even people on her detox regime were often unwilling to eat the sort of food she cooked and prescribed, all but Marius who shared her tastes. The *sortes* which he had discovered for her that morning – 'Two other precious drops that ready stood / Each in their crystal sluice' – they both saw as applicable to the glasses of juice which were to accompany the meal. Neither of them ever touched alcohol.

Marius arrived at six thirty. In the hallway he had encountered the Constantines and while he was talking to them the automatic doors opened to admit a young woman in very high-heeled shoes. She rang Stuart Font's doorbell, and when she wasn't immediately admitted, banged on the door with her mobile phone. This reminded Katie Constantine that hers had been stolen.

'While Michael and I were on the bus. We were upstairs

at the front. I was so tired I had my head on his shoulder and my eyes closed. My handbag was on the other side of me and someone must have put his hand in and taken my phone.'

Marius said that people who lived in poverty, as so many did, were more vulnerable to temptation than others.

Katie ignored this. 'I wouldn't care that much but all my snow photos were on it. And now the snow's stopped and I don't suppose there'll be any more.'

Inside Flat 2 Marius and Rose greeted each other with a chaste kiss. Marius had a mobile, though he seldom used it. Rose believed that they harmed the brain. Katie, she said, was still young enough to avoid lasting damage if she had the sense not to replace hers and she congratulated Marius on so often letting the battery in his run down. McPhee, who sometimes thought he was a cat, having spent his puppyhood among kittens, jumped on to Marius's knee and curled up there. Rose made a pot of pomegranate tea and Marius told her about the visitor to Flat 1 and her high heels which Rose said would cripple her in later life and make surgery for bunions more than probable.

It was dark outside but the street lamps shone with a brassy light on the last of the snow patches. Getting up to pour more tea, Rose called Marius to the window. On the opposite side of the street one of the young Asian people was walking up the path of the left-hand semi-detached house, carrying a heavy-looking bag of groceries in each hand. An older man followed him in, keeping some five or six yards behind him. Rose pulled down the blind.

'That house is called Springmead. I never noticed that before.'

'Nor did I,' said Marius, thinking of what his sister had told him and wishing he had never asked. Would he ever get over

49

this awkwardness? Yet in this pretty, faded woman, still slim as a sixteen-year-old, her voice still youthful, he could see the sweet shy girl he had made love to all those years ago. All she saw, he was sure, was an old man, tired, worn and ridiculous with his quotations from a poet no one read any more.

CHAPTER FIVE

Claudia was getting dressed. Stuart lay in bed, watching her despondently. This was the second time she had visited him since his encounter with Freddy and it was plain she knew nothing about their fight; plain too that, for all his fuss about his shoulder, the injuries Freddy had sustained were less than Stuart's own.

'I had to go to A & E,' Stuart had said to her.

If Freddy too had had to seek treatment in a hospital she would surely have told him. Surely she would have said, 'So did Freddy.' Why hadn't Freddy told her? More importantly, why hadn't he told her he had found out about her affair? Freddy had said to him that if he saw Claudia again, if he so much as spoke to Claudia, he would 'do worse'. What did worse mean? That he would damage his face or even kill him? Claudia was putting on her stockings in a seductive way. His dread increasing, Stuart started wondering why she even wore stockings. Few women did. He imagined Freddy walking into the room – he might have had another key cut, he might have innumerable keys – and abruptly he got up and went into the bathroom.

Freddy must be playing some deep game. Or perhaps, which would be worse, an ordinary sort of shallow game. I'm not going to tell her, I'm not saying a thing to her, Freddy might be telling himself, I don't want to warn her. Warn *him*, as I have done, so that if she wants to see him he makes it plain he doesn't want to see *her*. So that he sends her away, quarrels with her maybe, what do I care? Now totally covered by his camel-hair dressing gown, Stuart looked at himself in the mirror, then went into the living room where Claudia was sitting on the sofa, one leg crossed over the other to show her stocking tops, looking at the stain on the carpet.

'Is that blood, darling?'

Stuart said no, of course not, it was or had been hot chocolate. He had meant to clean it up. 'Claudia.'

'Yes, what? I don't have to go yet, you know. We've got at least another hour. You won't forget to have another key cut for me, will you?' While he was in the bathroom she must have seen the crate from Wicked Wine. 'Shall we have one of those bottles of champagne?'

'They're for my party,' he said in a repressive tone, and then, 'Claudia, we have to talk.'

'What on earth do you mean?'

What on earth did he mean? For a wild moment he thought of telling her he had to go away – his mother was ill and he had to be with her . . . his friend in San Francisco was ill . . . What sick person would want *him* nursing them? Instead, he managed, 'This is getting too much for me, this – well, relationship of ours. If I've got this degree of emotional involvement I need to be with you all the time.' He jibbed a bit at telling anyone he loved her when he didn't but now was no time for niceties. 'I love you, Claudia. I adore you.' Why did 'adore' sound so much less real than 'love'? 'I can't bear to let you go home to Freddy. If we're going to go on like this it's better we should part.'

'Oh, Stuart,' she said, pulling her skirt down over her knees. 'I'd no idea you felt like this.'

He was beginning to enjoy it. You rat, he said to himself, you heel. 'If I can't have you all the time, if I can't have you to myself, it would be better not to have you at all. It's going to break my heart, it's going to half kill me, but it's better for both of us – don't you see?'

She came up to him and put her arms around him, laying her cheek against his. Stuart nearly cried out at the pain of having his bruised back and shoulders squeezed. 'We don't have to part permanently, darling. Let's have a trial separation. We won't see each other for a – what? A fortnight? We'll still talk on the phone every day.'

With that half-measure he had to be content. At least, in the emotion of the moment, she had forgotten about the key.

Olwen's father had been a drunk and her mother, to keep her husband company, had been a heavy drinker. But Louis Forgan had held down a job, even led some sort of social life, while showing few signs of his addiction except to those who know about these things. Olwen and her brother accepted that there was always drink about, whisky mostly, but beer and wine as well. They accepted it as the norm and in friends' houses wondered why no bottles stood about in every room and the friends' parents never had a glass beside them. Until, that is, Douglas, who was a year older than Olwen, seemed to realise what was going on and announced at their evening meal that he would never drink another drop of alcohol as long as he lived.

Both of them had been encouraged to drink wine at table since they were nine and ten. Olwen blamed this custom for her own addiction and in the days when she read newspapers and attended to television, as well as simply having it on, had been made angry by articles and programmes which advocated giving children wine to encourage them 'to drink responsibly'. In her youth her longing for alcoholic drink worried her and made her actively miserable. She looked with wonder and near disbelief at Douglas who, living away from home, had adhered to his resolve, never touched beer, wine or spirits, and seemed perfectly content. Gargantuan efforts were made by her to follow his example and sometimes she did manage to go without for long periods. Her father died of cirrhosis, her mother suffered what her doctor called 'drink-related problems'.

While in one of her abstemious phases Olwen got married. Her husband was a social drinker and, knowing nothing of her family history, persuaded her that an occasional glass of something would do no harm. Olwen's first drink after doing without for six months was bliss. She had a second one with David and was back where she had been before she met him. For a long time she kept a bottle of red wine in the kitchen which she told him was for cooking. It was always the same kind that she bought so he couldn't tell whether it was the first bottle or the twenty-fifth whose level had fallen. She paid for it out of her own money for she had always worked as someone's secretary or, at one place, run the typing pool.

The marriage broke up, partly because David wanted children and Olwen was frightened at the prospect. She drank too much. Alone, she indulged herself and began drinking a couple of gins a day as well as the wine. While unaware of doing so, she must have learned from her parents how to be a heavy drinker without giving many signs of it to those not in the know. Bill wasn't in the know, he was a total abstainer, from taste rather than conviction. He didn't like the stuff. When they went out together he bought her drinks, said he liked to see her enjoying herself and admired her 'strong head'. Dreaming of Bill now, as she sometimes did, she saw him only as foolish, a mug, to have been so easily deceived. He was on the point of asking her to marry him – and this was the substance of her dream – before he told her that he had two children. In the dream he had five, though, she thought now, he might as well have had ten, his two were so much trouble. She woke up wondering, not for the first time, why she had married him and taken on all that caring and cooking and housekeeping and pretending to be indifferent to alcohol, pretending to like Margaret and Richard, pretending that she didn't need gin or vodka – it was all one – to keep herself sane.

Waking, she needed a drink but she had run out of booze. The vodka bottle she had put on the floor by her bed the night before had had at least two inches left in it. Or she thought it had, she remembered that it had. Perhaps she had drunk it before she went to sleep or had awakened in the night and drunk it. Plainly, it was now empty. She got up with difficulty and staggered to the kitchen where she looked in the drinks cupboard. Bottles were there, two gin bottles and one whisky, but they too were empty. She was aware of a fearful fatigue overcoming her so that, shuffling into her living room, she only just made it to the broken-down old sofa before collapsing.

Bright sunshine coming in through the window cast brilliant pane-shaped light patches on to her head and face. Cursing, she turned her face into the stained cushions. Her craving for a drink was strong now, almost violent. Although she would have been prepared to stagger along to Wicked Wine, holding on to fences and posts, using an umbrella as a stick, she knew her worn-out feeble body would never make it. If she phoned Rupert, could he be induced to come round or send someone over with a bottle of gin? The phone, like most small objects in her flat, was on the floor. She reached over, scrabbling for the phone before she remembered it would

55

be dead. British Telecommunications or whatever they were called had cut it off weeks ago because she had forgotten to pay the bill.

Any pride Olwen had once had was long gone. Keeping it through those two marriages, concealing the addiction and the smell on her breath and the unsteadiness of her walk, had been gratefully relinquished when she was alone at last and resolved on drinking herself to death. She eased herself off the sofa on to the floor and when she had crawled to the front door, pulled herself up by holding on to the handles on a built-in cupboard. She got the front door open, dropped heavily to the floor again, and crawled across to Flat 5. Her hammering with her fists brought Noor Lateef to the door with Sophie Longwich behind her. The sight of Olwen in a dirty pink nightdress covered by an ancient fur coat made them stare and then look away. Neither of them had ever heard her say more than 'Not really', and their reaction to what she said was as if Rose Preston-Jones's McPhee had given tongue to human speech.

'Could one of you go round the corner and get me a bottle of gin? Rupert'll be open now. It's half nine. I'll pay you when you get back.'

When she had recovered from the shock of it, Sophie, the more practical of the two, said, 'Shall I get you a doctor? I could call an ambulance.'

'I only want a bottle of gin.'

Noor, gaping, took a step backwards.

'It wouldn't be right to do that,' said Sophie. 'I'm sorry but I couldn't. You ought to have a doctor.'

Still on her knees, Olwen shook her head with all the violence she could muster, turned round and crawled back to her open front door. The girls closed theirs and inside stared at each other and at Molly Flint who had come out of the

56

bathroom, wrapped in a towel. They had all led sheltered lives; though a Friday- or Saturday-night session in a pub or club was requisite behaviour for all of them, though they indulged in some mild binge drinking at these times and saw others in a much worse way than they were, the sight of true alcoholism was new to them. They were a little frightened by Olwen's squalor, her rat-tail hair, her dirty nightdress, her swollen feet like slabs of beef in a butcher's window. The raw desperate face she presented to them was stripped of that control, that tidying-up and levelling-out which governs the features of the old, creating a mild and almost cheerful blank.

'If she'd asked us to get her some milk we would have,' said Noor.

'Milk's not like booze,' said Sophie. 'It wouldn't hurt her.'

Molly, reputed to be a philosopher, said, 'You don't know that. She might be allergic to milk. And it's not down to us to judge, is it? It's not down to us to be moralistic.'

'I'll tell you what we could do,' Sophie nodded decisively. 'We could go and get her a half-bottle of gin or even a quarter-bottle and when we've done that we could tell Michael Constantine about her and see what he says.'

The others said this seemed a good idea and they set about scraping together the requisite five pounds.

'You gossip too much,' Wally Scurlock said to his wife. 'You'll get yourself into trouble.'

Mrs Scurlock, whose name was Richenda, said, 'We've been through all that before, Wally. And I've told you, so what? And who's going to get me into trouble?'

'You'll do it yourself. You stand down there in the hallway shouting at the top of your voice that no one in this place goes out to work. Don't deny it. I heard you.'

'I'm not going to deny it. It's true. There's three of them students – or so they say. And not one of the others has what you'd call a job. Now when I was young and even more when you was young, in a place like this, six flats, everyone'd have gone out to work, nine-to-five jobs the lot of them – well, maybe the wives, some of them, would have stopped at home. Done their own housework in them days.'

'Then you'd have been out of a job,' said Wally triumphantly.

Richenda cleaned all the flats in Lichfield House, three in Ludlow House, two in Hereford House and five in Ross House. Her mother had cleaned flats before her and her grandmother before that, but they had dressed for the job, the former in 'slacks' and cotton blouse, the latter in an overall. Richenda told the residents that she wore what she called her ordinary clothes because she was no more going to get herself into a uniform than Wally was. If the ordinary clothes – a short tight skirt, tight cardigan over a low-cut T-shirt and stiletto heels – caused some astonishment, Richenda said they could take it or leave it. See what they'd get if they took on one of those single mums who put cards through the door offering cleaning services – their homes stripped bare and an open invitation to every burglar in north London.

She started at Stuart Font's, her intention to use no cleansers, no polish and no appliance but the vacuum cleaner. When Stuart pointed out the hot-chocolate stain she said, almost before he had finished his sentence, that this was a job for a carpet-cleaning firm. The woman he was 'carrying on with' phoned soon after that and though it was apparent as he moved from room to room, looking over his shoulder, that he wanted to be on his own, Richenda followed him, pulling the Hoover after her and listening carefully to his side of the conversation.

Wally Scurlock allowed ten minutes after her departure

before going out and carrying with him his garden tools in a large canvas bag. He was almost totally uninterested in other people unless they came into the category of those who interested him very much. Therefore, he no more registered Duncan Yeardon taking out of number 3 Kenilworth Avenue a box of papers for recycling than he noticed the cypress tree by Duncan's front gate. The young girl with a silk-smooth pale face and sleek black hair who emerged from Springmead was another matter altogether. Wally took in with hungry eyes her slender shape, long slim legs and the flower-petal hands that held a black plastic sack which looked far too heavy for them. He considered crossing the road and offering to carry that sack for her but dismissed the idea as soon as it came to him. Attracting attention to himself was pointless and possibly dangerous.

Ten thirty was the date of his self-made appointment and it was now twenty past. He walked past the church, designed by Sir Robert Smirke a hundred years ago but now called the Bel Esprit Centre and converted into a mini-shopping mall with cafeteria and children's play centre, and briskly up Kenilworth Avenue, a street of mixed dwellings, short terraces of three-storey town houses, detached and semi-detached villas, all interspersed with blocks of flats very much like Lichfield, Ross, Ludlow and Hereford but older. At the top was a round-about where there was a hairdresser's, a newsagent's, a building society branch and a shop selling fitted bathrooms, now in the process of closing down. Wally passed two exits and took the continuation of Kenilworth Avenue. Here, past Kenilworth Green and St Ebba's, the oldest building in the neighbour-hood by about six hundred years, was Kenilworth Primary School, its pupils about to come out into the playground for their mid-morning break.

It was a very long time since anyone had been buried in

the churchyard of St Ebba's but the graves were still there and the gravestones. Wally, whose family had its roots in Merton, had no connection with any burial place in this neighbourhood but he had fixed on Clara Elizabeth Carbury's grave for his particular attention. He liked the name and, more than the name, the location of her gravestone which was close up against the openwork iron gates dividing the churchyard from the school grounds. Clara, he would have lied to anyone who asked, had been his great-grandmother. By this time he had read the inscription so many times that he knew it by heart. *Clara Elizabeth, b.1879, d.1942, beloved wife of Samuel Carbury, Abide with Me, Fast falls the Eventide. RIP.*

The churchyard was on the whole not well maintained, most of the plots shaggy with long grass and the slabs overgrown with weeds. But Clara Carbury's was an example to all descendants of the dead, most of them negligent and uncaring, in that its marble kerb was clean and polished, its grass plot neat and weed-free and its stone urn sporting a well-pruned pot plant except when the local youth vandalised it. In spite of its trim appearance, created by himself, Wally squatted down to begin on it afresh, taking out of his bag a set of shears and, for the more precise work, a pair of scissors, a trowel and fork and a pack of polishing cloths. He had just begun snipping off the past week's growth of grass as a hairdresser might start to trim a short back and sides, when the Kenilworth Primary children burst out with shrieks and shouts into their playground. The girls shrieked, as Wally well knew, while the boys shouted. It was the former he was interested in and he could watch them run and jump, their skirts fluttering up in the breeze, almost without lifting his eyes from the trowel he plied to remove a non-existent dandelion.

Later in the week he would take himself a little further afield to Daneforth Comprehensive and the first year's netball.

There was no convenient churchyard in Daneforth Grove but a window in the stairwell of a nearby council tower block overlooked the school. Wally secured himself a vantage point at this window for half an hour on Wednesday mornings by dint of signing up for a local authority scheme called Salute4Seniors. All this involved was visiting a pensioner and chatting to him or her for twenty minutes, a breeze which meant he could afterwards spend an hour viewing the sub-teens at play. So far, no parent or other interfering busybody had spotted his weekly activities or, if they had, thought them other than innocent.

The young girl went first down the Springmead garden path to the summer house. Then came the boy. Watching them from his back-bedroom window, Duncan made up his mind that she and her brother must be meeting to have a conversation in their own language. They seldom got the chance to be alone together inside Springmead where the girl's middle-aged husband was no doubt very demanding, expecting her to wait on him hand and foot and the brother to toe the line. He hadn't seen the husband go out but prob-ably he had. Not nearly so many people seemed to go out to work as they had when Duncan was that age but that was very likely where he had gone. When he fantasised about people he usually gave them names and now he named the husband Mr Wu after a George Formby song about a Chinese laundryman and the girl and boy Tigerlily and Oberon. He saw them go into the summer house, looking over their shoul-ders before closing the door.

Duncan opened the window just as he had opened all the bedroom windows. The weather had grown mild, and though he had turned down the heating, the well-insulated house remained very warm. Soon he would be able to turn it off altogether. Duncan felt rather proud of helping to reduce global warming while at the same time keeping himself very comfortable and his electricity and gas bills down to a minimum.

Inside the summer house, Xue and Tao sat on rattan chairs, reading nothing, looking at nothing and not speaking. After a while Xue slid on to the floor and lay there, pressing her bare arms and legs against the cold tiles.

CHAPTER SIX

Never having practised, Michael Constantine didn't quite like the idea of attending a patient. It might be illegal for all he knew. 'If it happens again,' he said, 'you'd better call an ambulance.'

Sophie Longwich hadn't told him how she had bought a half-bottle of gin and handed it in to the woman who opened the door of Flat 6, a woman who looked to her scarcely human in her tattered fur and with grey hair transformed by neglect into dreadlocks straggled about her face. She was concerned for Olwen but at the same time she was frightened of her. Brought up by gentle courteous parents, she had been taught to respect those she still thought of as 'grown-ups'. They knew how to conduct their lives, the long years had instructed them in living, and when she found one who didn't know how, she felt shaken and bewildered.

Her flatmates had gone out, Molly to her art school in Hornsey, Noor to a business course she was attending in Wembley. Sophie had no lectures today at her South Bank university, and though there was a lot of reading she should be doing, she found herself unable to concentrate on Scott Fitzgerald and J. D. Salinger. Several times during the morning she went out on to the top landing and listened outside Olwen's door. At first there was only silence. She imagined

Olwen pouring herself a gin with something – orange or tonic or one of those things people mixed with gin. It didn't occur to her as possible that gin might be drunk neat. Olwen would be feeling better by now, would have had a bath and put on clean clothes. The idea of Olwen cleaned up and humanised comforted her. She could now allow herself to think about the five pounds the half-bottle had cost. Noor had a rich father who owned this flat, Molly's parents were comfortably off but she, Sophie, one of five children, had to live on her government loan, all to be paid back one day.

She read some more of *The Great Gatsby* and then she went back to Olwen's door. There was a sound of movement from inside the flat, then a crash that sounded as if something had been flung against an interior wall. She waited. Olwen spoke, cursing, apparently enraged, drumming, by the sound of it, her fists on the floor. Seriously frightened now, Sophie ran back to Flat 5 and into the bedroom she shared with Molly which happened to be the one furthest away from the landing and Olwen's door.

Nothing leads to the making of discoveries like an enforced change in one's lifestyle. Stuart, determined to escape from Claudia's phone calls, had begun going out a great deal. Long walks were taken, he twice went to the cinema, met his old friends Jack and Martin on Tuesday night, had a drink with an ex-girlfriend for old times' sake on Wednesday and next day even visited his parents. He had found that it was unnecessary to take his mobile with him. This was a revelation to him; it wasn't since his mid-teens that he had been anywhere without carrying it or one of its predecessors. But without it in his pocket the heavens didn't fall, retribution didn't descend on him, no vengeful illness struck him down.

It was even quite peaceful not hearing 'Nessun dorma' every five minutes, restful not having to speak to Claudia.

When he got home the messages were piling up, two from Claudia, one from his mother from whom he had parted three hours before, one from Martin inviting him to Sunday lunch with himself and his girlfriend. Stuart deleted them all and still lightning didn't strike him or the earth open. The results of his X-ray had come and revealed that no bones were broken. He knew that already. He studied his own image in the mirror, feeling calm and even cheerful. How handsome he was! Trying to think who he reminded himself of, he came up with José Mourinho, only a younger version, of course. Another way of getting away from the phones would be to join a gym. His figure was perfect but there was no harm in doing a bit of work to keep it that way. Besides, Jack had told him a gym was an amazing place to meet girls, all of them beautiful or they wouldn't dare strip down to leotards and prance about in public on elliptical cross-trainers.

At the end of the fortnight he was going to have to confront Claudia. Another discovery made through his new lifestyle was that he didn't really like Claudia. He fancied her, of course – any man would fancy her. But if he liked her or, more than that, *loved* her, Freddy Livorno's threats wouldn't have carried much weight with him. He would, he told himself, have defied that hectoring bully. No, Freddy had perhaps done him a favour. Instead of missing Claudia and pining for her as she and he too had thought would be the case, he was rather relieved and worrying only about how to stop her *coming back to him* when the two weeks were up.

Still, he felt that he had reached an important point in his life, a crossroads perhaps. Things were on the crux of change. Once before, when he had first moved in, he had consulted Marius Potter – on the recommendation of Rose

Preston-Jones – and applied to him for a *sortes* reading. Now seemed the time to request another. Stuart sat down in a strange chair with a rail padded in brown corduroy providing its back while Marius sat in a chair with a diamond-shaped seat and carved circular back and consulted the copy of *Paradise Lost* which lay on the marble table. Marius opened it at random, leafing through the pages with his eyes closed like a practised card sharper.

He opened his eyes but without looking, ran his fingers down the right-hand page, stopping a little more than halfway down. He read: "'Live while ye may, / Yet happy pair; enjoy, till I return, / Short pleasures, for long woes are to succeed!'"

'That's not very good, is it?' Stuart was dismayed.

'Well, I'm sorry.' Marius sounded genuinely contrite. 'That's the trouble with the *sortes*. You have to take the rough with the smooth. Come back tomorrow and you might get something more hopeful.'

'I don't think I will, thanks.'

The reading plainly referred to his relationship with Claudia and must mean that things were all right for him now but would change when she returned. Any pleasure would be short-lived and afterwards, misery. For the first time in the six months since he gave up, Stuart thought how much he would like a cigarette. Reminding him where addiction might lead, he encountered Olwen crossing the hallway, a clinking plastic bag in each hand. She wore her tattered fur. Her face was grey, her head wrapped up in a scarf of much the same shade. Everyone in Lichfield House had by now of course heard on the grapevine, which had its roots in Flat 5, of her near collapse, her apparent illness and pleas for someone to buy her alcoholic drink. Everyone had his or her own view of how this crisis should have been handled.

Stuart didn't care but still thought it incumbent on him as

a resident to ask her how she was. He recoiled a bit from her unsavoury ambience. 'Are you feeling better?'

'Not really,' said Olwen, though she knew she would be once she had swallowed her first gulp of the vodka which, February having started, would probably be the liquor of the month. She shuffled up to the lift. It was now four days since she had eaten anything and there was no food in the two bags she carried.

Still made uneasy by his *sortes* reading, Stuart decided a long walk would be a good idea. He would go up to that new gym which had opened on the borders of Mill Hill, see what it was like and maybe sign up. Back in the flat to put on a jacket, he heard 'Nessun dorma' repeating and repeating itself over and over in his bedroom. He let it repeat, slipped on his very handsome Burberry jacket and, having contemplated his reflection in the mirror to his great satisfaction, went out into the fresh air, leaving his phone behind.

It was rather a nice, pale grey, mild sort of day. A couple of small white flowers Stuart supposed must be snowdrops poked timidly through the earth just inside Lichfield House's front gate. The street was deserted but for hundreds of cars parked nose to tail along both sides. For the first time ever he saw someone go into the Bel Esprit Centre. Halfway to the roundabout, he passed Wally Scurlock trotting along briskly, very upright, very purposeful.

'Good morning, sir, and how are you today?'

Stuart said he was good, though he wasn't, not at all. The man coming down the opposite side was called Duncan something – Stuart had forgotten what. He looked like a paedophile, or how he thought a paedophile would look, furtive, covert, and wearing a raincoat. He cheered himself up a bit by reflecting on what Scurlock and the paedophile must think of him. How they must envy him, his slim figure, his handsome features and fine, luxuriant head of hair. Both the paedophile and the care-taker were bald.

When he had been to the gym and paid in advance for twelve sessions, the desire for a cigarette returned. Everyone said it would be a mistake to give in to it. You only had to have one and you were hooked all over again. Stuart walked past the hairdresser's, the building society and the now closed-down bathroom shop and went into the newsagent's. It was a large newsagent's, selling greetings cards and wrapping paper, sweets and cigarettes, as well as papers. Nothing alerted him as to what was to come, nothing said to him, go, turn round and leave now. If this was his fate, perhaps the most signif-icant moment of his life, as forecast by the *sortes,* he didn't recognise it. If this was to determine his death he knew nothing of it or that, like the sword of Damocles, it hung by a hair above his head. He had never heard of Damocles. All he thought about was cigarettes, which brand should he buy and would he need a disposable lighter or would matches do?

He saw that there were two people in the shop apart from the man behind the counter, a man and a girl. If he had thought about it he might have decided they were not together, for the girl who had her back to him was at the counter, waiting to be served while the man appeared to be choosing a birthday card. Then, taking her change, she turned round.

The song which tells of a 'lady sweet and kind, ne'er a face so pleased my mind' Stuart was unfamiliar with, but the senti-ment was his own. Never had a face so pleased his mind as this one. He knew with a seriousness and an intensity quite foreign to him that this was the most beautiful woman he had ever seen and if it were possible to fall in love at first sight this was what was happening to him. It was not a European face but seemed to belong in South-East Asia, pale-skinned with features of perfect regularity, the upper lip short, the mouth full, the eyes large, grave, thickly lashed, a dark golden brown. Her hair hung in two thick black curtains from a centre parting.

She looked at him and lowered those eyes, opening the pack of cigarettes she had bought. He stammered out a request to the shopman for the same brand and, completely disorientated, fumbled for change, dropping coins on the floor. He stooped down to pick them up and so did she, handing him a two-pound coin with a little nod.

'Thank you,' he said. 'Thank you very much.'

The man who hadn't bought a greetings card was standing quite near them now, watching her, not speaking. Because this man was in his forties, round-faced and because his hair was also black, Stuart decided he must be her father. Possibly a strict father, a Muslim as a lot of people from that part of the world were. He took his cigarettes and when he turned round the girl and her father were gone. To lose her now was the most appalling thing he could think of. He rushed out of the shop, staring wildly about, but he hadn't far to look. She was standing in the doorway of the bathroom shop, leaning against the boarded-up entrance, smoking.

He stared. Her eyes were turned in the direction of the old church and Kenilworth Primary School, so she wasn't aware of his gaze. Her father was nowhere to be seen. She was as slender as a reed, as the stem of a flower, cocooned in a black quilted coat. Her ankles, he thought with some exaggeration, were the circumference of another girl's thumbs. She finished her cigarette, stamped out the stub but, instead of leaving it on the pavement, picked it up in a tissue and put it into her pocket. He couldn't just let her go, he must follow her. That meant he must follow her dad too, for this man had appeared from out of the alley that ran between the building society and the hairdresser's and was hustling her along towards the next turning out of the roundabout.

One moment they were there, it appeared to him, and the next they had both got into one of the parked cars, the doors were slammed and dad was driving off. The car was a black Audi, he took that in, but it didn't occur to him to take its number until it was too late. There was nothing for it but to go home. On the way he smoked one of his cigarettes and it served to make him ask himself why he had ever given up. He could almost feel his swollen nerves shrinking back to normal. His mobile told him he had three messages, one from his mother and two from Claudia. Claudia had also left a message on his landline. This one he listened to. Why did he never answer his phone? Was he ill? Or had he gone away? In spite of the pact they had made, she would come round and see him if he didn't speak to her in the next twenty-four hours.

Stuart lit another cigarette and made himself a mug of hot chocolate. Why did women think they could make themselves more attractive by bullying and nagging you? He thought of the beautiful girl in the newsagent's, her eyes, her long slender hands, her full red mouth. She would never nag a man but be a sweet submissive companion. They had so much in common, both dramatically good-looking, a couple to be stared at, both smokers, not common these days. He knew now he never wanted to see Claudia again. Freddy Livorno could rest easy. No need for him to watch his wife, check up on her meetings, put private detectives on to her – or whatever he had done – for their affair was over. It was a pity he had spent such a lot of money on that necklace, but if that was all he had to pay to free himself, it was cheap at the price.

But how was he to find the beautiful girl?

*

70

On the first Monday in February it snowed. The snowfall wasn't like the one just before Christmas but a serious 'weather warning' event, as the media called it. Seven or eight inches fell that morning, blanketing the pavements and gardens, masking the cars in fleecy white. Panic ensued as motorways came to a standstill, airports closed, buses disappeared and the Tube was disabled. Cautiously, Stuart answered his mobile to Claudia. As if he had been begging her to come, she told him in a scolding tone that it was impossible for her to move out of the house that day. He realised this must be when their separation was due to end and he said rather too heartily that she mustn't think twice about it, of course she must stay at home.

The day now fixed for him and her to meet again was by coincidence the day before his house-warming party. Claudia was, of course, now not invited. She had understood this would be too awkward. Most residents of Lichfield House had accepted, as had Martin and his girlfriend and Jack, as well as two couples from Chester House whom Stuart had been introduced to by Rose Preston-Jones. They were clients of hers, one signed up for her detoxing programme, the other having acupuncture. Noor Lateef and Molly Flint had asked to bring their boyfriends. For all that, Stuart would have given a great deal not to have had the party. He could hardly understand now what had made him think a party a good idea. Of course, things would have been very different if he could have invited the beautiful girl, but since their encounter in the newsagent's he hadn't seen her again, though he had gone back several times on the chance that she would come in while he was there. One of the results of that had been his return to becoming a thirty-a-day smoker.

This snow put everything on hold. Almost everyone had accepted his invitations. Even the Scurlocks were coming.

Over the roar of the vacuum cleaner Richenda had said, out of the blue, how much she and Wally were looking forward 'to your thrash, Stuart'. He made his way round to Lichfield Parade to buy more champagne as well as wine and beer, slipping and sliding and clutching at snow-laden fences. At first he couldn't believe it, Wicked Wine was closed. Not simply closed but closed down. Like so many other businesses, Rupert's shop had suffered disastrously from the recession. Customers' needs were satisfied by the large supermarkets or remained unsatisfied. Stuart wondered if this provided him with sufficient excuse to cancel the party but decided that it didn't. No buses were running. The television told him that no Tubes were running but for the Victoria Line and that was no use to him. Like most people who didn't go out to work or who had decided to stay at home today, Stuart watched television, intent on weather updates. Snow fell all the morning, sometimes light and airy, sometimes thick and fast. In the lulls between snowfalls, children and parents with children came out of the houses with trays and doors and plastic bags and the occasional real sledge and tobogganed down Kenilworth Avenue.

Katie Constantine typed twenty-five pages of a historical novel about Perkin Warbeck. Her husband devoted his column to debunking Bach flower treatments with special vitriol reserved for the Rescue Remedy. He was trying to forget the letters which had arrived that morning, one of them from an eminent trichologist calling his statement that women who shaved their legs risked coarsening the growth totally false. Utter rubbish, wrote the hair expert, balderdash. This word Michael had never heard before but he understood it to be pejorative.

Molly, Sophie and Noor plodded down to the pizza place in moon boots where they had a very long lunch of margaritas, peach, anchovy and bacon pizzas and chocolate and vanilla yogurt which lasted from midday to three thirty. So no one was at home when Olwen rang their doorbell in the hope of finding someone to go shopping for her. Marius Potter whom she called on next let her in but refused her request to buy drink for her at the Kenilworth Avenue Tesco.

'Too slippery,' he said, 'and it's made worse by all those kids sliding up and down. I don't want to break my leg. I'm afraid you'll have to do without.' He thought of adding, 'For once', but he was a kind man and he only smiled.

Olwen knew herself to be even less able to walk on those pavements. The closing-down of Wicked Wine had brought her alternating depression and panic. Once this snow had gone she would place a weekly order with one of the wine shops in Edgware. If the delivery man laughed at her and gossiped about her, what did she care?

Downstairs to seek Rose and tell her about it, Marius encountered Stuart looking extra handsome in a bulky white sweater, jeans and moon boots and holding a Harrods carrier bag.

'If you're going to the Tesco,' said Marius in a satirical tone, 'I don't suppose you'd feel like fetching old Olwen a litre of her poison?'

'Are you serious?'

'Not really, as she might say. I mention it because she asked me.'

'Look across the road,' said Stuart, 'at those two houses, number 3 and number 5. The one on the left's called Springmead. Why isn't there any snow on their roofs? All the other roofs are covered but theirs aren't.'

'Ah, that's easily explained,' said Marius, the Luddite. 'They've got solar heating and the panels are on the roof of Springmead. The snow won't settle while you've got those panels.' And he went into Rose's flat to tell her about the explanation he had invented and Stuart had swallowed. But talking to Rose and being with her wasn't the same as it had been. The memory of their meeting so long ago and of that night they had spent together weighed heavily on him. He felt, obscurely, that he was somehow deceiving her, even cheating on her, a notion that would only go away when he spoke out. But suppose she too remembered that night, but remembered it with horror, and the man with whom she had spent it, with shame and, worse, dislike. Marius told himself sadly that there was no question she might have recognised him. His appearance now, scraggy, hollow-eyed and with thin grey hair, was a far cry from the stripling of the Hackney commune.

Stuart tramped up Kenilworth Avenue, carefully placing his feet in the oval indentations made by those who had gone before him like the page who trod in Good King Wenceslas's footprints. He was on his way to look for the beautiful girl.

CHAPTER SEVEN

Wally Scurlock had walked all the way up Kenilworth Avenue to the churchyard, was actually squatting down by Clara Carbury's grave, before he realised something was wrong. St Ebba's clock had struck, with a double stroke, half past ten, but no Kenilworth Primary School children had come out to play. Even inside gloves, his fingers were growing numb and his feet in wellies were icy. Perhaps the children were late because of the weather. The weather affected everything, spoilt everything. He paced a bit, slapping his upper arms with his gloved hands. It was supposed to warm you up but it didn't. St Ebba's struck three strokes for the three-quarters and then he knew. They had closed the school! That's what they did in snowy weather, they closed the schools. The comprehensive, visible from the pensioner's tower, would also be closed. Wally felt cheated of what he thought of as a legitimate and harmless activity, a pastime which saved him from the indulgence he truly – intensely, exultantly – preferred. He got slowly and stiffly to his feet.

The churchyard lay peaceful and silent under its thick and fleecy covering. No such silence had prevailed in this part of London for many years, the cars undriven, the buses stilled, pedestrians housebound. Wally knew what would happen if he went back along the snow-hushed streets to Lichfield

House and down into his basement flat. Richenda would be out cleaning. He thought with hatred of Richenda. With her great bosom and wide hips, her big painted face and lacquered hair, she was the antithesis of his desire, but it was because this was what she was that he had married her. A real woman, a big woman, was what a man like him should want. Except that when they had been married for no more than a few weeks he knew she wasn't. His imagination wasn't big enough to substitute, when they were in bed at night, one of these schoolchildren or the tiny lovely girl from Springmead for the pulsating bulk in his arms. Even with all the lights out, the blinds down, the curtains drawn, the imagined girl wasn't real enough to dispel Richenda.

Yet the girl was a grown woman. He could somehow tell that. Her breasts were tiny, her legs a teenager's, her back and shoulders narrow, but she was maybe twenty-five years old. If, knowing what he now knew, he could have found a woman like her, wouldn't she have saved him from the churchyard and the pensioner's tower, and more than that, much more, from what he was about to do?

Through Rose Preston-Jones's window he saw Richenda plying the vacuum cleaner. If she saw him she gave no sign of it. His feet were frozen, he could scarcely feel them any more. Another resentment welled up inside him as he made his way over to the stairs on his numbed feet. What sort of an architect must it have been to design a block of flats with a lift for the residents on the ground and upper floors but only a staircase for the caretaker's use? Going down was one thing but coming up, as he was obliged to a dozen, two dozen, times a day, was deliberate cruelty. It was bad enough now and he was only in his forties. And then there were the other blocks, Ross, Hereford and Ludlow – he was the caretaker for the lot of them, forced to go out into the open whatever

76

the weather to attend to some footling matter in another building.

Richenda had left him a note. She always left him a note. This one incorporated a shopping list and an order to call BT about a fault on the landline. It could wait. He could do those things after she got back. This he wanted and needed, had to have, must be done while she was absent, could only be done while she was absent. The flat was small, just a living room, bedroom, kitchen and bathroom. The computer was kept in the bedroom. He shut the door, wishing he could lock it – there was a key in the lock, but he dared not. If she came back and found that door locked, she would never rest until he had told her why. He wished he knew whether she had started at Rose Preston-Jones's and still had Stuart Font's to do, in which case she would be two hours, or had done Stuart's, was halfway through Rose's – to himself he called the residents by their given names – and would therefore be no more than half an hour. Would she go on to Hereford without coming home first?

He sat down, started the computer. When the pictures he wanted began he grew hot and his heart began to beat faster. No imagination was needed, none. He never downloaded, he was too afraid to do that. Besides, he couldn't print out because he had no printer and he was pretty sure, almost sure, that if you never downloaded these pictures they could never find out what you'd been doing, but there was no one he could ask. They could never find out the sites you'd visited, could they? But he longed to download just one or two – well, say six. Having them in print would make such a difference to his life. Being able to look at them without coming in here, without having to be sure to exclude Richenda, would make him *happy*.

And what harm did it do? he thought, as he moved from

picture to picture. It wasn't real. It was just pictures. Just photographs and videos, the stuff that dreams are made of.

Though more fell in great quantities in other parts of England, in London the snow froze, then began to melt. On Thursday morning it was raining. Olwen had never thought she would be glad to see rain. But she could go out in it, she wouldn't slip and fall over on wet pavements. As near as the now defunct Wicked Wine but a lot nearer than Tesco was Mr Ali's corner shop. Its proper name was Alcazar Foods but everyone called it Mr Ali's. Sophie had called it that the day before when Olwen had opened her front door to see her coming out of the lift and carrying a bottle of Sauvignon Blanc.

'From Mr Ali's,' Sophie said. 'He doesn't drink himself but he sells it.'

'Just wine?' Olwen asked, baulking at a more direct enquiry.

'Well, food and stuff. There was a woman in there buying something for cleaning drains.'

Olwen put on her old black coat, tied a scarf round her head and searched for an umbrella. She wasn't sure why she failed to find one – because there wasn't an umbrella in the flat or because she was trembling and shaking too much to look properly. No one was in the lobby and this pleased her because she knew none of them would do her essential shopping for her. She had asked them all and all had refused. Not rudely or scathingly and the sharpest response she had had was from Michael Constantine who told her that now was her chance to give up drinking.

The front path to the gate and the street was encrusted with old snow and grey ice in which footprints had made deep craters. The rain falling on it seemed not to have washed any of this away, though it was possible now to see dark paving stones in the hollows. Wally Scurlock should have swept this earlier in the week, not left it till today. He would never do it now but rely on the rain doing it for him. Olwen set off, pressing her boots into the declivities, surprised to find how slippery the uneven surface still was. There was nothing to hold on to except the box hedge and that was no more than eighteen inches high. She was not only unsteady on her feet but weak from lack of food.

She could see ahead of her that the pavement in Kenilworth Avenue wasn't much better than the path in here, worse perhaps where the children had hardened the surface by tobogganing on it. She had almost reached the gate when she fell, sliding over backwards and hitting her head on the brick border of the path. It was Rose who found her no more than two minutes later. She had come out with McPhee because dogs need to be exercised whatever the weather. Rose called an ambulance before she even touched Olwen. Then, covering her with her own warm winter coat, she sat down on the low wall, shivering and hugging herself, waiting for the paramedics to come. MacPhee, less conscientious, ran around her in circles, tangling his lead between her legs and yapping, for a walk deferred makes a dog's heart sick.

Michael came out on his way to the post office and pronounced Olwen probably concussed. He noticed what Rose hadn't, that she had a cut on the back of her head which was bleeding into the snow.

'Shall I give her some Rescue Remedy?' Rose asked him. 'Or would my own herbal elixir be better?'

'Have either of them got any booze in them? Because if not I reckon she'll spit them out.'

Rose thought that a dreadful way for a doctor to talk. It just went to show how much better a practitioner of alternative medicine would be in this situation. The ambulance came after ten minutes and two paramedics, a man and a woman, took Olwen away to hospital. Rose waved cheerily to her as they moved off and then she took McPhee round the block, eagerly anticipating as she picked her way through ice and dirty snow and puddles how, when she got back, she would tell Marius what Michael had said.

A taxi took Stuart to the Tesco and brought him home with a back seat full of drink, crisps, nuts, cheese and biscuits. He had also bought two hundred cigarettes. It was expensive, adding greatly to the cost of this party which now he dreaded, though he had no intention of offering cigarettes to the guests. His little fridge was too small to take more than two bottles of champagne and two of white wine at a time. He could put some of it out in the snow if any snow was still there by Saturday. His mother, who phoned five minutes after he got back, thought it would be.

'I'm sorry, darling, but there's no way Daddy and I can come all the way to where you live in this weather.' Annabel Font always said 'where you live' to avoid naming Stuart's suburb. 'We've had such an enormous lot of snow out here. Of course you do in the country.'

Loughton might be on the edge of Epping Forest but it hadn't been 'in the country' for about seventy years. Stuart let it pass. He was so enormously relieved that his parents wouldn't be at the party that he had immediately been put in an ebullient mood. 'Oh, don't worry about that,' he said. 'There'll be another time.'

'Well, I should hope there would, Stuart. I'm quite surprised that you haven't asked us before. After all, you've been there for three months – or is it four? A long time anyway.'

Stuart said nothing, his jolly mood waning. 'Any more thoughts on a job?' his mother said.

'I've told you, I'm not thinking about jobs until at least April.'

'That attitude is all very well in times of financial stability, Stuart – I'm quoting Daddy – but it's positively dangerous now. Do you know what Maureen Rivers told me? Her son wrote a hundred and seventy-three applications before he got his present job. Of course, it's a very good job.'

Stuart could hear 'Nessun dorma' playing in his bedroom.

Claudia. He said goodbye to his mother as soon as he could, lit a cigarette and went back to the wine and the food. The table up against the front window was the best place to set it out, he thought, and let the guests come into the kitchen for drinks. Where would he put the glasses? He suddenly realised, standing there at the window, that he only possessed about six glasses. He would have to buy some – more expense. Where would it all end? At this thought, this unanswerable question, he looked up and saw, on the opposite side of Kenilworth Avenue, the beautiful girl. She was walking along with her father a little way up to the left, coming in this direction. Party, drinks and glasses forgotten, he pulled on the heavy sweater he had just taken off and plunged out of the flat, out of the lobby, into the icy-cold air. The girl and her father had disappeared.

Apart from the blow to the back of her head, there appeared to be very little wrong with Olwen. Her concussion was short-lived and there was no permanent damage. Her step-daughter Margaret came to see her in the hospital. Olwen had no memory of telling anyone at Lichfield House that she had a stepdaughter or indeed any relatives but Margaret said she had had a phone call from someone called Katie.

'When you come out of here,' she said in a tone and form of words expecting the answer no, 'I don't suppose you'd think of coming to us for a few days.'

'Not really,' said Olwen, then recollecting that this was what she said only to her neighbours, 'No, thanks. I shall be OK at home.'

Margaret and her brother had so much resented Olwen coming into their lives when Margaret was eight and Richard six, trying to take the place of their dead mother and sleeping in their father's bedroom, that they had done their best to make her life so miserable that she would leave. They succeeded in making her life miserable but she didn't leave. She stayed because she wouldn't be beaten and because, if she didn't love Bill, he certainly seemed to love her. She gave up her job and stayed at home to look after the children. They were rude to her and even physically violent, they stole from Woolworths; when she was eleven Margaret told her father Olwen had a boyfriend she had seen her kissing and when she was fourteen that Olwen had sexually assaulted her. How much of this their father believed Olwen never knew but his attitude towards her changed. He told her to get another job – being with the children was obviously bad for her. So Olwen went back to work and almost as soon as she did so Margaret and Richard ceased to be the children from hell (as she called them to herself) and began to behave like civilised beings. Both went off to university and then to homes of their own and when they came home, as they occasionally did, they behaved to her as if they had always had a pleasant and equable relationship. But Olwen had had enough. At the age of fifty-eight she asked for a divorce and got her decree absolute on the day she became sixty.

All those years, for the sake of her marriage and for the children, she had severely controlled her drinking, having no more than a couple of glasses of wine a day. But when Bill went away, as he occasionally did on his own to visit his sister and her husband in Lancashire, she binge-drank for the whole weekend. The term wasn't current at the time and she didn't call it that. She had no name for it. It was just the time when she drank all day until she passed out and, coming to next day, drank again until nightfall. As far as she knew, Bill never suspected.

But when she was alone again, living on her own and with her two pensions, with a sigh of relief that was very nearly happiness, she had settled into a permanent binge drinking and thus ending up here, in this hospital. Margaret knew nothing about her alcoholism, none of them ever had. Like hundreds of people, she had slipped in the snow and injured herself. But she never had any sort of accident before and probably never would again – or not until another bad winter. Margaret thought herself exceptionally unselfish and caring to have come to visit her at all.

'Well, I expect you'll be all right on your own, won't you?'

'I'll be OK,' said Olwen. 'I'm going to have a sleep now.'

It was only by composing herself for sleep and closing her eyes that she could handle this terrible deprivation, because in the past it was only while she was asleep that she wasn't drinking. She thought about Mr Ali's shop. That girl had bought wine from him. Did he also sell spirits? Olwen thought of all the corner shops she had ever been in in various parts of London. The ones that sold wine had also sold spirits. She held on to that, trying to sleep. A different ambulance from the one which had brought her took her home on Saturday morning. It wasn't really an ambulance at all but something called a people carrier which, appropriately enough, was full of people all being dropped off at various locations in north London. Olwen asked the driver if he would drop her at Mr Ali's shop.

'Can't do that, darling,' said the driver. 'My job is to take you home, right?'

'I'll only be a minute.'

In not at all a 'darling' kind of voice, he said, 'Sorry, darling, but it's no.'

The other people in the bus made fidgeting grumbling noises in fear of his changing his mind. He got down at Lichfield House and helped Olwen up the still-unswept front path, on to which more snow, rain, hail and sleet had fallen since she was last there. He took her as far as the lift, summoned it, checked she still had her key and saw her off up to Flat 6. The lift door opened and there stood Molly Flint with a long-haired boy who had a ring in his nose and a stud in one eyebrow, waiting to get into it.

'Not really' was useless for this urgent request. 'If you're going out would you go to Mr Ali's and see if he's got any vodka? Gin will do if he hasn't got vodka.'

The boy was shaking his head furiously and Molly said, 'Sorry, I can't,' thinking of Sophie who had never got her five pounds. 'I can't. I'm late.'

Carrying two boxes, each containing six wine glasses from John Lewis, Stuart was on his way to meet Claudia in a Starbucks. He had responded to her latest message, cravenly denied that any of the others had reached him, and faced up to this meeting which had been arranged for a long time. His only stipulation was that it shouldn't be at his flat.

None of this was enough to save him from the wrath of Freddy Livorno. Doubting that Stuart had taken his warning sufficiently to heart, Freddy put his little gizmo back among the dried flowers. Claudia's call to Stuart was rapturous. She must be in a bad way, Freddy thought furiously, if she was that excited about meeting her lover in a coffee shop. Could she come to his party tomorrow night?

'We'll see about that,' Freddy said aloud.

CHAPTER EIGHT

The beautiful girl must live somewhere in the area. He had seen her walking with her father along Kenilworth Avenue. Of course, that might only mean that they were visiting friends in the neighbourhood, but that a friend's house was nearby would hardly account for her shopping at the newsagent's on the roundabout. No, she and her family lived locally. Enquiries among his neighbours and perhaps at the shops in Kenilworth Parade would surely locate her.

Stuart was thinking about this all the time he was having coffee with Claudia at the Euston Road Starbucks. Afterwards, he could barely have repeated a word she had said, though he vaguely remembered something about her falling in love with him. What he did recall was her asking, quite humbly and pleadingly for her and for the second time, if she could come to his party.

'Oh, all right, I suppose so,' he said very ungraciously. He was surprised to learn that there are some women, and Claudia was evidently among them, who like you more and *want* you more if you treat them unkindly. It was a revelation. After they had parted he was thinking that he must put this into practice in the future but not, of course, with the beautiful girl. If he was ever lucky enough to find her – and he must, he must – he would never be cruel to her, but treasure her, cherish her, treat her like the exquisite jewel she was. He had been home no more than five minutes and was smoking his first cigarette of the day, when Claudia phoned him on his landline to say that she'd definitely come to his party. She was longing for it.

It was a fine clear day but very cold again. Little patches of frost lingered in shady spots. He pushed the long table close up against the window, set out some plates on it and arranged the new floral paper napkins in two neat piles. Richenda had told him he should have napkins and that the ones he already had, patterned with Christmas trees, wouldn't do. More people were about than usual, doing their emergency shopping before the next snowfall, forecast for the following night. Wally Scurlock was coming up the path, carrying a small bottle of something in a translucent red plastic bag. On the doorstep Stuart saw him encounter Rose Preston-Jones, taking McPhee for his walk. He went back to the kitchen, made himself a large mug of hot chocolate and began stuffing as many bottles of champagne and wine into the fridge as it would take. The coldest place on the exterior of his flat was the windowsill of the spare bedroom where some optimistic builder had fixed a window box. Stuart put the remaining two champagne bottles and four of wine into the box. They would stay cold there. Proud of his resourcefulness, he lit another cigarette and contemplated himself in the spare-room mirror. There was no doubt that a handsome man's sexiness was enhanced by a cigarette. He posed, first with the cigarette hanging from his mouth, then holding it negligently some few inches from his face. It was no wonder really that Claudia was in love with him.

*

Without a drink, Olwen had made it through the night. That is, she was still alive. She found some stale bread at the back of the fridge, removed the pale blue mould and ate a slice of it with the scrapings from the bottom of a marmalade jar. There was nothing to wash it down with but water and when she had drunk that she was sick.

If asked (by that inner enquirer to whom the secrets of all hearts may be told), she would have said she was afraid of nothing unless it was being denied access to drink. But she was afraid this morning. Ice lay on the puddles on the path. The pavements weren't being gritted. The whole country was running out of salt which, apparently, was an essential ingredient of grit. Next time she fell she would break something, she was sure of that, and breaking something meant only one thing to her: many weeks of drink deprivation. Wearing her fur coat, she made her way down in the lift and, standing at the top of the stairs to the basement, called out to Wally Scurlock. Eventually, when she had called a dozen times, he came up.

The modicum of respect with which the Scurlocks favoured the residents of the four blocks wasn't extended to those they deemed unworthy. These included a couple in Hereford who lay in bed each day till noon, a man in Ludlow they suspected of being a transvestite and, of course, Olwen.

'Yes, what is it?' Wally came wearily up the stairs.

'Will you go down to Mr Ali's and get me a bottle of vodka? Or gin would do.' Olwen realised some politeness was required. 'Please?'

'It'll cost you.'

For a moment she thought he was referring to the price of the vodka but it soon dawned on her that he meant his fee. She always carried a lot of money on her which she withdrew, two hundred at a time, from the cash machine outside the post office in Kenilworth Parade. 'Five pounds?'

'Ten,' said Wally. 'I want it in advance.'

He wasn't long about it and within a quarter of an hour the treasured bottle was standing on the draining board in her kitchen. Until that moment Olwen hadn't been certain that Mr Ali sold spirits, but this was confirmation. Still, for the first time since she had moved into Lichfield House she was coming to understand that she would have to cut down. She must make this bottle last her until Monday by which time the ice might have gone. The first glorious glassful poured, she sat down on the sofa and decided she would go to Stuart's party. At first she hadn't even considered going but, when she came to think of it, drink would be there, possibly only wine, but four or five glasses of it would eke out the vodka . . .

Stuart had asked the neighbours opposite, putting notes through the doors of three houses. This was not because he wanted Duncan Yeardon, the Pembers or Ms Jones and Mr Lee at his party but because this way it was possible that he might find out from one of them where the beautiful girl lived. He had had a reply only from Duncan but perhaps it wasn't done round here to write acceptances to a drinks party invitation.

The three girls were in two minds whether to go to the party but the bitter cold was getting them down. Whether to go and thus miss meeting friends (who probably wouldn't turn up) at a wine bar in the Haymarket was discussed by Molly and Sophie throughout the day. Noor, of course, could come and go as she pleased. The prince would pick her up in his white Lexus.

'Stuart's very attractive, isn't he?' said Molly.

Sophie lifted her shoulders. 'Yeah, but I think he's gay.'

'Is he?'

'Every time you see him in the lobby he's looking at himself in that mirror. Should we take a bottle?'

'If you want. Mr Ali's got Moldovan Chardonnay at three ninety-nine.'

The Constantines were going. They had said they would and not to turn up when they had said they would was against their principles. The party was due to begin at seven thirty and Rose Preston-Jones had invited Marius Potter down for an early supper. Sorrel soup began the meal, the main course was a walnut pilaf with sprouts and chestnuts and the pudding grapefruit yogurt. McPhee climbed onto Marius's lap and licked his left hand.

Rose had asked for a reading of the *sortes* before they went across to the party and Marius had brought *Paradise Lost* down with him. His eyes on Rose, thinking how very much prettier she looked than those who plastered their faces with make-up, he opened the book at random. The sentence he read slightly embarrassed him but it made his heart beat faster too, and there was no escape from reading it aloud.

'"Henceforth an individual solace dear: / Part of my soul I seek thee, and thee claim / My other half."'

It was foolish to feel awkward of course. Rose had blushed becomingly to match her name. His own embarrassment would have been less but for those Hackney memories. When the colour came into her cheeks she looked more like that girl of long ago so that he could hardly understand how he hadn't been able to place her when first he moved in.

'Let's go across to Stuart's, shall we?'

Claudia was the first to arrive. Must have been the only time in her life she'd actually been early for anything, Stuart thought. She congratulated him on the window-box refrigerator, opened a bottle of champagne and helped herself. She of course had brought nothing. He would have been amazed if she had. Marius and Rose came next, then Mr Lee and Ms Jones who were called Ken and Moira, complaining about the cold. The sister of one of them had skidded on the ice in her new BMW that morning, the car was a write-off and if she hadn't been wearing her seat belt . . . Duncan Yeardon arrived as Moira was describing the accident and contributed experiences of his own when he worked for the AA or the RAC or something like that back in the dark ages. Stuart started worrying when they all rejected wine in favour of sparkling water in case he hadn't got enough.

'They'll just have to have tap,' said Claudia, who had taken over the running of the party as if she were his wife.

No fear of this in Olwen's case. She homed in at once on to the Sauvignon, pouring herself a tumblerful. Eyebrows were raised at the sight of her, for she was wearing a dress. Memories of the few parties she had attended, mostly the office kind, had come back to her a couple of hours earlier as she reached about halfway down the vodka bottle. She had worn a dress to those parties, she still had that dress. It was in a cupboard some-where. The flats in Lichfield House were well appointed with cupboards and she opened hers one after another. Rubbish fell out, old newspapers, unwashed clothes, dozens if not hundreds of empty bottles, green, brown, clear glass, a single blue one that must, once, have contained Bombay Sapphire gin. They rolled across the floor.

The last cupboard held clothes, the ones she had worn before her tracksuit days. At first she couldn't see the dress and, fumbling along the shelf at the top in case she had rolled it up and stuffed it there, her hand came in contact with a bottle. A full bottle of Absolut vodka. Tears of joy came into her eyes and ran down her cheeks.

She remembered then. She had hidden it there in case of just such an emergency as had come about in these past freezing days – hidden it and forgotten it. For a moment the tears were also for her anguish when she had been utterly deprived and no one had helped her, but finding the dress, black, ancient, in desperate need of dry-cleaning, its hem coming down at the back, put an end to crying. A long swig of vodka once the dress was over her head, and she was off down in the lift to celebrate her find at Stuart's party.

The tumbler of wine in her hand didn't stop her helping herself to champagne when Claudia came round with the tray and they all toasted Stuart's 'happy house'. By that time Jock and Kathy Pember had come. Molly and Sophie with Molly's boyfriend arrived late but this, as Sophie's father used to say, was 'par for the course'. A good deal of the champagne had gone before they got there but their Moldovan Chardonnay was received gratefully by Stuart who kissed all three of them, thus convincing Molly that he wasn't gay, after all. Further confirmation, to her dismay, was provided by Claudia who clung closely to him, kissing his neck.

The Constantines drank white wine, liberally diluted with water from the kitchen tap. They talked to each other and occasionally to Marius Potter and Rose Preston-Jones. Rose said she wanted to ask Michael something. Michael groaned inwardly as people were always asking him something, usually what they were to do about their weight or their headaches or their sinuses. Rose, though, had a question which had nothing to do with ill health. Due no doubt to a diet of *Paradise Lost*, she wanted to know if it was true what someone had told her, that men had fewer ribs than women on account of Eve being made from the one taken out of Adam's side.

Suppressing an urge to scream and stamp, Michael said gravely that it wasn't true. Men and women had the same number of ribs. He was watching Olwen with concern and already longed to act like a conscientious barman and say, 'I think you've had enough.'

Until now he hadn't quite realised how deep into alcoholism she was. He had seen the bottles she carried in but had no way of knowing how long they lasted or how many people had shared them with her. She hadn't been drunk when she arrived, but then she was probably never drunk in the usual sense of the word. You might equally say that she was *always* drunk. He had been near enough to her to detect that she smelt – no, stank – of gin. He had read somewhere that in the past women like her used camphor to mask the smell. She smelt of mothballs, the camphor was on her clothes, but not enough to cover the heady odour of spirits. In the past half-hour she had refilled her tumbler of wine three times. His thought that she had had enough was an understatement. But, anyway, you can't go up to a fellow guest at a party and say that. He fixed her with a disapproving eye but, as he had feared, she took no notice and poured another glass of wine.

Among the latecomers were Jack with his girlfriend and Martin. Stuart had never met Hilary before. As much a connoisseur of women's looks as he was an admirer of his own, he was very disappointed in her appearance. No make-up, hair in need of a wash and figure in need of a diet. He was surprised at Jack, but perhaps someone who looked like him couldn't be very choosy. They had brought lager, he and Martin, which Stuart thought, but didn't say, would very likely never be drunk.

'Is that stain blood?' were almost the first words Jack said.

Hilary gave a little scream.

'Of course not,' said Stuart shortly.

It was just after nine. Noor arrived at five past with the prince who was wearing a white silk turban with a feather stuck on it with a jewelled pin. They each brought a bottle of very good claret. The party, Claudia whispered to Stuart, linking her arm in his, was going well. People were enjoying themselves. The Constantines and Duncan Yeardon had also brought bottles of wine and there was no shortage of drink. Everyone – or those who thought about them at all – had given up on the Scurlocks. This brought a certain amount of relief as no one knew how to address them, still less what to talk to them about. Just as Stuart was deciding that they had changed their minds, they arrived, Richenda in a minidress and knee-high boots, Wally greeting everyone with these words: 'Now I know I'm only the caretaker and I hope I show a proper respect to one and all but when we meet on a social occasion like this one to which Mr Font has been good enough to invite us, I suppose no one will object if we use Christian names. No one object? Right. Thanks very much, Stuart, for asking us.' And he set down another bottle of Mr Ali's Moldavan Chardonnay on the table.

'Come into the bedroom,' Claudia said rather haughtily to Stuart as if she intended to discuss with him in private the manners of his latest guests.

Lamblike, Stuart went. Almost before the door was closed she had seized him in her arms and clamped her mouth on his. Resistance was impossible – and ridiculous. But he had no intention of letting her get him into bed. Not with all those people a mere matter of feet away.

'Later,' he was saying, because he couldn't think of anything else to say, when he heard a door slam in the street. This was followed by footsteps pounding up the path. Claudia moved a little away from him. He stood very still. The footsteps made an unnaturally loud noise as if the man who was crashing across the floor of the lobby intended a disturbance. Stuart's front door received a kick, then it burst open, smashing against the wall and causing one of the women to scream.

The unmistakable voice of Freddy Livorno, deep, strong and very loud, said, 'Where is he? Where is my wife's lover?'

'Oh God,' Claudia whimpered. 'Oh God, I don't believe it.'

'I do.' Stuart wanted to get under the bed and hide. But it was no good, he had to go out there.

Freddy was standing just inside the front door which had closed behind him, brandishing a cudgel thick as a tree branch. He stood like some hero of ancient days, Belisarius perhaps or Joshua, a huge man grasping a lethal weapon. The party guests stared. Olwen took a more than usually huge swig of her drink. When he saw Stuart, Freddy advanced a little, taking perhaps two strides forward. He had left a couple of square yards of empty space between himself and the door into the hallway and Moira and Ken took advantage of this by slipping out of the flat in silence. Molly and Sophie were far too fascinated, not to say hoping for better things to come, to move from their corner where they had been gossiping with Marius and Rose. The expression on Wally's face, compounded of fear and fascination, was that of a man who has come for a normal sort of booze-up and found himself precipitated into a Roman orgy.

Perhaps because he had an audience, and he always enjoyed being looked at, Stuart approached a little nearer to Freddy and said, 'How dare you burst your way in here – you're trespassing.'

'I'll trespass a bloody sight more. Where's my wife?'

'In the bedroom.'

'In the *bedroom*? You dare say that to me?!' Also perhaps enjoying being the cynosure of all eyes, Freddy addressed the company. 'Ladies and gentlemen!' The words were absurd but no one laughed. 'Ladies and gentlemen, I don't know who you are or why you're here, but this man, your host, this miscreant and villain, is an adulterer who has been shagging my wife.'

95

This raised gasps from Kathy Pember and Duncan. 'I could have used a stronger word but out of respect for your feelings I abstained. You will want to know what I intend to do. I will tell you. I intend to kill this man.'

Without a word, Marius Potter slipped away, unnoticed by Freddy, keeping to the rear of the spectators until he was out of the front door. Alone in the lobby he did something which, in his hippie days when he despised the 'filth', the 'fuzz', he would have scorned even to consider. He was old now and things had changed. He dialled 999 and asked for the police. Now he had done his duty, should he go back upstairs to his flat? No, because it would be most unchivalrous to leave Rose there, possibly in danger. While he was thinking about it, Duncan Yeardon came out of Flat 1 and with an embarrassed smile at Marius slipped out of the automatic doors into the night, followed by the Pembers. He had left Stuart's front door ajar. A loud scream from inside fetched Marius through it.

In his absence various things had happened. The girls from Flat 5 and Olwen had shut themselves in the kitchen. Claudia was nowhere to be seen but was probably still in the bedroom. It was Richenda who had screamed when her husband, attempting to intervene between Freddy and Stuart, had been pushed to the ground by a great shove from Freddy. Stuart stepped over him, said to Claudia's husband, 'Now, listen, we can talk about this. Look what happened last time. We both got hurt.'

'You alone will be hurt this time.' Freddy picked up the heavy glass celery jar which Stuart had transferred to the mantelpiece. He thrust it into Richenda's arms with a 'Here, take that. Put it somewhere. If you don't want to witness a murder.' To the rest of the company who remained he said, 'You had better leave now.' He stepped aside to let them pass and when Wally, limping, had moved off into the lobby, turned swiftly, raised his stick and brought it down with vicious strength on Stuart's head. Or tried to. It struck his upper arm instead with a dreadful sickening sound of breaking bone. Stuart screamed, 'Not my face, not my face!'

Claudia came out of the bedroom, running to him.

'Get out of the way,' Freddy yelled and struck Stuart again, hitting the back of his neck this time and felling him. He dropped the stick and rubbed his hands together as at a job satisfactorily done.

Stuart sat up, Claudia kneeling beside him. 'He's broken my spine,' he shouted. 'I'll never walk again.' With that, he struggled to get to his feet and stood there, swaying, holding on to the furniture. 'My arm's broken.'

'Yes, but not much else is, more's the pity.' Freddy picked up his stick and surveyed the room. Everyone but Stuart and Claudia had gone. 'However, that will do for now. Next time, if there is a next time, I shall kill him.' He turned to his wife. 'Come along,' he said. 'Home, you.'

She obeyed him. As they were getting into his car, parked in Kenilworth Parade, a screaming of sirens and flickering of blue lights announced the arrival of the police. 'Let's get outta here,' said Freddy, smiling.

CHAPTER NINE

'What's that stain?' the younger of the two policemen asked.

'It's not blood,' said Stuart.

The policeman didn't say he would be the best judge of that but he looked it. They had been told something in the nature of an affray was going on in this flat but there was no one here except the owner, though plenty of evidence in a full ashtray, empty and half-empty glasses, mangled cheeses and biscuit crumbs that visitors had been here. Stuart had told them he didn't want to press charges.

'Sure of that?'

He hadn't been at all sure but he had thought about it while they went over the flat. If he pressed charges any possible witnesses had disappeared. Claudia had gone off with Freddy without even asking how he felt or saying goodbye. He, Stuart, would look foolish if this got into the papers as it would. It would be a different matter if Freddy were to be sent to prison for ten years, say. The most likely outcome would be that Freddy got a suspended sentence or even a couple of weeks' community service. Seeing that he was a solicitor, that would probably mean spending a similar time working for Citizens' Advice for free.

'I'm sure of that,' he said.

'That arm needs seeing to,' said the younger one, passing him the phone so that he could call an ambulance.

In his day, Duncan thought, it would have been called 'conduct likely to lead to a breach of the peace', but what it was now he had no idea. He was very glad he had escaped when he had. Among other causes for relief was the warmth inside his own house. Stuart's flat wasn't exactly cold but you could call it cool, the temperature probably no more than, say, sixty-eight. Duncan had never managed to convert Fahrenheit into Celsius (or centigrade as they used to call it when he was young) without doing a complicated sum that involved multiplying something by something and taking away 32. He didn't know what the temperature was in here, he had no thermometer, but he guessed at least eighty. And that was fine, that was what you wanted when it was minus five outside.

The police had come, he had seen them arrive from his window, and, standing there in the glorious warmth while a thin sleet fell against the windows, he expected to see them emerge with Freddy handcuffed. But nothing of that sort happened. They came out alone just as an ambulance arrived. Then Stuart appeared, pushed along in a wheelchair, his left arm in a sling made out of a Burberry scarf. Duncan recognised the check pattern even through the rain and snow mixture. Why did you have to be in a wheelchair when it was your *arm* that was injured? Some health and safety rubbish, he supposed. One thing was sure, that young man was certainly not gay. Very much the reverse, in fact.

It had been an exciting evening but now it seemed to be all over. Twenty past ten, time for bed really. Duncan drew the curtains, keeping more of the lovely heat in. He bolted the front door, went into the kitchen to fetch himself a glass of water in case he got thirsty in the night and, pausing at the foot of the stairs, noticed something unexpected. The wallpaper was coming off, just beginning to peel away from the staircase wall. Would heat do that? He supposed it would. It was a sign to him to get rid of the wallpaper, he had never liked it, and redecorate the place. Do it himself in what they used to call distemper but didn't any more, one of those new whites, apple white, almond white, or maybe the absolutely pure white he really preferred. He went on up the stairs to bed.

I n the Lichfield House gossip ratings, Olwen's drinking took second place to the repeated turning over, thrashing and dissecting of the assault on Stuart Font. Richenda Scurlock said to her husband that she didn't mind how many sexual partners single people had, that didn't hurt anyone, but when you were married it was a different thing.

'Not your business,' said Wally, who was still limping from a badly bruised leg sustained when Freddy pushed him over. 'You ought to be thankful they don't want you for a witness.'

'They don't want you either.'

'No, thank God.'

Wally was thinking of the sites he visited. He was innocent, he thought, he had done nothing, and what Stuart Font got up to was nothing to do with him, but suppose the police had come down here, suppose they had just looked at his computer and because they were experts been able to . . . They hadn't and they weren't going to. Thank God. He didn't want the police anywhere near these flats. Who had called them? he wondered. Some interfering busybody, probably that Dr Constantine – if he was a doctor.

Richenda must have said something to the three girls because they seemed disappointed at not having a chance of going into court. 'But if a guy goes into another guy's place,' said Molly, 'and, you know, like beats him up with a stick, he can't just get away with it, can he?'

'Apparently he can,' said Marius Potter, not sorry that no one had asked him who called the police.

Halfway through Sunday morning Katie Constantine said to her husband, 'Isn't it lovely, Michael, now you've qualified and something like this happens you can say to everyone, "I'm a doctor!"?'

'Except that I don't feel like a doctor because I haven't got a job. You can't be a sort of disembodied doctor. I wouldn't even dare say I was one.' He sighed and went back to reading all the letters he had had in response to the article he had written about St John's wort being useless as a cure for depression. There had been even more emails, most of them unfavourable and several abusive. All troubled him because, like most people, he hated being vilified and called names in print, but the one that frightened him was from a professor of psychiatric medicine at some university. The professor pointed out that Michael's piece was inaccurate because recent research had shown that St John's wort did ameliorate certain types of depression if used with care and therefore could no longer be called alternative medicine. This was worse than the trichologist. There was also an email from the features editor enquiring if he would like to respond, in other words defend himself. Michael hadn't answered this and didn't intend to because he had no defence.

Stuart's arm had been put in plaster. Weeks would pass before he could use it again. He told his mother the party had been a success but he had slipped on the ice next day and broken his arm.

'But there isn't any ice,' she said. 'The rain has washed it all away. Round here, at any rate. I suppose it may be different where you live.'

Nothing had been heard from Claudia. Stuart wondered a little about how Freddy's visit of Saturday evening had come about. Had Claudia *told* him she was coming to his flat? Or had he overheard her phoning him? He wondered but not for long. However you looked at it, he had had a lucky escape. If Freddy's aim hadn't been so poor, he, Stuart, would be dead by now.

On Monday morning one of the girls from Flat 5 called on him to ask if there was anything she could do to help. It was Molly Flint but he didn't know that or had forgotten and didn't bother to ask. Molly weighed about a stone more than she should have done and in his mind he called her 'the fat one'.

'You could unload the dishwasher,' he said. 'I managed to fill it but taking the stuff out and putting it away is hard with only one arm.'

'It must be. Where shall I put these glasses?'

'They're new. Maybe you could find a place for them in one of those cupboards. And when you've done that you could make me a mug of hot chocolate. Don't worry about the cleaning. Richenda will do that.'

Molly put all the glasses away very tidily, reloaded the dishwasher with the plates Stuart had left lying about, made the chocolate and brought it to him with some Duchy Original lemon biscuits on a plate.

'Oh, thanks,' said Stuart. 'Tell me something. Have you seen a very beautiful girl around here, Thai or Vietnamese or something, about twenty, always about with her dad? I wondered if you knew where she lived.'

'No, sorry, I don't,' said Molly sadly.

'Pity. I think I'll go and lie down now. I've got a bit of a headache where that animal hit me.'

Claudia hadn't phoned because Freddy had broken her jaw. Or it felt as if he had. On Sunday morning he maintained total silence, making no reply to her taunts and indignant questioning. Then, suddenly, he turned to face her and fetched her a blow across the face.

'You don't want to press charges,' he said to her while he was driving her to the A & E department of the nearest hospital. 'When they ask you who did this you reply, like Desdemona, 'Nobody, I myself, farewell.' That is, you write it down since you won't be able to speak for a bit.'

Claudia began to cry.

'In my opinion,' said Freddy, 'things were a lot better when domestic violence was a private matter between husband and wife and the police just took it for granted.'

This was not the first time Mr Ali was visiting Saudi Arabia but this time he was taking his eldest son with him and there was no one to run the shop. Olwen, arriving with her carrier bags, found it closed. She shuffled back to the post office where there was a telephone kiosk. This kiosk had several times been broken into by vandals and the phone cable pulled out of the wall but at the moment it was intact. Olwen asked the man behind the counter for the Yellow Pages. A receipt left behind by a customer served to make notes on with the pencil attached to the wall by a length of string.

Making phone calls requesting things or responding to requests was something she had been doing for the various firms who had employed her all her life. There was nothing new in that. What was new was the attitude of the wine shops. The first two she called wanted a credit card number plus expiry date before they would deliver anything. Olwen hadn't brought her card with her. At the third number she called they suggested she come in to select her gin and vodka but that was impossible. They were in Edgware. The woman in the fourth shop said they never delivered anything.

People who came into the post office looked at her curiously, amazed to see someone who apparently had neither landline nor mobile. On her way back to Lichfield House, she met Wally Scurlock coming back from St Ebba's churchyard. The weather was improving, the schools were open again and, while ostensibly tidying up Clara Carbury's grave, he had spent a pleasant twenty minutes watching the pupils of Kenilworth Primary School at play.

'Would you get me a bottle of gin and one of vodka from the Tesco?' Olwen said to him. 'I'll pay you.'

'I should just about think you would, madam.'

'Ten pounds.'

'Twenty,' said Wally. 'It'll have to wait till this afternoon. I haven't got time to go back up there now.'

Passing the front windows of Hereford House, he had seen his wife plying the vacuum cleaner in one of the ground-floor flats. This sight brought him the addict's inner surge of excitement at the prospect of being alone to indulge his vice. What he had been doing at St Ebba's or sometimes did at the pensioner's tower window was self-indulgent entertainment – but no more than that. It paled beside the near ecstasy of watching those sites. While the schools had been closed and when Richenda was cleaning flats here or in one of the other blocks, the computer had drawn him as a magnet draws a needle, initially a soft tug, then a violent attraction that clamped him to the screen.

Once he wouldn't have believed himself capable of finding one site after another with such expertise. But he had learned that nothing teaches you a skill like a burning desire to acquire that knowledge. On the icy days when going out at all was a chore to be avoided, he soon found ways to access more graphic and *harder* films, permitting himself to see activities he had never dreamed possible. The playful pupils of Kenilworth Primary couldn't compare with this.

But Wally was not entirely without a conscience. He dealt with it mainly by his fear of the law and also by telling himself – incongruously – that what he did was harmless. These were photographs, these were videos, it wasn't *real*. Your actual police (as he put it to himself) coming into the building had frightened him more than he let on to himself at first. Far more than he let on to Richenda. He had been waking up in the night in a sweat, imagining what might have happened, what they might have done. This fear sent him scurrying back to the grave in St Ebba's churchyard where, as he squatted down, shears in hand, by Clara Carbury's grave, he told himself this was better than the computer, this was entirely innocent, no more than a childless man indulging his love of children by watching their games. But he knew it wasn't that and it wasn't better.

Now, for the first time since Stuart's party and the police visit, with that familiar and wonderful feeling of breathless anticipation, he sat down at the computer, pressed the start key and then moved the mouse on to the one for Internet Explorer.

'Other joy / To me is lost. Then let me not let pass / Occasion which now smiles.' This was Marius Potter's *sortes* reading for 13 February. The occasion referred to could be St Valentine's Day which would fall next day. He had thought of buying a card and had taken a look at those on offer at the Kenilworth Parade newsagent's but they were all so vulgar, hearts with arrows through them, pink bows, glasses of champagne, bunches of roses. Even these last were unsuitable to send to Rose. Perhaps he should send flowers and then visit her on this auspicious day.

He was going to tell her. He had made up his mind.

But it wasn't so easy, he found himself thinking a few hours later. Suppose her memory of their night together was different from his. If she looked back to it at all it might be that she remembered it with distaste and regret. Probably, like the rest of them in the commune, she had been promiscuous, free and easy, doing no one any harm by her behaviour and none to herself. But she had only stayed there for one night and though she had seemed to enjoy herself as much as he had, there was her rapid departure next morning to be taken into consideration. It was almost as if she had fled from him and from that house, the scene of a yielding to temptation brought about only by the use of an unfamiliar drug.

And now he confessed to himself that time had brought many changes in his own attitude to life. It was bound to have done. With a lifetime of teaching behind him, he was still the intellectual of those days, loving the classics, devoted to poetry, still a socialist, a campaigner against nuclear weapons, a health freak and advocate of alternative medicine. But the view he took of sexual matters had altered radically. To him now the idea of having sex with a woman one had just met was nauseating. Indeed, most sexual encounters seemed distasteful and he could barely remember when the last one he had experiencd had taken place. Years ago certainly and then with a woman who had come back out of his past and expressed a wish to resume their relationship. It hadn't worked, it was over almost as soon as it had begun.

But he could conceive of a love affair with the right woman and he was half ashamed to confess that he saw this in a romantic light. No doubt it was the result of reading so much poetry. He imagined himself meeting someone who would *love* him and, smiling derisively to himself, thought that she would have to love him, for to look at he was now far from an object of desire. But it was impossible and would never be. He and Rose must continue as they were, friendly acquaintances – perhaps a little more than that – and he would never remind her of what had happened thirty years before.

He wasn't going to tell her, after all. Not now, not tomorrow, not ever.

So his idea of sending her a dozen red roses on the following morning must come to nothing. He would go down, ask her out for coffee, or more probably green tea, and say nothing about its being St Valentine's Day.

CHAPTER TEN

Stuart dared to venture out now that the pavements were free of ice but he found that a broken arm – though less of a hindrance than a broken leg – inhibits walking to a certain extent. He mostly stayed at home, feeling sorry for himself. There had been no word from Claudia. In fact, 'Nessun dorma' was seldom heard in Flat 1 these days. Only his mother, who knew nothing of the fracas which had ended the party, still called him and she preferred the landline. He guessed that Martin and Jack, or more likely Jack's girlfriend Hilary, had been inclined to rethink their friendship with him after hearing Freddy Livorno, particularly the bits about him being a villain and a shagger of his wife. Nothing had been heard from them and no calls had been made from the Pembers or Duncan Yeardon to thank him for inviting them. Perhaps they were embarrassed. Molly Flint came regularly to make him cups of chocolate and wash dishes and run errands, and when he went out to pick up his post he had encountered Marius Potter who uttered his usual formal greeting. But he had the inescapable feeling that Marius's smile was amused rather than sympathetic.

*

Taking a taxi to a wine shop in Cricklewood, getting the driver to wait and then drive her back home had grave drawbacks. Due to her lack of a phone, Olwen had to use the post office phone box or hail a taxi in the street, not easy in Kenilworth Avenue, and once one had been secured, get the driver or the shop proprietor to carry a crate of spirit bottles back to the cab. She did it once but with great difficulty and when the crate had been deposited in the Lichfield House lobby, she had to ask Mr Scurlock to carry it up in the lift for her. The effort of it, the energy it demanded and the strain of all that talking and asking and pleading was almost too much for her. When she was back in her flat, the first bottle opened and the first glass poured, she lay down on her sofa, groaning with exhaustion and admitted to herself she was too weak for this, she could never do it again.

Wally Scurlock had charged her ten pounds to carry the crate up. That plus the taxi fare there and back and the waiting came to twice as much as it cost to employ him to go up to Tesco and bring her back two bottles of gin. Of course she got more by the crate but maybe she could persuade the caretaker to bring three bottles at the time.

'Not for twenty bloody quid I couldn't, madam. I'm not like some, I haven't got no car. I have to carry it and it's nearly pulled my arms out of their sockets.'

Olwen hated having to speak to him. She hated having to speak to anyone. 'Thirty pounds for three bottles, then.'

'Correct me if I'm wrong but I thought I'd explained I can't carry three bottles. Two bottles is my limit and that'll cost you thirty quid. Like every-bloody-body else, I've had to put up my charges.'

Considering the flat was hers and she paid no rent, her pension plus the retirement pension had always seemed quite adequate to her needs. After all, she ate very little, she bought practically nothing but drink. But in the face of Mr Scurlock's demands her bank account was diminishing at a rapid rate. The last time she had been to the cash dispenser, always walking with a stick now as well as hanging on to bushes and fences and lamp posts, she had found that if she were to draw out her customary £200 she would be overdrawn. Taking £150 instead, she nevertheless gave Wally Scurlock thirty pounds to fetch her two bottles of vodka.

Next door to the Tesco, on the other side of the car park, was a store called IT Heaven where they had a sale on. Wally brought Olwen's vodka and, carrying it in two plastic bags, wandered over to have a look at what was on offer. He hadn't intended to buy anything but, thanks to Olwen, he was very flush at the moment and the price reductions were, frankly, ridiculous. It would be imprudent *not* to buy one of those printers. Wally told himself that if you had a computer you really needed a printer as well. Suppose the computer crashed, as they sometimes did, and all the emails were lost, as might happen if not transmuted to paper. He went in and bought a small printer in a nice shade of pale grey with blue trim.

It took him a while when he got home to make it work – that is, to attach it to the computer and program the computer to accept it. But in the end he succeeded and then he realised he had no paper. Well, he wasn't going back up there or traipsing all the way over to West Hendon. He'd buy the paper next time that old soak wanted another couple of bottles of her poison. One of her poisons. It wasn't as if there was anything he wanted to print out. Any images he wanted to look at he could just as well see on-screen.

*

The wallpaper came off very easily. In places it was only necessary for Duncan to take hold of an edge and peel it off. When he placed his hand on the exposed plaster it felt pleasantly warm. Looking back on the various homes he had had, his parents' house, the first flat he shared with Eva, then the cottage out in Essex, he couldn't recall anywhere that the central heating was as efficient as here. Now March had come in and the sun shone every day, he had turned off all but three of the radiators and still he had to open the casements wide and the French windows.

At the DIY store beyond the Tesco and IT Heaven, he bought almond-white eggshell-finish paint, a sheepskin roller and two small brushes for doing the fiddly bits. The man who was the caretaker for the flats opposite came out of the Tesco carrying bottles of spirits. By the shape of the bags Duncan could see they were spirits, one bottle of gin and one of whisky. The man must be an alcoholic, not at all suitable for a responsible job like his. Duncan thought of doing something about it but postponed any action until he had finished painting the hall and stairwell. He often thought of doing something about things but when the time came he seldom did.

'Leila has opened a boutique in the Bel Esprit Centre,' said Molly, pouring hot milk onto the cocoa powder, sugar and milk mix in the new mug she had bought Stuart. 'Me and Noor and Sophie are going in there to have a look.'

'Who's Leila?' said Stuart for something to say.

'I don't know. Some woman. She put a flyer in our pigeon-hole. That's how I know she's opening this morning. We can't afford to buy anything but we thought we'd take a look.' Stuart's beauty made Molly shy of asking anything of him but she took courage. 'You want to come?'

'I don't like going into crowds, not with my arm.'

'I don't suppose there'll be a crowd. It's not Oxford Street, is it?'

A place like that, Stuart thought, was a kind of Mecca for young women. Would it attract the beautiful girl? 'I may see you there,' he said not very graciously.

He spent a long time at his front window, watching for the beautiful girl. Once he had seen her father, walking along the street alone. Once he had seen that same man driving the black car with a woman beside him but whether it was her he couldn't tell for the woman had a thick black scarf wound round her head and neck. After Molly had gone he stationed himself at the window, holding the hot-chocolate mug which had a scarlet heart pierced by an arrow on it, unaware that it was a Valentine's gift from her. The street was empty, no crowds of eager women queuing up at the Bel Esprit Centre. But looking across to the opposite side of Kenilworth Avenue, he saw the face of Duncan Yeardon at one of his windows. It wore, he thought, a wistful lonely expression, and having no desire to be seen in the same light, he moved away and eased himself into the heavy pale blue sweater, the only garment for the upper body he could presently wear with ease.

It was a very warm day for mid-March so that Stuart almost decided to go for a longer walk later. But Leila's boutique first. He mounted the front steps and the glass doors parted for him. Apart from a coffered ceiling and a dark brown wooden arch or two, nothing much remained of Smirke's ecclesiatical interior. A door on the left led into the Holistic Forum where Rose Preston-Jones did a stint twice a week; another to an acupuncturist, while on the right an arch led to the Recreation Arena and the Yoga Room. Ahead of him, above an open door, was the word *Leilaland*. Inside, he could see something very near the crowd he had anticipated, milling about among racks of clothes. There was not a man in sight. Not subdued by this but wary of a knock to his arm, Stuart approached the open door, suddenly confident that the beautiful girl would be here. It was her sort of place, the diaphanous wispy bits of chiffon and lace masquerading as dresses made for her.

Holding up his right hand to protect his left arm, he moved cautiously in among the racks, looking this way and that for his quarry, his head well above most of those of the women in the room. Molly and Noor and Sophie were soon spotted, each of them concentrating on tops and trousers and shifts with the kind of attention their parents and teachers would have liked to see them give to their studies. There was no sign of the beautiful girl.

When he first came in he had attracted stares as the only man there, or more probably because of his looks, but the clothes and the price tickets were more of a lure and soon they left him alone between a table laden with folded sweaters and a tall cabinet like a bookcase full of costume jewellery and artificial flowers. He moved about carefully. Afraid for his arm. Staying seemed pointless and he was turning to leave when a door at the back of the shop opened and Claudia came out with a middle-aged Asian woman. He felt disorientated, for a moment doubting his own eyes, then he remembered something he usually managed to forget, that she was a fashion journalist. She must be visiting this place and interviewing this woman for her newspaper's women's pages. At the same time a visual memory came to him of that enormous thug Freddy Livorno. But before he could escape Claudia had found him.

'How sweet of you to follow me here, darling!'

Useless to deny it. He stared helplessly at her and then his eyes fell. She was a good-looking woman, no doubt about it, but not in the same league as the beautiful girl.

'Did you see me from your window? How is your poor arm?' Without waiting for replies, she seized him by his good arm and said, 'There's a lovely little cafe at the back of the arena. Come and buy me a cappuccino.'

Buy *her* one, Stuart thought. Typical. But he went with her through what had once been the nave of this 1890s church and into the chancel which, long stripped of its altar and communion rail, now held a dozen scarlet tables, four dozen scarlet chairs and a long glass counter laden with food and drink.

'Imagine,' said Claudia when her cappuccino and his hot chocolate had come, 'what I found when I knocked over the bowl of dried flowers behind my desktop. You'll never guess. All those dusty old flowers fell out and so did a little *device*. A gizmo for spying on people's conversations. I don't know how it works but I can guess. It picks up anything that's said within earshot.'

'What about it?'

'*What about it?* It's been planted there by Freddy. It means he's heard everything I've said to you all these months. *And* I found a nasty little thing he's fixed on to my computer so he can read all my emails.'

'That's why he broke my arm,' Stuart said indignantly, his irritation with her just as much as Freddy.

'Exactly. But I know how to outwit him. I put the thing back among the flowers and I'll never send another email that isn't absolutely innocuous. But when I speak to you I'll do it from my bedroom or my office or in the garden.'

Where he might have more of these hidden devices . . . 'Better not speak to me at all,' said Stuart, and his upper arm which hadn't pained him at all for a month, claimed his attention with a sharp shaft of agony. 'Better we don't speak.'

'Then how are we to carry on our relationship?'

'We're not.'

'Now, sweetheart, you don't mean that. You're not well yet. I've not been well – he hit me too, you know. Well, you don't know. But he did. I thought he'd broken my jaw and he meant to but he hadn't. He did frighten me a lot and that's why I didn't call you. Then I found that horrid little thing among the flowers and I was *scared*, darling, but I've got over that. Let's go to your place and just lie down quietly on your bed for an hour. I haven't got to be back till one.'

So they lay down quietly on Stuart's bed and nothing much happened. Stuart found that it wasn't only walking which was inhibited by a heavy plaster weighing down one's arm. If it had been the beautiful girl lying beside him he was pretty sure he wouldn't have allowed a broken leg and a fractured skull as well as a broken arm to impede him, but it wasn't, it was Claudia. He went out into the street with her when she left and up to the Watford Way to find her a taxi. Cabs were more frequent and the drivers more obliging since the recession had begun, but still it was several minutes before one came. At least he wasn't going to have to pay for it, Stuart thought, walking back into Kenilworth Avenue.

He had turned through the gateway to Lichfield House, was walking up the path, when something made him turn his head. What? Some instinct, some stroke of fate, some spiritual summons of the object of passion to the lover? Whatever it was, he turned round and there, on the other side of the street, mounting the shallow steps to the front door of Springmead, was the beautiful girl followed by her father. In their hands they carried shopping bags which they had evidently brought from the black Audi that was parked at the kerb. By inserting a key in the lock and opening the door the beautiful girl told Stuart *she lived there*. She and her father *lived there*. Stuart, riveted to the spot – a phrase he had read but never previously experienced – watched her walk into the house, watched the man walk in, but instead of closing the door behind him, drop his bags and return to the car. The beautiful girl, now turned round to face him and her father, showed Stuart the full extent of her beauty, her lithe and slender shape, her swan's neck, her incomparable face and jet-black hair, piled like a geisha's in smooth coils on top of her head. She faced him and her father but for no more than a moment, then she closed the door.

Stuart had been holding his breath. He expelled it in a long exhalation. She lived opposite, she must do. Why otherwise would she have let herself in with her own key? Her father drove off. No doubt he was putting the car away in a garage they must have somewhere round the back. Silently, Stuart said to himself, 'Thank you, Claudia.' If it hadn't been for escorting Claudia round the corner to find a cab he might never have found out where the beautiful girl lived. Well, if not never, not for a long time. Thank you, Claudia. He stood in the sunshine, the pain in his arm quite gone, until the three girls appeared from the church, all carrying bags labelled *Leilaland.*

'We've spent zillions,' said Noor. 'Well, our Visa cards have. I'm crossing my fingers Daddy will pay. Are you all right?'

'I'm absolutely fine,' said Stuart.

It was April before the plaster came off his arm. In the weeks before that happened he found himself making plans for his future all dependent on that day coming. Everything was on hold until then but when it came and the removal of this great chunk of rock, grubby now and fraying at the edges, had taken place, he would do several decisive things. Make it plain to Claudia that their affair was over and refuse to listen to her cajolements; think seriously about getting a job and start looking for one in earnest; go across the road, ring the bell of Springmead and meet the beautiful girl.

Claudia had had flu. That kept her away from him for about ten days, and after that, when she was better, she and Freddy went to Greece on holiday. The moment she came back – well, it felt like the moment – she phoned. 'Nessun dorma' rang once more through Flat 1 Lichfield House, but she assured him that she was phoning out in the street, actually standing in the entrance to Angel Tube station. She arrived and it was quite a lot like old times, but even then he was telling himself that it couldn't go on. The truth was that even at the height of his lovemaking he heard Freddy's voice saying, 'I'll do worse . . .' and he thought about that heavy stick smashing his face, breaking his nose, mashing up his mouth. Oh, no, no, no. Freddy was a demon. Stuart wouldn't put it past him to have had spies with recording devices lurking in Angel station.

CHAPTER ELEVEN

S tuart's teens had been free of acne and any facial erup-
tion had been rare, but there had been the occasional
spot. One of these, on his nose, he still remembered
with horror. He had been seventeen and already conscious of
his looks, a vanity fostered by his mother who often spoke
of him as 'my handsome son' or 'my good-looking boy'. The
spot was so distressing that he had wanted to take time off
school but his father had put his foot down.

'I could understand it if you were a girl, Stuart.'

Since then there had been various small disfigurements –
'pink eye' dyeing one retina red, a chipped tooth and the wait
until the crown could be in place. Now he was appalled by
the sight of his left arm when the plaster came off, the skin
white, scaly and wrinkled like he could imagine (but had never
seen) the arm of an old person, someone like Marius Potter,
for instance. The weather was warm but the state of his arm
made wearing a tight royal-blue T-shirt impossible. 'Nessun
dorma' was repeating itself hysterically from his bedroom where
he had flung the mobile on his bed. Whatever Claudia might
say, he had a horrible feeling that Freddy was sitting in his
solicitor's office also listening to that ringtone and waiting for
him to answer it. Waiting for the incriminating evidence which
would be enough to fetch him down here with a lethal weapon.

He moved his arm up and down from the elbow like someone doing 'curls'. It felt a bit stiff but it didn't hurt. He was young, the skin would rejuvenate itself – wouldn't it? Once it was back to normal he would go to one of those fake-tanning places, there was one up at the roundabout, and get himself done a lovely golden brown all over. Or maybe find himself a sunbed. But no, those things gave you cancer.

He had rather gone off hot chocolate. Perhaps it was something to do with the way Molly made it – not like his mother did – or else it was the stain on the carpet that Richenda had said was impossible to eradicate. Now he preferred cappuccino. Able to use his arm and hand as if he had never been injured, he made himself a mugful, grated some white chocolate and sprinkled it on the top, and took it to his front-facing window. Stuart was as frequently stationed at the window as the Lady of Shalott and as assiduous a looker in the mirror. But as he drank his coffee he told himself the time had come to stop gazing and act.

Today the weather was warm enough to dispense with the pale blue sweater, but wearing a long-sleeved T-shirt wasn't much to his taste. He possessed one in navy-blue and white horizontal stripes but he seldom wore it. Going into his bedroom to find it and see what it looked like on, he was met by 'Nessun dorma'. He switched off the phone, a daring step to take and one he could barely remember ever taking before. Although the place had been quiet before, once that key had been pressed it seemed to him to be followed by utter silence. It made him feel a little uneasy. He pulled the striped T-shirt over his head, contemplated his reflection in the mirror in the black-matt frame and decided he was satisfied.

Now the time had come he felt inclined to put it off. Not for long, maybe just for half an hour. So a walk first. Again he went unaccompanied by his mobile. It felt strange, the way, according to his mother, a woman feels when out without her handbag. The sky was a clear cloudless blue, the sun very warm, and the trees were coming into leaf, a fresh bright green. Other trees he didn't know the name of were a mass of pink and white blossom. He walked up as far as St Ebba's, round Kenilworth Green and back at the roundabout and made an appointment at Embrown to come in for an all-over tanning session the following afternoon. Varying the walk by returning via Chester Grove, he walked past the parade and noticed that Design for Living had closed. Another casualty of the recession. No more putting it off, Stuart, he told himself. The time has come. But what was he going to say to whoever came to the door? That was something he had given no thought to. Maybe simply say that they were neighbours, he had seen them about and would they like to come over for a drink? It was the kind of thing people did. His mother had often done it when new people moved in. Of course it would involve him in more expense and more preparation but all that was worth it to meet the beautiful girl. And they might say no, thank you for asking, but you must come to us.

All Duncan Yeardon's casement windows were open. As if it was high summer instead of only April. He could smell the paint from halfway up the path. Stuart thought of DIY as essentially something you did when you were too old to do anything else and Duncan's activities didn't interest him. Few people's did unless they were young and attractive.

In spite of the sunshine, blinds were down at all the Springmead windows, slatted blinds made of some kind of thin wood, and not a single window was open. The front door was painted black with 'SPRINGMEAD' on it in silver capitals. Stuart wasn't usually very observant but he noticed the lack of a letter box. That was strange. He wouldn't have been surprised to learn that not having a letter box was against the law.

There was, however, a bell. He pressed it and heard chimes from inside. No one came. Perhaps they were out. The absence of their car meant nothing, as when they weren't out in it, it was kept in a garage.

He rang the bell again. This time someone appeared from the side of the house. The gate was opened between Springmead and number 7 and the beautiful girl's father came out. With him was a girl, but not the beautiful one.

He had a clipped jerky accent and his voice was rather high-pitched. 'Yes? What is it?'

Stuart felt awkward. He hadn't expected to be treated like someone distributing flyers. 'I – I mean, I'm a neighbour of yours. I live over there. In those flats. I wondered – I wonder if you'd – well, if you'd like to come over for a drink some-time. You and your –' he found himself using a phrase he thought he would never utter '– the two young ladies.'

This one was very different from the beautiful girl, being short, rather squat and with big coarse features. Her hair was jet black and long but not glossy and her eyes looked malev-olent, perhaps because they were sunk in fleshy folds. The man said something to her in what was presumably their language, said it in a sibilant whisper. She turned away and went back the way she had come.

The man looked down before he spoke. 'You are kind,' he said, 'but no, thank you. We don't go out. We stay in our own place. Thank you.'

He didn't wait for Stuart to go but followed the girl, closing the side gate behind him. Stuart looked round to see Duncan Yeardon standing on the other side of the dividing fence, holding a mug in one hand and a paintbrush in the other.

'I just popped out for a breather,' Duncan said. 'Do you fancy a cuppa?'

'I don't drink tea.'

'You can have coffee if you don't mind instant.'

Stuart made no reply but went inside. He didn't remark on the heat. Dust sheets and pieces of newspaper covered the hall floor and half the staircase. Duncan brought him a mug of thin coffee in which curds floated.

'Do you know the people next door?'

'I've seen them,' said Duncan. 'They keep themselves to themselves. There's that bloke you were talking to and two girls and a young chap. Well, I suppose that girl lives there too. I've never seen her before. I call the other girl Tigerlily.'

'The beautiful one?'

'Well, she's pretty. I wouldn't call her beautiful myself but there's no accounting for tastes.'

'Tigerlily,' said Stuart in a dreamy tone.

'That's not her real name, mind. I made that up or got it out of a book or something. I call her Tigerlily and the boy Oberon. Mr Wu, as I call him, is her husband.'

Stuart was appalled. 'Are you sure?'

Remembering that this was a relationship he had himself invented, Duncan said no, he wasn't. 'I mean, he's not her husband. He's not called Mr Wu either. That's just my fun.'

Stuart put his half-empty mug on the floor because there was nowhere else and said he must be off. 'I need to rest because of my arm.' Duncan hadn't asked him about it, an omission he resented. Outside the Lichfield House gate he met Wally Scurlock, carrying a bottle of gin and a bottle of vodka.

'Not for my consumption, sir,' said Wally, 'so you needn't look like that.'

'I wasn't looking like anything. They're for Olwen, are they?'

'I perform this little errand for her, yes. You wouldn't care to take it on, I suppose?' Wally had been on the point of saying that Stuart had plenty of time because he 'did fuck all' but decided it would be going a bit far. 'She'll pay,' he said.

'I've got a bad arm,' said Stuart. 'I'm convalescing.'

His encounter with Rose (or Rosie as he then knew her) came back to Marius with almost total recall once he had found the right place for her in his memory. He had just finished his degree, it was in classics and he had got a first. And in those days, as he told himself, a first *was* a first. Six months off and then a year at teacher training college. The six months he spent at the Hackney squat as part of a commune with people called Storm, Anther and Zither (not their real names), Simon Alpheton the painter, who wasn't famous then, and a woman named Harriet something. Rosie had arrived one morning, brought there by Storm whose girl-friend was her friend. Well, it was more like the middle of the afternoon as no one ever got up before late lunchtime. She was rather shy and quiet and looked a lot younger than her real age. He remembered her extreme slenderness and her long pale hair.

No one in the commune ever did anything. They sat around on the floor in the evenings and sometimes long into the night, smoking pot, passing damp brown joints round the circle, picking things up – a green glass ball, an ostrich egg, a string of beads – and stroking them, cooing over them and making sounds of wonder as if they were priceless objects. Why did they? He couldn't remember, and now he felt ashamed of wasting his time. But he had done it with the rest of them and so had Rosie who sat next to him.

She had been allotted a mattress in Harriet's room. No one had a bed. It was summer and hot. In some of the rooms the windows had been boarded up because the glass was broken but not in his. It was quite airy in his room and quite clean. He had always kept his living places clean, much to the derision of the others. That night no one wanted to go to bed because of the heat – except Rosie, who got up rather unsteadily and asked where she was to sleep. He said he would take her to Harriet's room, but when they were out in the passage – that house was a maze of passages – she looked trustingly at him and said she didn't want to be alone. He was used to the place but he could see that to a newcomer it could be more than intimidating. It could be frightening. Darkness prevailed. Cobwebs hung everywhere, grey veils swaying in the draughts from the broken windows. Bulbs were in only a few of the light sockets, burnt-out candles stood about in cracked saucers, old Indian bedspreads were draped over some of the mattresses and pinned up at some of the broken windows. He put his arms round her. She was trembling but warm and soft.

'Let's go into my room,' he said. 'It's better there. It's nice there. And there aren't any spiders.'

'I don't mind spiders,' she said.

After all these years he remembered that. He had meant to lie down beside her and not touch her again, but he couldn't keep to this resolve, partly because she so evidently didn't want him to. The lovemaking was lovely, he remembered, protracted and repeated, and they fell asleep in each other's arms, something he had read about happening to couples as quite a normal common thing, but it had never happened to him before. They moved away from each other later, surely another normal thing. But in the morning – the afternoon, really, when he woke up – she was gone.

Storm had brought her so it was to him he had gone. Who was she? Where was she? But Storm was too far gone on an acid trip, out of his head on the stuff, even to know whom he meant. And Storm's girlfriend had broken up with him and disappeared so she was no help. Marius had asked the other people in the commune but no one knew Rosie's other name. She was just Rosie and they talked of ships passing in the night. Why had she come in the first place? No one knew. That wasn't the kind of thing they enquired about. They were there to escape from questions of that kind – what are you doing? Why are you here? What time is it? When are you going to get a job? Who's that girl?

Within weeks he went off to his teacher training and he forgot her. Or thought he had. There had been other girlfriends, even a fiancée. He had never married but he wasn't enough of a sentimentalist to attribute his singleness to his night with Rosie. But now that total recall had come to him he stayed away from her. Being in her company embarrassed him.

When Claudia arrived at Lichfield House it happened that several of the residents were either on their way out or reaching home. This was because the time she had chosen was five thirty in the afternoon. Stuart himself was returning from his tanning session at Embrown and Michael Constantine from a meeting with the features editor of his newspaper. The Scurlocks, together for once, were on their way to visit Richenda's mother in the Royal Free Hospital, and Marius Potter was off to a house in Mill Hill where on Tuesday evenings he tutored a seventeen-year-old for her Latin A level. Duncan Yeardon wasn't there but, having finished his decorating for the day, was whiling away the time until his dinner by watching Lichfield House.

He saw the arrival of the tall blonde woman whose husband had broken up Stuart Font's party and Stuart Font's arm. She got out of a taxi, had an argument with the driver and flounced off up the path. The door opened to receive her as it had opened for that medical chap two minutes before. Stuart appeared next, looking as if he had been on a long holiday in the Caribbean, but stopped outside the Bel Esprit Centre to stare at Tigerlily and Mr Wu who had just got out of their car. Stuart waved and called out hi and wasn't it a lovely evening but Mr Wu hustled Tigerlily into the house and quickly closed the front door. Duncan was beginning to enjoy himself.

The man who looked like an old hippie – Duncan called him Ringo – came out, then went back as if he'd forgotten something. Stuart trailed slowly up the path, obviously fed up about Tigerlily not talking to him. What was going on there? Before he could provide an answer, the wife of the madman who had injured Stuart appeared, the glass doors opening for her and almost precipitating her into Stuart's arms. The word Stuart used was uttered so loudly that Duncan heard it clearly from his open window – and deplored it as unnecessary and a sign of the times. The doors stood open, kept in that state by the press of people all standing on the threshold. That caretaker chap and his wife pushed their way through, the caretaker or porter or whatever he was shouting that they'd break the door mechanism if they went on like that.

Inside the lobby of Lichfield House Claudia was hanging on to Stuart, holding his arm and clutching his other shoulder. She had lost all control and begun shouting at him that he needn't think he could treat her like that, never answering her calls, ignoring her after all they'd been to each other. Duncan could no longer hear her and barely see anything now the doors had closed. Regretfully, he turned away to think about cooking something for his supper.

*

Stuart unlocked his door and pushed Claudia inside. He didn't want her there but it was a preferable alternative to the scene she was making in front of Marius Potter and Michael Constantine.

Once inside, Claudia demanded drink. She needed it. Surely he had a bottle of wine in his fridge? He told her she would have to drink it warm, and while she was taking a long swig, he resolved to be strong and decisive. A break must be made. She set down her glass, said, 'You've been away. You'd never get a tan like that in this country.'

'In Barbados,' he lied. 'And I'm going back there.' He began fabricating. 'Tomorrow. I'll be away a long time.'

'Oh, darling, is that why you didn't answer my calls?'

He weakened. Instead of telling her all was over and they were never to see each other again, as he had resolved to do, he agreed with her. That was why. 'Where does Freddy think you are?'

'Oh, God knows. Who cares? Let me come to Barbados with you. That'll be the start of leaving Freddy. You don't know how I long to see the back of him.'

This was worse than he had ever dreamt of. 'Listen, Claudia, you tell Freddy I'm in the Caribbean. Or tell him I've moved – anything. Don't you realise he more or less threatened to kill me?'

'Yes, but it's all talk, darling. Oh, darling, let's go to bed.'

Claudia admired his beautiful tan, something which once would have gratified him, but he didn't much enjoy himself. It was the last time, though, he made up his mind as she was dressing that it absolutely must be the last time. When he was going about with Tigerlily – something he must make happen – Claudia would get the message, she would give up, she would have to.

By now it was dark, the street lights coming on. He saw

Claudia out, found a taxi waiting hopefully in the parade and put her into it. On his way back he saw the black car, its headlights on, pulling away from outside Springmead with Tigerlily's father at the wheel. He was so excited he could almost feel the adrenalin surge and he ran up the steps and rang the bell. The place was brightly lit behind its slatted blinds. He heard the chimes the bell made, pressed it again, it chimed again, and the door was opened.

Tigerlily stood there, beautiful in her white dress, her hair in two thick black plaits. Even Stuart, not known for his sensitivity to other people's feelings, saw her look of horror. She put one slender hand up to cover her mouth. Behind her, instead of some sort of hallway or room, was another door which she must have closed behind her. It was made of thickly chased glass, apparently coloured green, unless there was a green curtain behind it.

'I came to ask you over for a drink,' he said, adding when the look remained unchanged. 'You and your father and your sister, of course. Any time you like. I'm always there.'

She began shaking her head. She took her hand away from her mouth, said, 'No, no, no . . .' Then, taking a step forward, she laid one hand on his arm, looked up the street to the right and the left. 'Are you good man?'

No one had ever asked him that before. He nodded. 'Yeah – well, I hope so.'

It was what she wanted. 'I come,' she said. 'Please. Tomorrow.'

The door was shut. Amazed at his success, quite dizzy with it, he walked down the path to the gate as Tigerlily's father's car appeared from the corner of Kenilworth Parade. The man had seen him and pulled in to the kerb. Stuart also ran, across the road, causing a van driver to brake and curse, plunged into Lichfield House and the sanctuary of his flat.

CHAPTER TWELVE

The impossibility of living isolated in this world when you have an addiction and when you have cut yourself off from almost all means of communication, was now borne in upon Olwen. It was something she had not allowed for. When adopting this new ideal life for herself, she had supposed she would always be able to go out to buy her own drink, that wine shops would always be in easy reach and in that failing to pay her phone bill she had nevertheless thought she would be able to use someone else's landline or mobile to ask British Telecommunications for reconnection. Now she realised that everyone in Lichfield House was avoiding her, except Wally Scurlock and he kept in touch only because she paid him.

Even if she had been able to get on the phone again she had insufficient money to pay some wine shop in Edgware or Hendon to deliver to her. As it was, she had been forced into the near-intolerable position of being unable to call on Scurlock for fresh supplies. With the aid of her stick in one hand and clinging on to fences with the other, she had managed the walk – the struggling, dragging, crawling – to the cash machine in the Kenilworth Parade post office. There she found she had thirty-four pounds and some odd bits left in her account. The pensions wouldn't come in until the 24th, which was the middle of next week. She staggered back home, wondering if an appeal to Scurlock would be any use. Unlikely. Last time she had tried it he had refused point-blank. She could empty her account and offer him twenty pounds to fetch her a bottle of gin but he was bound to say no. It wasn't worth making the journey for only one bottle, he would say.

She had perhaps three inches of vodka left in the bottle and half a bottle of gin. Cutting down, making it last, were alien concepts to Olwen. Of course, she had done that in the past – her whole life had been arranged around having a drink, putting off a second drink, waiting an hour, having a drink and another one, exerting all her will to have no more till next day. But the very point of coming here, of cutting off all ties, of putting the past behind her, had been to drink all she wanted, every drop she wanted, until she died. And she had been happy doing that, she thought as she contemplated the two bottles, really happy for the first time in her life, whatever the abstemious might say.

The terrible nightmare of tomorrow loomed in front of her. As a dry desert it appeared, a brown sunless plain where nothing grew and nothing moved. She poured herself two inches of gin, murmuring, make it last, make it last.

Turning off his central heating, Duncan opened all the windows in the house. Appreciate the weather, he told himself, don't moan about it. The cloudless sky and the hot sunshine were surely more suited to July than April, and then he remembered how, two years before, April had been just like this, April had been the summer, and afterwards it was cold and wet until September. His painting finished, he set up his garden furniture, a white-painted metal table and four chairs, one of them a cushioned recliner.

From time to time he heard the twittering voices of Tigerlily and the girl he called 'the other one' and occasionally the high-pitched gutturals of Oberon and Mr Wu. Those three chairs looked very empty and he considered putting his head over the fence and inviting whoever might be out there to join him for a cup of tea or a glass of wine, but then he thought better of it. Instead he asked the Pembers from number 1. They knew all about Tigerlily, Mr Wu, Oberon and the other one, only she wasn't Tigerlily's sister but her stepmother. Or so they said. The family came from Hong Kong and ran a family mail-order business from Springmead: garden plants, seedlings, seeds, annuals and perennials as well as vegetables, very much in demand in these hard times. Moira Jones that Duncan called Esmeralda and Ken Lee at number 7 had told them all about it. Ken had a Chinese mother himself. Hadn't Duncan noticed?

Rose's three clients of the morning had gone and the fourth and last one was late. Sitting in one of the two small rooms of the Holistic Forum, she felt the onset of depression, once familiar to her, but rare since coming to live at Lichfield House. McPhee would have comforted her, his pretty fluffy face, his muscular furry body in her arms, but obviously a dog had no place here in this temple of hygiene, all white-and-peach tiles, peach carpet, opalescent washbasin and crystal flagons of what Marius – very kindly and sincerely – called 'magic potions'. The health and safety people wouldn't allow a dog in.

Of course really she knew the cause of her depression – the lack for the past fortnight of Marius in her life. Not McPhee who would be waiting for her when she went home in an hour's time, not on account of the credit crunch keeping a lot of clients away. No, it was because Marius no longer rang her doorbell, no longer phoned, no longer invited her. She had been a fool to bank so much on it, to read more into his visits than was actually there. He was very clever, highly educated, a mine of history and classical lore, he knew about everything, while she was very ignorant about all but alternative medicine. He had seemed interested in that too but no doubt he had got bored with it – and her. She felt too low, and the lowness was increasing, to take steps herself. Suppose he snubbed her? Suppose she went up in the lift and knocked at his door and asked for a *sortes* reading and he said he was too busy?

The client came. She was a large woman wearing tight white trousers and tight green T-shirt. Rose thought she had seldom seen such an expression of misery on anyone's face.

'Shall I work out your BMI, Mrs Hayley?'

The client asked what a BMI was and when Rose said it meant body mass index a dark red blush spread over Mrs Hayley's sad face. 'If you must.'

Rose got her on to the scales, calculated her height and fed the information into her computer.

'Well, what is it then?'

'Thirty-two,' said Rose. Two tears welled in Mrs Hayley's eyes and trickled down her cheeks. 'Please don't be upset. We can deal with this, you know. I'm going to let you have some of my herbal tincture to take three times a day. I want you to drink plenty of water before meals and I shall give you a diet sheet.'

'They used to say "fat",' said Mrs Hayley. 'I didn't mind that. But "obese", that's awful. It's obscene. That's the trouble, the word *sounds* like "obscene".'

'Yes, but it doesn't mean the same thing.'

Rose knew that was a feeble thing to say. She knew that sound was all and that some people rarely saw the printed word.

Mrs Hayley, she suspected, was one of them. That reminded her of Marius, to whom the printed word meant so much . . .

The green herbal tincture was handed over along with the diet sheet and a booklet of simple exercises. Mrs Hayley paid and when she had gone Rose closed up. McPhee was waiting for her inside Flat 2, rapturously waving his feathery tail at the sight of her. She picked him up and hugged him hard. One of the lovely things about McPhee was that he never minded how tightly you hugged him.

'What would I do without you?'

McPhee wagged his tail even more vigorously. Rose put his lead on him and took him out for a walk round Kenilworth Green.

It was by chance that Olwen discovered that Mr Ali had returned from his pilgrimage and his shop was open once more. Her front door was ajar, she was just inside it, bracing herself to venture out and find Wally Scurlock, when she heard two of the girls talking outside their own flat.

'That Asian man is back if we need more Coke.'

'You mean Mr Ali.'

'Yeah, whatever.'

'You want to remember I'm Asian,' Olwen heard Noor say. 'You want to show a bit of respect.'

They began arguing, Sophie shouting that no one called her a racist and got away with it and Noor countering that no one would if she watched her mouth. Olwen pushed her door open and came out. She stood on the threshold, leaning on her stick, but leaning unsteadily, her whole body faintly trembling. The sight of her in her moth-eaten fur coat over the same black dress she had worn for Stuart's party silenced them.

'Are you OK?' Sophie asked.

'Not really.'

Molly would have asked if there was anything she could do to help but Molly was down in Flat 1, making Stuart's bed, bringing him her version of a cappuccino and offering to take over Richenda's cleaning job. The two girls looked again at Olwen and Noor said to Sophie, 'I'll see you out the front,' and departed for the lift.

Olwen said, 'If you're going round to Ali's and you'll get me a bottle of gin and one of vodka, I'll give you ten pounds.'

Remembering the five pounds she had never had back, Sophie said, 'You mean you'll give me the price of the booze and ten pounds? And what about the fiver you owe me?'

Well brought up as she had been, Sophie would never have dreamt of talking in that tone to any of her parents' friends (or come to that, her grandparents'), but Olwen, through her lifestyle, had forfeited all deference. As Noor had put it, Sophie wanted to show a bit of respect, but it didn't occur to her to do so. Olwen hesitated but she had to go on. It was a matter of life and death to her.

The date was the 23rd and on the following day her pension would come in. There was no help for it, she would have to trust Sophie, for she could already tell that this girl would be a lot cheaper to employ than the caretaker. Scurlock was already charging her thirty pounds to fetch two bottles of spirits. 'Will you do it for ten?' Olwen said harshly.

Sophie knew she should refuse. She could see Olwen was killing herself. All the strictures against heavy drinking were known to her, as they must be known to everyone who looked at television or the Internet, not to mention glanced at a newspaper. Olwen was a living (barely) example of what drink did to you. But ten pounds for simply buying what Olwen wanted when she was going to Ali's anyway . . .

'OK, if you want.'

The next step terrified Olwen but being without a drink terrified her more. 'You'll have to go to the cash machine in the post office first. Get the money out.'

'Tell me your pin, then.'

'Come in.'

So Sophie went into Flat 6. She expected it to be dirty and even untidier than hers and she was surprised that it wasn't. Its barrenness struck her, the lack of furnishings, the bare walls, the absence of any signs of eating, no clothes lying about, no curtains or blinds. She was reminded of when her parents and she and her brothers and sister had all moved to a new house, and until their household goods arrived, lived for twenty-four hours with just their beds and a sofa and the TV. But the smell there had been of floor polish and air freshener while here it was of gin.

Olwen had sat down, had sunk down, into the sofa where her ancient scuffed black leather handbag lay. From it she produced a credit card. This card was almost the last thing she now possessed that brought her into participation in the present-day world, unless you counted the television remote which had ceased to function for lack of batteries.

'You'll have to tell me your pin,' Sophie said again.

Olwen would never have dared disclose that to Wally Scurlock. She didn't know how far she could trust Sophie but did she have a choice? The bottle on the floor by her feet contained about an inch of gin and that was all she had. She turned her eyes slowly on to it as someone in a broken-down car in the desert might look at the last of his water.

'Seven-five-two-nine,' she said.

Sophie didn't write it down. She would remember it.

"'He for God only, she for God in him,'" Marius read when he opened *Paradise Lost* at random. For once, perhaps for the first time, he slammed Milton shut and nearly threw him on the floor. Ridiculous, sexist stuff, he thought. And Milton had had three wives! If he and Rose were together, they would have a totally equal partnership, loving and giving ... He caught himself up. That could never be. He could never remind her of that night they had passed together and which had so evidently slipped her mind. Or, probably, hadn't slipped her mind, but had rather slipped into that chronicle of brief sexual encounters everyone keeps, many or few, not to be entirely forgotten perhaps but recalled as having been spent with a handsome boy whose long hair was chestnut-coloured, whose body was muscular and whose face was smooth.

His phone rang. 'Oh, Rose,' he said, his heart beating faster.

'I was wondering if you'd like to come down for supper this evening.'

'So sorry but I can't. I've got a new pupil at seven.'

'Some other time then.' Her voice sounded sad.

'Of course.'

And he went off to teach Roman history to Penelope Moore-Knighton in Edgware.

She must learn to make it last. Olwen knew this. She knew her plans and dreams to drink as much as she wanted and whenever she wanted were doomed to failure. Only a wealthy person could do that. A rich woman would have servants who asked no questions, who had the use of a car, who would buy what her employer wanted by the crate or simply order it on the phone. You could probably buy it online, she thought, though what she knew of the Internet was fast receding out of her fuddled brain. As for her, when she started on this strange enterprise of hers – she knew how strange it was – she hadn't calculated that she might lose the ability to buy drink herself, simply to walk out of the place and buy what she wanted. And she hadn't counted on the recession closing wine shops nearby. How long, for instance, would Mr Ali last?

Meanwhile, Sophie Longwich had brought her the bottle of gin and the one of vodka and returned her card. What she had forgotten to ask for was a receipt from the cash machine. Sophie called it a 'hole in the wall' and had said nothing about a receipt, which probably meant she hadn't one. Olwen worried a bit about Sophie having her pin number, but when she had twice filled a tumbler with gin and drunk it down, she worried less. Nor did she worry too much about what she had resolved the previous evening: to reduce her alcohol consumption by a half. That would be bearable, wouldn't it? She could manage that. Tonight, though, she would drink what she wanted and think about economy tomorrow.

Tomorrow is another day. She vaguely recalled Scarlett O'Hara saying that from the days, now long gone, when she read books and watched films. I'll worry about it tomorrow, for tomorrow is another day.

CHAPTER THIRTEEN

Tomorrow had come but no Tigerlily with it. Stuart wondered if he had dreamt her promising to visit him but he knew it had really happened. The kind of dreams he had weren't of girls asking him if he was a good man. Was there anything he could do? He remembered how her father had stared at him and remembered too how ignominiously he had retreated. Since that evening there had been no sign of her or of any of them. Remembering what he had told his mother about April, though April was nearly over, he sat at home with newspapers' appointments pages in front of him and applied for jobs, made uneasy by the brevity of his CV.

'Nessun dorma' rang out frequently from the bedroom. He never answered it but Molly did, humbly telling Claudia that she was his cleaner and, in response to frantic gesticulations from Stuart, that he had gone out. His mother also phoned. He spoke to her and heard that a woman journalist called Claudia Livorno had called her to ask if her son had changed his phone numbers. She needed to get in touch because she wanted to interview him in connection with a story she was writing.

'You didn't tell her, I hope.'

'Well, of course I did, Stuart. That is, I confirmed the

numbers she had. They were both right. Surely you'd like to have a piece about you in the papers.'

His mobile began to play that tedious tune while they were still talking. Stuart let it play but gave up applying for jobs. On his way out he told Molly he hoped she realised he couldn't afford to pay her. Molly, who had never thought payment a possibility, took a phone call on her own mobile from Carl wanting to know why he never saw her these days. She fobbed him off with promises but not caring very much.

It was a lovely sunny morning, almost the last day of April, and all Duncan's windows were open. Stuart rang the doorbell. He knew Duncan would ask no questions but simply invite him in for one of his cups of watery coffee which, he hoped, would be drunk out in the garden. For a moment he thought his new friend must be out but the second time he rang the bell Duncan came to the door. Things then followed their usual pattern. The kettle was boiled, the water poured on to a very small amount of instant coffee, semi-skimmed milk added and custard cream biscuits arranged on a plate. Duncan always asked if Stuart would like to have his 'elevenses' inside or outside and Stuart always said outside. He had taken to visiting Duncan regularly. Duncan had never asked what prompted this sudden interest in himself and his garden but now, carrying the tray out through the French windows, he did ask. Or, rather, guessed right.

'You're hoping to get a look at Tigerlily, aren't you?'

'Yes, well, sort of,' said Stuart.

'You're more likely to see her on a cold grey day. They don't like the heat, that lot. Her and her sister and brother or whatever they are, they come outside to get cool.'

'But why?'

'They have to keep it hot in there. It's a real hothouse. They raise orchids, you see. They're specialist orchid growers and they've got a flourishing business supplying plants to all the garden centres in west London. Got their work cut out, they have.'

Stuart, who had always loved warm weather, now longed for the kind of grey day he would have said was typical. But an area of high pressure lay over the south-east of England, creating what was almost a heatwave. Even he realised that he couldn't keep calling on Duncan for coffee without some reciprocation, so he had him over for six o'clock drinks along with Ken Lee and Moira Jones. Molly arrived too, bringing Sophie with her. It was quite a party. Sophie regaled them with tales of the drink she was buying for Olwen but she said nothing of the ten pounds a time.

Stuart worried all the time that Claudia might turn up. She didn't – but nor did Tigerlily. He was in no doubt that she had meant to come but been prevented by that autocratic father of hers. They must come from one of those Far Eastern families where all power was vested in the parents. He wasn't well endowed with imagination, but still, he could picture her tending the delicate orchid plants, pinching off shoots from the thin supple stems, winding a tendril round a support, watering from a teacup-sized can with a long pointed spout. Her long glossy hair would be fastened back with a tortoise-shell comb and tied with a white ribbon.

The fine weather lasted for another three days. Then it clouded over and the rain came, pouring down all night. In the morning the temperature had dropped to ten degrees Celsius and a sharp wind was blowing. Stuart went across the road to Duncan's but found that while his host was very willing to give him coffee and biscuits, he refused to have it outside.

'May is a treacherous month,' he said – meaninglessly, as far as Stuart was concerned.

No longer attempting to keep the true purpose of his visits from Duncan, Stuart opened the French windows and stood outside on the step, coffee in hand. From there he had quite a good view of the Springmead garden, the summer house and the gate into the back lane where the garage must be. There was no one about but then, just as he was thinking that it was too cold even for hothouse dwellers, Tigerlily came out and with her the other girl, followed by the father. He and she went out through the back-lane gate, no doubt to the garage, leaving Tigerlily to make her way to the summer house.

She was on the steps leading to the little pink-painted door when something made her turn her head. It must have been him willing it, Stuart thought, it had to be. Their eyes met and she mouthed, 'I come later. Evening time.'

He could hardly believe his luck. He watched her go in through the pink door, and almost at the moment she closed it behind her, a boy of about eighteen – older maybe but those people always looked younger than they were – came out of the house and walked down the path to the summer house. Her brother, thought Stuart, left to guard her. I wonder how she'll manage to get out this evening, but she will this time, I know she will.

Xue, whose name means 'snow' symbolising purity, and Tao, whose name means 'great wave', sat on the floor in the summer house, savouring the cool air. They didn't speak to each other. They had nothing to say except things which must never be said. Tao, who could sleep anywhere and for very short periods, lay down and closed his eyes, but Xue stayed awake and thought of the tiny ray of hope that might be offered to her.

*

There was no scene this morning, no involvement of the other residents. All was peaceful in Lichfield House and there was not a soul about, yet Claudia had got in and was sitting on his bed, counting on his mobile the messages she had left.

'Oh, darling, where have you been?'

'Having coffee with a friend. How did you get in?'

'What a way to speak to me! Like I was some sort of intruder. If you must know, there was a fat girl here, dusting the place. Anyway, she had a duster in her hand. I told her I was your partner. I must say she looked a bit stricken but she let me in and then she went. Don't tell me you're having some sort of relationship with her?'

'Of course I won't tell you that, Claudia. Of course I'm not. She sort of cleans for me and she doesn't charge anything so I've given Richenda the push.'

'You really are something else, Stuart Font. Aren't you going to give me a kiss?'

Stuart looked at her. Why had he never noticed before how coarse her skin was, how dry and frizzy her long pale hair? Why had he never seen the muffin top starting round her waist and the lines that encircled her wrists? He glanced at himself in one of the mirrors. He looked years younger than she was, ten, fifteen years younger. How old was she anyway? She had never said.

'You'll have to go, Claudia. I'm busy.'

'You what? You're never busy.'

He realised that the crunch had come. Now he must tell her their affair was over. He couldn't have her getting in his way when dramatic events were about to unfold. Not her or that ridiculous Molly Flint. Tonight Tigerlily would come and an adventure might be about to happen. He might have to take her away somewhere, hide her from her father, even marry her. The prospect excited him. His life had become intolerably dull.

'It's over, Claudia,' he said, a new firmness in his tone. 'It was good while it lasted.' The clichés rolled out. 'I'll always remember the good times we had. You'll always have a place in my heart.'

She got up. 'If you don't change your mind by this evening – say 6 p.m. – I'm going to tell Freddy I came here to end it and you – you raped me.'

New-found courage aided him. 'He won't believe that. He'll know you can't rape a woman who never says no.'

She came at him then, sharp nails extended. They had scratched his face before he succeeded in grabbing her round the waist and pinioning her arms behind her back. She struggled and kicked, catching him on the shin with one of her high heels. That made him yell but he held on to her, marched her across the floor and forced her out of his front door. Katie Constantine, collecting her post, watched with interest. Stuart slammed the door shut. The bolts on it had never been used but now he used them, to no purpose but to make himself feel safe. Claudia pounded on it with her fists – and by the sound of it, with her feet too – shouting and shrieking as she did so. Stuart went into his bedroom and closed the door.

He scrutinised his face in the Design for Living mirror with all the anxiety of a model concerned about tomorrow's photo shoot. The bruising on his forehead was long gone but the marks on both cheeks looked like what they were – scratches from eight sharp nails. His shin was bleeding, the blood coming through his jeans. When he had dabbed Savlon on his face, stripped off his jeans and put a plaster on the wound Claudia's heel had made, he lit a cigarette and lay down on his bed to think about Tigerlily.

What was the set-up over at Springmead? If they had been

Indians or Pakistanis, he would have accepted that the two girls would have marriages arranged for them and allowed to know no other men but prospective bridegrooms. Surely Cambodians or Vietnamese were Buddhists, though? Stuart found his knowledge in these matters shaky in the extreme. But someone had said they came from Hong Kong. He thought he had read somewhere that Malaysia was a Muslim country. Could they be from there? But if the girls were Muslim and their father was strict, how did it happen that they didn't wear scarves over their heads when they went out? Then he asked himself why Tigerlily had agreed to come. The easy answer was that she was attracted by him, something that Stuart never found hard to believe. More difficult to understand was what she had meant by calling him a good man. Girls weren't usually interested in men because they were good. It was a puzzle and not one that he was likely to solve by talking to her. She seemed to have almost no English.

But this deficiency bothered him very little. He wasn't much of a talker himself and on the whole he preferred women without much to say. Talking only led to trouble. Look at his mother. Look at Claudia and her constant phone calls and Freddy's little gizmos. No, if you wanted speech you had only to turn on the TV.

His mobile began playing 'Nessun dorma'. He put a pillow over it.

Sophie regretted telling the others about shopping for Olwen. That had been a mistake. Noor was away a lot, anyway, staying at her boyfriend's, while Molly only wanted to talk about Stuart. What a beautiful voice he had, how handsome he was and how graceful.

'A guy can't be graceful,' said Sophie.

'Why not? Stuart is.'

'If you miss any more lectures they won't take you back in October.'

Molly ignored her. 'I'm making myself indispensable to him. He's getting to a point where he can't do without me. If you're going to the shops, would you get me some Kenya mountain blend coffee? Stuart doesn't like instant and I can't blame him.'

Sophie said she would, but she said it grudgingly. She had so far been to Mr Ali's for Olwen's gin and vodka and now had paid his shop three visits in the past ten days. It was becoming embarrassing. Young as she was, Sophie already knew that the excuse 'I'm getting it for a friend' is believed by no one. This time she must go further afield. Walking up to Tesco was no great hardship but carrying the two heavy bottles back would be, especially with the added burden of Stuart Font's coffee. Ten pounds a time was nothing really. Olwen ought to understand that she was a student and couldn't really spare the time from all the reading she was expected to do. If she was going to make all these trips – she hadn't realised how frequent they would be – she needed to be better compensated.

Tesco had its own cash machine on the wall by its petrol station. Sophie had intended to draw out of Olwen's account enough to cover two shopping trips – the cost of four bottles of spirits and twenty pounds for herself. She could do with twice that, she thought, she could do with forty pounds if she was going to repay Noor what she owed her for lunches and the cinema and that top she had bought at Leilaland. Everyone borrowed from Noor, she was so rich, but even she was starting to get funny about it, reminding Sophie of her debts each time she came back to the flat.

Standing in front of the cash machine, whistled at by a

tanker driver, Sophie thought she might draw out forty pounds now and that would cover her next ten-pound payments. When the time came, she would just draw the cost of four bottles of gin and vodka but nothing for herself. With a haughty glance at the tanker driver, she keyed 7529 into the machine and then the sum she wanted. It would be gratifying to repay Noor without even being asked.

You entered Kenilworth Green from Kenilworth Avenue by way of a kissing gate. When Rose first heard the name, in the days when she and Marius were at ease with one another, she asked him what it meant and he showed her how when the gate was opened by someone entering it was necessarily closed to someone leaving. Trapped in the wrought-iron loop with the gate between them, the girl could be kissed by the man over the top of it. Rose thought Marius might have suited the action to the word and kissed her but he didn't.

The path from the gate led into a little park perhaps two acres in size, a grass plot, occasionally mown, surrounded by fine tall trees, horse chestnuts now in the full flowering of their white candles, cherries whose shed blossom lay thickly around their roots, oaks coming into leaf, a copper beech or two, red-gold in leaf buds. In the centre of the plot stood the slender green cones of two swamp cypresses and half a dozen hornbeams, their inverted heart shapes natural to them but looking man-made. There was a seat under the hornbeams, one under the chestnuts, and a third in the far north-eastern corner near a see-saw and two swings. Sometimes, when those using the swings and the see-saw were girl children and the Kenilworth Primary School pupils had gone in to their lessons, Wally Scurlock took his trowel and his shears to another grave and knelt down to stare through another gap in the hedge.

One afternoon at the beginning of May he had an unpleasant shock. Two girls, aged perhaps six and seven, were on the swings while another, older but no more than twelve, sat on the seat, looking at a picture book. Wally clipped at the long grass under an ancient gravestone, looking up from time to time at the swinging children. Both were wearing T-shirts and full skirts and the little breeze blew their skirts up almost over their heads when the swing reached its highest point. He moved closer to the hedge and squatted down to peer through the gap.

Suddenly, without warning, the one on the seat slammed her book shut and strode towards the hedge. And he saw that she was no child. Small and thin though she was, pigtailed and short-skirted, she was a grown woman of thirty or more. He got quickly to his feet as she shouted at him.

'What the hell d'you think you're doing? Pervert! Paedophile! Child molester!'

Wally was trembling but he defended himself. 'I don't know what you mean. I'm working on the graves, that's all I'm doing.'

'Like hell it is! I'll have you know I come here every time my daughters come and I'll be watching for you. If ever I see you again, looking at kids, I'll see to it you go to prison for a long, long time.'

'I've done nothing,' Wally said. 'I didn't even notice your kids.'

'I haven't got my mobile with me. If I had I wouldn't be arguing with you, I'd be calling nine-nine-nine and the police would be here before you'd turned round.'

Wally didn't wait to hear any more. He put his tools into the bag and made his escape, not running but trying to maintain some dignity. The trouble was that he was shaking all over, his legs trembling so badly that he couldn't have run. He could only just walk. And when he was out in Kenilworth

Avenue and allowed himself to look back, the woman and her daughters were still there, but worse, much much worse, so were Rose Preston-Jones and that dog of hers. A long way away, right up by the chestnut trees, but not at all far from the little girls who were now kneeling on the grass to fondle the dog while their mother was talking to Rose. No prizes, said Wally to himself, for guessing what they were talking about. Thank God that woman didn't know his name. But had Rose seen him before the woman spoke to her?

There was nothing to be done. Yet he had done nothing. He had only looked. When did he ever do more than look? Even with those Internet images he only looked and they were only pictures. Where was the harm?

Amanda Copeland, whom Rose slightly knew through her daughters' fondness for McPhee, had told her about the paedophile watching the girls, about his lecherous expression (her words) when their skirts blew over their heads in the wind. That was upsetting enough but even worse was when Rose looked over her shoulder towards Kenilworth Avenue and saw Wally Scurlock scuttling home with his bag of garden tools. Of course she couldn't be absolutely sure that the man Amanda had seen and shouted at was Wally, not sure enough, for instance, to tell the police, though as they said in the courts she was certain beyond a reasonable doubt. But she said nothing to Amanda, only sympathised.

'I've seen him in the cemetery before,' Amanda said. 'He was cutting the grass round another grave. Or that's what I thought he was doing, but now I think he had his eye on the schoolchildren.'

Rose put McPhee on his lead and started for home. Connecting Wally with Amanda's allegations had disturbed her more than she had thought possible. Like most people, like nearly all women, she was shocked and horrified by paedophilia. What was she to do? Anything or nothing? If she had actually seen Wally squatting beyond the hedge, peering at the children, she would have gone to the police. More than that, she would have phoned the police from Kenilworth Green, for, unlike Amanda, she never went out without her mobile. But she hadn't seen him until he was walking past the fence, a hundred yards away.

If only there was someone whose advice she could ask.

Her parents were still alive, up in Manchester, but they were very old, cared for by her sister, and though she visited as often as she could, she knew that their reaction would be the kind of shock that put up a barrier to any reasonable discussion. The same went for her sister. Mary? Wendy? Other friends and acquaintances she sometimes saw such as Anther and Zither, now respectable and with normal names? Unless they were much changed they might even sympathise with paedophilia in a detached kind of way. She shuddered. There was only one person to consult. A few weeks ago she wouldn't have hesitated but have called Marius even before she got home. Things were different now.

At home, with McPhee snuggled up on her lap, Rose sat by the window. She saw Wally Scurlock come in. He had taken his time about it, dawdling on his way back. Her eyes followed him as he came up the path, hoping somehow to gather from his demeanour and the expression on his face, when he turned once to look back, evidence of dreadful proclivities.

Molly Flint came in with two heavy bags, then Noor with a tall dark young man who looked as if he might be an Eastern prince, the son perhaps of a raja or nawab. Rose wasn't consciously watching for Marius, but when he appeared, returning perhaps from a tutoring session, she put McPhee gently on the floor and went slowly to her front door. From there she heard his footsteps cross the hallway on his way to the stairs. No lift for him, ever.

She gave him five minutes to climb the stairs and five minutes more to get inside his flat. Then she went out into the lobby and up in the lift.

CHAPTER FOURTEEN

'Oh, Rose,' Marius said in what sounded to her like a cold tone. 'Come in' followed reluctantly.

'Am I disturbing you?'

He intended to say that he was rather busy, but the sight of her, so pretty and fragile, so apparently troubled, went to his heart. He thought that if he wasn't so old and skinny and grey, a tiresome old pedant, how much he would love to take her in his arms and comfort her. 'What is it? Is something wrong?'

'I suppose so. Well, yes.'

'Would you like some tea? I could make white tea. Or Earl Grey?'

She nodded. 'I'd like that. One or the other, it doesn't matter.'

Although he had only gone into the kitchen, she was absurdly afraid that if she let him out of her sight he might disappear. She followed him. He put the kettle on, the tea bags into two mugs, and then he turned round, his face set and his eyes narrowed as if he had come to some momentous decision. He *had* come to a decision – he was going to tell her. In those few moments he had decided and he would never change again, as cravenly he had last time. Now, for some reason, was the moment. If she failed to believe him or denied it or was shocked, if she was affronted, so be it. The point was that he couldn't go on the way he had been.

'Rose,' he said. 'Rose, I've got something to tell you.'

His gravity had frightened her. 'What do you mean? What is it?'

'Rose, we've met before – long ago – in a commune – in Hackney. I've known for ages. You won't remember. I am very changed. It sounds ridiculous. But I was young then and it wasn't ridiculous then. Oh, Rose . . .'

There are different kinds of laughter. The laughter of sheer mirth, the laughter of incredulity, the laughter of cynicism – and the laughter of pure joy. This last was Rose's laughter and when it had subsided into a smile, she said, 'Of course I know, Marius. I recognised you the first time we met, the day you moved in.' The kettle began to boil, shaking and juddering and exuding steam. 'You haven't changed – or not much. I have, I know. That's why I thought you didn't recognise me.'

'Why didn't you say?'

'Because I'm an old woman now and then I was young.'

'But you haven't changed at all,' he said, and as he said it he thought, that's love, time is the test of love. It alters not in his brief hours and weeks but bears it out even to the edge of doom . . . He took her in his arms and when she made no resistance, held her close, his lips against her hair.

They forgot about the tea. Rose, for a while, forgot about Wally Scurlock. She sat next to Marius on his aunt's old grey sofa. 'You see,' she said, 'you were so handsome – still are – and when I woke up in the morning and saw you asleep, your face on the pillow, I thought what a lovely face it was and how sweet you'd been to me. And I began to think what you must think of me – well, you didn't know me, we'd never really met, and still I went to bed with you . . .' she turned her face away '. . . and when you woke up I thought, he'll despise me, he'll think me so cheap and never want to see me again and I got dressed and left, not saying goodbye to anyone. I just left.'

'And I tried to find you and never could till in the end I gave up. Rose, no one knew your surname except my sister and she'd gone off to America. You were sitting on a bench in Victoria Park and you told Storm you couldn't move into the room you were renting till the next day. But he didn't know where the room was or anything else about you.'

'I haven't seen Storm since but I do sometimes see Anther. He's called Terence Tate now. That's his real name.'

'You and he . . . ?'

'No, nothing like that. There's not been anything like that in my life for a long, long time.'

'Nor in mine,' said Marius in a low voice, and then, 'I love you, Rose. I think I've always loved you. Certainly I've known it since I first moved in here.' He kissed her cheek and then her mouth. 'What shall we do? Now I've found you I don't want to let you out of my sight.'

In later years Rose sometimes said that she and Marius had been brought together by the behaviour of a paedophile and Marius said that out of the vile came forth sweetness. But that evening, when they at last had that white tea in Rose's flat – Marius wasn't thinking of leaving it before the next day – he was more shocked than he would have expected by what Rose told him.

'You hear about it all the time and you read about it but still it never seems quite real.'

'Amanda Copeland wouldn't make something like that up, darling,' said Rose. 'She's a sensible woman – much more sensible than me.'

'You are sensi*tive,*' said Marius, 'which is better.'

'And of course I'm not absolutely certain it was him. I couldn't swear to it. Do you think we should consult the *sortes?*'

'I'm fed up with *Paradise Lost*. When I was miserable about you I threw Milton at the wall.'

'I know you did. I picked him up off the floor and brought him down with us in my bag.'

So Marius opened the book at random, ran his finger down the page and read: '"Abandon fear; to strength and counsel joined, / Think nothing hard, much less despaired."'

'It doesn't seem to mean much,' said Rose. 'I'm sorry, darling. It usually does. I'm not criticising.'

Marius laughed. 'It usually *doesn't*. It's only a game. But perhaps it means that we should just do nothing. Not yet, anyway. Or almost nothing,' he said thoughtfully.

Rose looked enquiringly at him.

'I'd suggest the police if he'd done anything but he just looks. We should keep an eye on him, watch him but no more. Not yet. If I get the chance,' he said, 'I will drop a hint, tell him not to do it. I will try to be subtle about it.'

'You won't have to try,' said Rose. 'And now I am going to cook us some delicious asparagus and after that prawns.'

'I intended not to leave your side for even a moment but you won't mind if I do for ten minutes, will you? If I go up to Mr Ali's and buy a bottle of champagne? We don't drink, I know, but tonight is the night to break the rule of a lifetime. Oh, and Rose, do you still not mind spiders?'

'I quite like them. Why do you ask?'

More frightened than he had ever been in his entire life, Wally was experiencing the extremes of fear, those which paralyse the nerves and muscles so that ordinary walking is difficult. Staggering through the roundabout, he had doubted if he would make it to Lichfield House. He might actually have fallen, lain prone in the gutter with his tools scattered about him. People must be staring at him as he leaned against the blank window of the now abandoned bathroom fittings shop, they would take him for a drunk, turned out of the Kenilworth Arms for disorderly behaviour. In fact, there was no one to see until Duncan Yeardon emerged from the newsagent's. Duncan had glanced in his direction and turned away, embarrassed.

Wally would have liked to sink to the ground and close his eyes but that was impossible. He made a gargantuan effort – walk, keep walking, don't give in, you'll be OK in a minute. And this time it wasn't so bad. He took deep breaths, he walked, not attempting to do so at his usual pace. If Duncan turned round he would think Wally was walking slowly in order to avoid catching up with him, which was also true. Duncan crossed the road and paused to talk to the man from Springmead who had just got out of his car. Their backs were to him and Wally, taking advantage of this, made his way into Lichfield House as fast as his weak legs would carry him.

Downstairs in the basement flat he poured himself a small brandy from the half-bottle Richenda kept for emergencies. A wonderful quick-spreading warmth started in his chest and flowed up to fill his head. That was better. That was both calming and stimulating. What was he going to do? First ask himself what had really happened and what it amounted to. Because of Rose Preston-Jones, that friend of hers, that woman – that savage wild hysterical woman – would know where he lived and no doubt his name. It was too late to stop Rose telling her, it had always been too late. The question was, would either of them tell the police? Who was the more likely? Rose, he thought, Rose who knew him. He must give her some sort of explanation. Finishing the brandy and rinsing his mouth out with Listerine, he went back upstairs and rang Rose's bell. No answer. He rang again but by then he knew she was out. Could she have gone to the police?

If she had they would come soon. They would search his flat and take away his computer. Wally knew his wisest course would be to dispose of his computer, either smash it to bits with the heavy mallet he had in his toolbox or take it out of here, out of Lichfield House, get on the number 113 bus which went down through St John's Wood, and drop it into the canal from the bridge in Lisson Grove. He knew the area, he'd once lived in Penfold Street. But to destroy his computer and with it all the pleasure and excitement it contained, to that he couldn't bring himself. Not yet. There would be time, wouldn't there? Perhaps he could hide it. His flat had a bathtub in the bathroom but no shower. All the others had showers as well as bathtubs. This was something Wally bitterly resented. It told him the designers or architects or whatever of Lichfield House believed that the caretaker and his wife belonged to a different species from that of the middle-class residents, one whose members needed total immersion to cleanse them of their inherent dirt.

The base of his bath had been concealed by hardboard panels, held in place by screws. A nasty cheap job, Wally had thought and had covered the panels with tasteful black-and-white marble-effect vinyl and the screws with chromium nuts. They would never look there. He removed the nuts and one of the panels. Inside was a space just big enough for the computer. He laid it carefully on the floor and was screwing back the last nut when he heard Richenda's key in the front door.

'You'll never guess who I've just seen go into Rose thingy's flat. Together, I mean. Her and old Potter.' Gossip always put her into a good mood.

'So what's new?'

'I'll tell you what's new. They was *kissing*. Like young ones.'

Did that mean Rose was too preoccupied to trouble herself with him? Hope struggled up into his throat on an inhaled breath.

First her dad had got out of his car and was talking to Duncan Yeardon. Then he went into Springmead and was inside for a long time, so long that Stuart began to think he wouldn't come out again. But the car was still there by the time the traffic warden, still writing down numbers in his book at twenty-five past six, went off duty. Stuart stood inside his front window, smoking and drinking his fourth cappuccino of the day. Twenty minutes passed and he was halfway through another cigarette when Marius Potter appeared from the automatic doors. Even Stuart, not the most observant of men, noticed the spring in his step. What's got into him? he wondered. Must be off to tutor one of those poor kids in horrible Latin verbs or some such rubbish, and he remembered the teacher who had come to him on Wednesday evenings, trying to drill Caesar's invasion of Britain into him. But no, Marius was back in minutes, carrying what was unmistakably a bottle of champagne, wrapped up in dark blue tissue paper. Hypocrite, thought Stuart, him and that Rose always going on about the evils of alcohol.

At that moment, as the automatic doors opened for Marius, Tigerlily's dad came out of Springmead with her sister or stepmother. The two of them got into the car and shot off in the direction of the main road. Dusk was coming early because it had been a dull day and lights were already showing in some of the houses when the front door of Springmead opened and Tigerily came out. She paused on the step and looked to her right and her left. Then she came quickly to the gate and crossed the road. Although she must have seen Stuart at his window she gave no sign that she had. He heard the swoosh of the doors, a light footstep in the hallway and then his bell rang.

She slipped inside immediately he had opened it. He would have liked her to be dressed in diaphanous white or ankle-length black but she wore what he liked least – jeans and a loose white shirt. She was still wonderfully beautiful, her almond-shaped black eyes grave and steady, her hair hanging loose and water-straight from a centre parting.

'Hi,' she said. 'Hi.'

He took her hands, led her into his living room. 'What's your name? I call you Tigerlily.'

'Ti-ka-lee-lee,' she said, and she smiled. She's Chinese, he thought. That's what she is. She peered into his face, touched with a forefinger the scorings on his cheeks Claudia's nails had made. 'You cut?'

'It doesn't matter.'

She smiled a very small smile. Then she astonished him. 'Ti-ka-lee-lee name go in passport.'

What did she mean? 'No,' he said, 'must have real name for passport.' Involuntarily, he was speaking pidgin English. 'Sit down. You like drink?'

She shook her head, refusing seat and drink. 'You good man,' she said, a statement, not a question.

He smiled, nodded, because he didn't know what else to do. He was mystified. If only she would sit down, so that he could. But she stood there, stock-still, her eyes turned to the window. 'What do you want, Tigerlily?'

'Ti-ka-lee-lee,' she said again. 'Want passport. You get?'

He knew then. It had been going on since he was a child, since before he was born. A friend of a friend of his mother's had married a man from somewhere in Asia to give him British citizenship. It had been easy then. Would it be as easy now? Somehow he doubted it.

'You want you and me get married?'

She didn't understand. She shrugged, held out her hands, palms upward. 'Passport,' she said. 'I make photo.'

If he married her she wouldn't get a passport at once. He knew that much. His thoughts rushed almost too fast for him. She'd get something called right of residence, wouldn't she? He could find out, the Internet would tell him. But *marry*? When the time came where would he find a lovelier wife? Wives, in his experience, were like his mother and Claudia, good-looking, bossy, constantly talking, over-emotional, greedy. Tigerlily was none of these things except the first – and that in abundance. 'Sit down,' he said again and this time she did.

She perched on the edge of his sofa, still watching the window, clasping her knees in her slender white hands. Flip-flops were on her feet but her insteps were so arched that she might have been wearing high heels. Women from her part of the world, he thought, made good wives because they liked waiting on men, making themselves beautiful for men. They weren't always arguing or asking for things. Vaguely he remembered seeing pictures of geishas kneeling at men's feet, holding up trays of food and drink. Or was that Japanese? But marriage – it was a big step.

He said carefully, 'I look after you, Tigerlily. You savvy?' Where had he got that ancient word from? One of his father's friends maybe or that caretaker? He tried again. 'I care for you. Understand?'

She was smiling, nodding.

'We must meet again.'

How to tell her where? Somewhere he had a London A–Z. There weren't many places it could be and he soon found it in the cupboard part of his bedside cabinet. She looked at the map he showed her – this part of north London – and her face was full of wonder. It took him a few minutes to make her see where Springmead was, where he was and the extension of Kenilworth Avenue with Kenilworth Green and St Ebba's Church. The church was marked on the map by a cross and when he pointed to that she nodded, managed, 'Understand.'

'Today is Friday.'

This was beyond her comprehension. The procedure he had to go through was like looking for the A–Z but worse. At last he found the calendar of English beauty spots his mother had sent him along with her present at Christmas. How well he remembered the letter that came with it, especially the bit about never seeing him and never being invited to his new home, so she had to send his present. The calendar he had never hung up and he found it at last in a drawer under some shirts he never wore.

He knew at once that she couldn't read the names of the days. Of course. She couldn't read – what was it called? – yes, Latin script. 'Today,' he said, 'Friday. Yes?'

'Friday.' She made the *r* into an *l* as he had heard the Chinese did. 'Good,' he said. He counted on his fingers, 'Saturday, no. Sunday, no. Monday?'

She moved her head slowly from side to side, said, 'Monday, no,' and she shuddered. 'No Tuesday.'

'Wednesday?'

For the first time a 'Yes'.

'Wed-ness-day,' she said. 'Good.'

'Wednesday at Kenilworth Green.' He said it again, over and over again, and then he showed her the time on his mobile. It said 19.31. 'Same time?'

Another nod. 'Same time Wednesday.'

'Kenilworth Green.'

She got up, looked him in the eyes and made a little formal bow. He was enchanted. 'Will you give me a kiss, Tigerlily?' He formed his lips into a kissing shape.

She shook her head violently, turned away her face, and quickly she was gone.

Well, he wouldn't want a wife who'd kiss a man the first time she met him. A wife? The word made him flinch a bit. He thought of his parents' reaction if he turned up with a Chinese wife. But he never did turn up, did he? They'd probably never meet his wife, never have to know he'd got one. He went to the window. It was getting dark and Tigerlily's father had his headlights on as he turned into Kenilworth Avenue. The girl got out of the car first. This one looked years older than Tigerlily. It must be an arranged marriage Tigerlily wanted to escape. He hadn't known the Chinese were Muslims. No doubt other countries and other religions had arranged marriages. But why did she want a false passport? She must have a passport already but perhaps her father held on to it and wouldn't let her have it.

Of course there was no way he could get her a passport, he wouldn't know where to begin, but he could marry her. She would have to get a new passport then, wouldn't she? He realised she hadn't told him her name. That must be the first thing to get out of her on Wednesday. And was he saying that once they had met on Kenilworth Green she would never go back to Springmead? Perhaps he was saying that. He must be. That brought him unease and a shiver went through him. He suddenly thought of the responsibility he was taking upon himself, the decisions he would have to make, the cost of it all, for he would have to take her somewhere and not here to this flat. A hotel? And then what? Go to a registrar somewhere and give their names, make a date for the wedding? But to be alone with her in a hotel where there was nothing to fear from her father, to have a safe quiet dinner with her, to drink champagne as those two old people must be doing, to go up to their bedroom together . . .

CHAPTER FIFTEEN

'I never wanted to own a house,' said Marius. 'I think that was because I was on my own, but when there are two of you having a home means a lot. The idea of it. And that ought to be in a house, not a flat. Even if it's a very little house.'

'It would have to be that, darling, because a mansion is beyond our means.'

'Would you think of selling both our flats and buying a house?'

'I'm already thinking of it,' said Rose. 'Would you like some pomegranate tea? It's a beautiful colour, a bright pink, and it's very sweet but I'm afraid it's got sugar in it. Do you remember that about the time you and I first met they were saying sugar was poison? Someone called it "white death".'

Laughing, Marius said, 'Yes, but no one ever died of eating sugar, did they? I *like* the taste of sugar much better than aspartame or whatever it's called. And we shall never get fat, you and I. Do you want to get married, Rose – my darling Rose?'

'It used to be against my principles and I don't think they've changed. I'm sure it used to be against yours.'

'Indeed. Still, I think we'd better. When we've got our house we shall need to protect the one who survives against inheritance tax.'

'Oh, Marius, I don't want to survive you. But then I don't want to die first and have you be unhappy without me.'

'It's a dilemma, isn't it?'

'Let the *sortes* decide, darling.'

'"Fair couple,"' Marius read, '"linked in happy nuptial league."'

'Well, that's pretty clear for marriage, isn't it?

'I cheated,' he said. 'I knew exactly where to find it.'

They had done nothing about Wally Scurlock beyond watching him and twice going up to St Ebba's churchyard. But on those occasions Wally hadn't been there and the only odd thing they discovered was that one single grave was well kept when all the rest were derelict and overgrown.

Sophie's heart gave a little jump and her throat grew dry. The cash machine had told her there were insufficient funds in Olwen's bank account to meet her request for £50. She had taken it for granted that Olwen had plenty of money, a more or less inexhaustible supply. This was something she assumed in the case of all 'grown-ups', for although Sophie was nineteen, the age at which her grandmother had twice given birth, she thought of herself, if not quite as a child, as a teenager without responsibilities or much in the way of resources. She was young, therefore carefree, immortal and free. Or this was how she had thought of herself and of circumstances until this moment.

It was not quite yet the middle of May and although Sophie knew little of financial matters, somehow she had become aware that most salaries, pensions and other sources of income are paid in at the end of the month. Olwen might be, as Noor said, several bean sprouts short of a Chinese takeaway, but she knew how much money she ought to have in the bank.

People usually did know that, Sophie thought in an increasing panic.

Empty-handed, she walked away and sat down on the low wall which surrounded the Tesco car park. Her own bank account should be in a healthier state than it had been for a long time. The balance of her grant remained in there plus the money Daddy and Mummy had paid in for her birthday present. As to her steady milking of Olwen's account, she had given up that rule of taking only £10 for herself each time. First there had been the £40 she owed Noor. Then, because it really was stupid of Olwen to think £10 a time was adequate – these old people were all out of touch when it came to the cost of living – she had taken £20 twice and £30 once. It was only at this point that she realised that the increasing amounts she was helping herself to were responsible for her present predicament.

None of what she had taken remained. She had spent it as she went along; on clothes, on new CDs, on one of those tiny iPods in a beautiful sapphire blue. But she couldn't go back to Olwen without the vodka and the gin. Miserably, she got up, went back to the cashpoint and drew out £30 from her own bank account.

The children who went to Kenilworth Primary School were out in the playground, running around, shrieking and yelling. The girls shrieked and the boys yelled. That man who was the caretaker for the flats was in the churchyard, doing something to a grave. Sophie thought she would tell Noor and Molly that he was a vampire who dug up bodies and sucked their blood. Noor, who was very superstitious, might believe her. The caretaker wasn't looking at what he was doing any more but staring at the children. Probably planning on grabbing one of them to suck *his* blood, thought Sophie, warming to her fantasy.

Olwen let her in about five minutes after Sophie rang her doorbell. These days she moved increasingly slowly, holding on to whatever she could grab, and of that there wasn't much. Sophie, as requested, brought her a cut white loaf and some sliced salami. Olwen wasn't hungry, she never was, but she thought her new feeling of sickness and savage stomach pains might be due to lack of food.

'How are you?' Sophie asked, the enquiry prompted by conscience. 'Are you feeling better?'

'Not really,' said Olwen.

'Would you like me to make you a sandwich?'

Olwen repeated her usual rejoinder and pushed the door shut almost before Sophie had backed through it.

Replies had come to Stuart's job applications. All were negative, some polite, some taciturn. A lot of companies simply failed to answer. April had gone by and he was still as far from getting a job as ever and still as far from acquiring money. He sat down at the computer and looked at the blank screen.

The drone of the vacuum cleaner irritated him but, apart from that, he barely noticed that Molly was there. He was preoccupied with plan-making. However he was going to 'rescue' Tigerlily, he must have somewhere to take her on Wednesday night. To bring her back here would be impossible. They needed to go somewhere her father and maybe the rest of the family would never think of looking. The kind of hotel he had originally had in mind wouldn't do. It had to be some middle-grade suburban place. For one thing, he had to consider the cost of it. He couldn't help thinking how much easier all this would be if Tigerlily was more proficient in English so that he knew specifically what she was afraid of and what she wanted – apart from being with him. Of this last he was pretty sure.

Were there any such hotels up here? Probably, but he didn't know where. From taxis he had squired Claudia about in, he had noticed a big old hotel in Cricklewood that had once been a pub but very much refurbished, and another newer one in Kilburn on the borders of Maida Vale. He should book a room in one of those. And then he must decide about marrying her. It was a big step but where would he find a sweeter lovelier girl? To do it would be a good deed, for it was surely what she wanted. Stuart admitted to himself that he didn't know how you went about getting a passport. Of course he had one himself, he was English, so without difficulties in this area. And if a foreign girl married such a one, such a British-born stalwart, would she automatically also become English, a citizen, a subject of the Queen, with a fine dark red British passport? Somehow he didn't think it was that easy. There was more to it. But she would get right of residence, surely? These were matters he must look up on the Internet. And then, when that was done, find a registry office and a registrar and – well, put their names down. He didn't actually know her name. When they met on Wednesday at seven thirty on Kenilworth Green he would get her to say her name. That must be his first priority. Once she was married to him they couldn't forcibly marry her to anyone else. At least he knew that this was true.

He started the computer and googled 'Passports'. Molly had finished with the vacuum cleaner and was standing behind him asking him if he'd like a cappuccino.

'You know, I've like gone off them. I think I'm back to hot chocolate.'

'We haven't got that much milk but I could run up the road and get some.'

'You do that,' said Stuart absently, and added, 'there's a good girl.'

Molly, who should have been at college, was standing in a queue at Mr Ali's when Carl phoned her. It was the third time he had phoned that morning.

'There's like someone else, isn't there?'

'So what if there is, Carly? It's not like we were engaged or anything.'

'Maybe you weren't, Moll, but I was.'

'Oh, come on. It takes two to be engaged.'

'It's that Stuart, isn't it? The one that had the party?'

'So what if it is, Carly?' Having got to the top of the queue, Molly ended the call and bought her milk. On her way back, she met Katie Constantine.

'Did you know two flats in Lichfield House are on the market?'

'Which two?' Suppose Stuart was going to sell his flat and move, Molly thought, and hadn't bothered to tell her? 'Not Stuart Font's?'

'Not so far as I know,' said Katie. 'That Mr Yeardon who lives over there told me.' She waved a vague hand. 'Funny you have to hear it from someone who doesn't even live there, isn't it?'

'Yes, but which ones?'

'Number 2 and number 3. That's Marius and Rose. Michael says they'll be lucky to sell what with this credit crunch.'

Molly felt happy to have a piece of news for Stuart. But when she told him he barely seemed interested. He was occupied on his computer, printing out reams of stuff. She stood behind him sadly for a minute or two and then she went off to wash up his chocolate mug. Stuart had discovered many websites dealing with eligibility for a British passport, marriage to a British citizen, right of residence and right of abode. Everything seemed to be all right if you married this British citizen before 1949 but that would make you about eighty now. The first of January 1983 seemed another significant date. He didn't know why. All that was clear was that Tigerlily wouldn't become a British citizen and thus have a British passport just because she was married to him. On the other hand, suppose it was true she came from Hong Kong? Had Hong Kong once been part of the Commonwealth? His father would know but he didn't want to ask his father.

The day was fine if rather windy. He went out for a walk to think about it, watched by Molly from the window. Fresh air – or the diesel-scented fug which passed for it – was supposed to clear one's head, and as Stuart passed through the kissing gate into Kenilworth Green, he found that it was having that effect. A plain fact had emerged from all that circumlocution and bumf. Getting married to Tigerlily wouldn't help her get a passport. She would have to get on to the Home Office herself and ask what to do, a procedure which would no doubt entail holding the phone line for about three-quarters of an hour while listening to Handel's 'Largo'. Marrying him would be no short cut. Much as he told himself he adored Tigerlily, he couldn't help feeling relief that he wouldn't have to marry her. All he need do was take her to a hotel that night, hide her from her family and find some-where for them to live. Maybe rent a flat on the other side of London while renting out Flat 1 Lichfield House. That way he wouldn't be much out of pocket.

Sitting down on the bench under the blossoming chestnut trees, he indulged in delightful fantasies: he and Tigerlily sitting side by side, her hand in his, watching TV, he at the computer while she cooked delicious Chinese meals, she

bringing him a glass of chilled white wine or possibly champagne on a Chinese lacquer tray, kneeling in front of him like
the geisha in the picture, he and Tigerlily entwined on a big
low white bed.

The wind blew apple and chestnut blossom on to the grass
like snow. He thought how there had been snow on the ground
when first he saw her. She was the loveliest girl he had ever
seen and soon she would be his. But not, luckily, his wife.

CHAPTER SIXTEEN

The police had never come. They hadn't phoned him. This must mean that the woman who looked from a distance like a little girl – but with her wrinkled face not the kind of little girl he might fancy – hadn't told the police. More to the point, Rose Preston-Jones, who knew him, hadn't done so either. And Rose would soon be moving. She hadn't bothered to tell *him*, of course, he was only the caretaker, only the person responsible for the welfare of everyone in the four blocks. Wally had seen the advertisement in the window of an estate agent's, which had just opened where Wicked Wine used to be, her flat for sale and the one that belonged to Marius Potter.

It looked as if he was safe. He would be more careful in future. Better stay at home, at least for a while, and as soon as Richenda went out cleaning, visit his favourite sites on the computer. Once she had gone he unscrewed the nuts on the vinyl panels and lifted out his Toshiba, glad now that he hadn't opted for the alternative and dropped it into the Regent's Canal. Pleased with himself and his escape from those women, he did something he had wanted to do for a long time but hadn't quite dared. He printed out the choicest pictures, spent ten minutes or so contemplating them, and then put them away in the space where the computer had been.

At ten twenty-five this Wednesday morning he walked across the road to his new friend's house. Duncan Yeardon had encountered him while they were both shopping in the Tesco, they had got talking, recalling their meeting at Stuart's party, and Duncan had invited him over 'for a coffee' and a look at his new decorations.

The coffee was thin and had the consistency and flavour of Bisto gravy, a favourite of Richenda's. Wally ate a Marie biscuit and remarked that Duncan kept his home very warm.

'Not me,' said Duncan. 'The heating's been off for weeks. It's the insulation. Wonderful insulation this place has got, enough to warm the cockles of the hearts of those climate-change people.'

Wally didn't know what he was talking about. As far as he knew, cockles were a kind of downmarket shellfish. He was looking at Duncan's newspaper which lay open on the arm of a chair at a story of a man who had been abusing children in Thailand and who had been watching hundreds of child pornography websites. There was a picture of the police taking his computer away while the abuser stood by, running his hands through his shoulder-length hair. Wally didn't want to talk about it and was commenting on the beauty of his host's back garden, visible through wide-open French windows, when Duncan said, 'These men make you sick to your stomach. I tell you what I'd do to them. I'd cut their – well, neuter them, like what they do to animals.'

Wally knew he ought to agree but somehow he couldn't. He needed to put up some sort of defence.

'Abusing kids is bad, of course, that's terrible, but there's no harm in watching films, is there? They're not real, they're just pictures.'

He was amazed at Duncan's response. 'Just pictures, are they? How d'you think they got those pictures, then? Real kids had to do those things, didn't they? Real *children* had to be made to do those things.' Duncan's voice was shrill with indignant rage. 'Trafficked kids, probably. Slave kids had to be forced to do that.'

'You want to calm down,' Wally said, and added, 'It's not me you want to get mad at. I don't make the bloody films.'

And Duncan did calm down. 'Bloody is right,' he said in a sad voice. 'I wonder how many die when those things are done to them, I just wonder.'

Wally didn't stay long after that. He wouldn't have much more to do with Duncan Yeardon. The man had made him feel vulnerable and frightened all over again. Was it true all that stuff he had said about children being forced to do those things? A lot of people believed that children enjoyed sex and wanted it just like adults did. Or it could be computer-generated, couldn't it? The really sadistic stuff, the cruel tortures, they couldn't be real but made up of bits of film sort of mixed up on a computer. Wally didn't know how but it must be something like the way they made dogs dance and rabbits sing for the commercials. It wasn't real animals and watching it was just harmless fun.

Michael Constantine was having a drink with his features editor. It was this man, midway between an acquaintance and a friend, who had got him his job. Their meeting would have been for lunch, Michael knew very well, if he was in favour. As it was, various difficulties which had come up were being pointed out to him; for instance, the large number of emails the newspaper received, drawing attention to discrepancies in Michael's articles. Lately there had also been tweets of a derisive or insulting nature.

'Surely a bit of controversy is good,' Michael said on his

second gin and tonic. 'Argument, discussion, all that sort of thing. A lot of this stuff is opinion, after all. What I write is my opinion. It's not as if we're talking about errors.'

'Well, as a matter of fact we are,' said the features editor, who never drank anything but water at lunchtime. 'That piece of yours about solar panels under the heading "Powerful Stuff", you don't seem to know the difference between kilowatts and kilowatt hours. Apparently it's a confusion between power and energy.'

Michael didn't say anything.

'That's halfway to understandable, I see that. But saying under the same heading that solar panels on a roof can heat up a house so that snow won't stick to its roof – well, that's simple fantasy, isn't it?'

Michael remembered picking up this piece of information from Marius Potter who had grinned at the time as if he knew it was – well, simple fantasy. 'I'm sorry. I must have been having an off day.'

The features editor laughed heartily to take the sting out of his words. 'Don't let it occur again, will you?'

Molly was always in the flat these days, it seemed to Stuart, at least a couple of hours each day. He several times tried to get rid of her by reminding her in an entirely uncharacteristic way that he was concerned about her missing college. She always said that she was on her way there, she had just 'popped in' to perform some essential task.

'I like you to have everything looking nice,' she said, smiling and putting her face too close to his.

These past weeks he had needed to do nothing for himself, not even pick up a mug from the floor or empty an ashtray.

She had scolded him once about his smoking but stopped when she saw his frown and had one herself when he offered her the packet. She made his bed and changed his sheets, cleaned the bath and scrubbed the tiled walls of the shower, waxed the floors and cleaned the windows. Once, in an impulsive moment after she had fetched his clothes from the dry-cleaner's, he had said, 'I don't know what I'd do without you.'

Her bright flush and adoring eyes told him not to say anything like that again. As an unpaid housekeeper she was a treasure but her presence in his flat had its downside. He disliked her being there while he changed his clothes, even though he shut himself in his bedroom. It meant putting on a dressing gown to go to the bathroom, and when he did, there she was putting bleach down the lavatory pan.

'Time you went, Molly,' he said, but to not much effect.

'When I've ironed the tea towels.'

Not even his mother ironed tea towels. He dressed himself with care in a snow-white shirt, laundered by Molly, black slub silk trousers and a blue denim jacket he had just bought in Hampstead. When he emerged from his bedroom Molly asked him if he was going somewhere nice.

'A hot date,' said Stuart.

'Have a good time.' Molly's tone was doleful.

She opened the front door for him like a maid. He gave her a quick kiss on the cheek, the first time he had ever touched her. But she ought to have some reward for all she did, poor thing. He smiled to himself, shaking his head, as someone slipped out through the automatic doors. No one he knew, whoever it was. He was carrying a small blue suitcase. It was of the softest, sleekest leather, the shade of a summer sky at dusk and in it he had placed a change of underwear, a clean shirt, a toothbrush and razor and various

.

other essentials of daily life. Some hours before he had phoned the Crown Hotel in Cricklewood and booked a double room for himself and Tigerlily.

But he was less happy about the forthcoming encounter than he had expected to be, because he had realised that what she must want of him was a *false* passport. It was obvious when you thought about it. Stuart was afraid of breaking the law. Apart from this, he didn't know how to go about it. Was it rather like getting hold of a handgun? You went into a pub in somewhere like Brixton or Harlesden and got talking to dubious-looking characters until one of them offered you what you wanted? Once, when he had been in such a place, he had been offered heroin and that had frightened him a lot. Well, he thought it was heroin. The dealer had offered him 'Big H'. Was he to go through all that again? Perhaps he need not think about it now. Or think about Claudia.

She had phoned him the previous evening. 'Where are you?' he had said, afraid of Freddy.

'Oh, he's out. Don't worry about him.'

But he did worry. The phone call turned into an argument, she saying she had to see him, he trying to tell her once again that their affair was at an end, but finally agreeing, knowing this was a promise he couldn't keep, to see her on Friday evening. St Ebba's clock struck seven just before he reached the roundabout. There, in the newsagent's, was where he had first seen Tigerlily. It had been love at first sight, he thought. But if only he could have just chatted her up a bit, asked her out and let everything take its normal course. She might be moving in with him now instead of his having to go through this horrendous business of passports and hotels and hiding from her dad or uncle or whoever he was. As for Claudia, when she turned up at the very expensive restaurant he said they would meet at, for the first time he wouldn't be there. Perhaps that would teach her. He was disconcerted when, as he approached the kissing gate, 'Nessun dorma' sounded again.

'Where are you now?' said Claudia's voice.

She must have heard his sigh. 'Does it matter?'

'I only wanted to tell you that I phoned the restaurant and they said you hadn't made a booking. They said that if you don't we shan't be able to get in, so I did. In your name, of course. You didn't tell me where you are now.'

He ended the call and switched off the mobile.

It was still as light as at noon. The chestnuts and the apple trees had shed all their blossom and it lay in billows of white and pink on the grass. After a while he sat down on the swing as St Ebba's clock struck the half-hour. Seven thirty. The swing had been made for people a lot lighter than him and it creaked a bit. He swung up and down a little, remembering from childhood that you placed your toes on the ground and pushed to make the swing rise higher. Better not do too much of that in case he broke it. Now to have a go on the carousel, spin it round a bit. He looked at the time on his mobile: seven forty. Which way would she come? Through the kissing gate or along the path from Chester Grove? He walked a little way along the path. No one was about, no one at all. When he turned round, walking back and emerging once more on to the green, he expected to see her coming through the gate, running perhaps because she was late. The green was empty yet for a single rabbit which hopped under the fence and came out on to the grass where it began eating a weed with yellow flowers.

Stuart returned to the swing. He felt he was being watched, yet when he turned round to look into the churchyard he could see no one. It was still daylight, but among the gravestones and under the dark evergreen trees, darkness had almost come. Nothing moved. He got off the swing and went up to the fence. There was no reason to suppose she would come through the grounds of St Ebba's and find herself having to climb over the fence, but still he stood there, peering in among the tree trunks, the sensation of someone watching him now overpowering.

He was afraid. Of what he didn't know. The stillness? The clear bright sky from in which the sun had gone but where distant stars showed? St Ebba's struck eight and the brazen notes sounded ominous. The kind of breeze that comes with dusk rustled through the new leaves and the last of the blossom, sending a shower of petals on to the grass. How long was he going to wait for her? Another half-hour? It was five past eight. The invisible eyes were still fixed on him. He turned his back on them, walked towards the see-saw, sat down on the low end of it, astride like a rider. Behind him came a crunching sound, like someone stepping on underbrush in a wood. He turned round then, certain it was Tigerlily, come at last.

Sophie was the only person who had come shopping on foot. To balance herself, she had got the checkout girl to put the vodka in one carrier and the gin in another. Cars were queuing up to leave the car park and one driver shouted at her when she rushed across the exit in front of his Honda. She never liked passing St Ebba's after dark, the churchyard was full of strange-shaped shadows and small things that moved. The small things that moved had eyes, so they were only wildlife, mice and squirrels and things, she supposed, but she always hurried past and past the green too. This time, though, something big moved among the graves and if it had eyes they held no green or golden glitter. Sophie ran, the carrier bags swinging and banging against her legs, heading for the safety of the roundabout.

Olwen was drinking the last of her last bottle of gin when Sophie rang her bell. She made her way to the door, forced now to call out that she was coming because all movement took her so long. It also caused her pain, in her back and especially in her knees. Her legs were so swollen that, without her usual opaque stockings, they looked like shiny red bolsters. A wheelchair was what she needed, she thought, but how to get one, who to ask and where to go – always supposing she could go anywhere – all that was beyond her. She got to the door and opened it.

Sophie, young and fit, looked at her in horror. She had been afraid outside St Ebba's but this was another kind of fright – the fear of madness. Olwen reminded her of a woman in a film she had once seen about the female inmates of what they called a lunatic asylum. She had the same misshapen body, the same straggling grey hair, and her clothes had almost become rags. As for her legs and feet, Sophie took one look and that was enough.

Inside, handing over the two bags, she said what she hadn't meant to say, what she had intended to put off saying for at least another two weeks when Olwen's money would come in. 'I can't do this for you any more. There's no more cash in your account.'

Olwen said nothing.

'You can hear me, Olwen, can't you? I'm not going shopping for you any more. I've not got the time and, anyway, like I said, there's no more money.' Sophie thought of the money, now amounting to £70, she had drawn from her own account. 'I'm spending my own,' she said, 'because you haven't any more. Do you understand?'

'Not really' would have done for a reply to this but Olwen didn't say it. Six months before, when she was still able to fetch her own drink from Wicked Wine, she had had a good idea of how much money she had and how much went in at the end of each month. Now her ability to make such calculations and retain some idea of them by a simple subtraction had gone. Working out how much drink she could afford had gone too. She stared at Sophie and, holding on to the back of the only chair in the place, slowly raised her head and lowered it, a single nod.

'OK, so long as you know.'

The nod came again.

Sophie had once had the sad task of bringing the news to a friend that her beloved dog had been run over. Her friend's initial reaction had been the same as Olwen's, a single nod, as if she were stunned. The dog's owner had soon burst into sobs and Sophie expected something like this from Olwen, but nothing came. Awkwardly, she stood there for a moment, not knowing what to do. Then she opened the door and let herself out, saying, 'You take care.'

Alone again, Olwen drank some of the gin straight from the bottle. With difficulty she screwed the cap on again before falling backwards into the soft cushions of the sofa.

There were no lights on Kenilworth Green but a gibbous moon had risen behind the squat outline of St Ebba's nave and its small square tower. It shed a pale, faintly glowing light on to the grass and the fallen petals. Michael Constantine, out for an evening walk with Katie, saw in the distance a patch of whiteness on the green. He asked Katie if she could see anything lying on the ground.

'Only the flowers on the grass. Shall we take a walk round?'

'I'd rather go home to bed,' said Michael. 'I'm feeling a bit low. Depressed, I suppose. Maybe I'll do my next piece on depression.'

CHAPTER SEVENTEEN

D uncan Yeardon's angry reproof had shaken Wally more than he realised at the time. For the rest of the day and half the night he had dwelt on the things Duncan had said. Only half believing them did nothing to take away his unease. As a fat man, worried about his weight, eats chips and chocolate for comfort, so Wally went up to Kenilworth County Primary to be consoled by the sight of innocent unharmed children. Rather, he went to St Ebba's churchyard with his usual bag of tools, reaching there as Kenilworth Avenue was filling up with the cars of mothers unloading their young. School opened at eight thirty in the morning and the children ran around in the playground until the bell rang to call them in at nine.

Wally looked his fill, undetected by any parents. When the bell rang and they began to go in, he crossed to the other grave he ostensibly tended, the one close up against the Kenilworth Green hedge. There was no one on the green. No children would be there until after three thirty when school came out, but Wally found he liked looking at the swings and the see-saw and the carousel. The association they had with those little girls fired his imagination and he could almost see them there, their skirts flying up in the breeze. Something else he could also see and he came closer to the fence.

It was a low hedge, composed of thornless shrubs, mostly

privet and box, and easily climbed over. Wally climbed over it, fearfully approaching what lay on the grass between the see-saw and the carousel. The body of a man lay face downwards. It wore a blue denim jacket and black silk trousers and in the middle of its back was a wide uneven bloodstain, more than a stain, a dried pool of blood. Wally recoiled but not perhaps as much as anyone with a different history might have done. The days when he had worked as a hospital porter, no more than a few weeks, stood him in good stead. He had seen bodies before, he had even moved them out of the wards where they had died. So, because curiosity was getting the better of him and he wanted to see the dead man's face, he knelt down on the still-dewy grass and turned him over.

It was still a handsome face, though now apparently composed of parchment-coloured wax. Stuart Font's cerulean eyes, dulled now, stared sightless back at him. Wally had not expected to be shocked but he was shocked. He even felt a little sick, something he never had in the wards. He should go home now, get away from here, maybe never come again. The green was still deserted but, as he got to his feet, he saw someone come in through the kissing gate. Whoever it was had a dog on a lead. Rose Preston-Jones? Wally was beginning to think of Rose as the bane of his life, his nemesis or the opposite of a guardian angel. But it wasn't Rose, it was a much larger woman and the dog was much larger than McPhee. Wally turned, clambered over the hedge and ran out of the churchyard.

When Molly had begun taking over Richenda's duties, she had begged Stuart for a key to his flat and eventually he had given her one. This key she used to let herself in on Thursday morning at eight. It was so early because, after she had made hot chocolate and breakfast toast, tidied the kitchen and dusted the living room, she intended to go to college. Of course she had rung the bell first, rung it twice. She supposed he was still in bed and she tiptoed into his bedroom. Once or twice, when she had arrived early, this had happened and she had stood by his bed, doing what she loved to do, watching him sleep. But this morning he wasn't in bed. He wasn't in the flat at all.

She remembered what he had said to her the evening before, that he had a hot date. He must have spent the night with this woman, this Claudia, whose husband had crashed into the party and made all those threats.

'I hope he's OK,' Molly said aloud to the empty flat. 'Oh, I do hope nothing's happened to him.'

'I wouldn't want to give up my days at the Bel Esprit Centre,' said Rose. 'I get more clients there than I do at home and it's much more lucrative.'

Marius took the hand that wasn't holding McPhee's lead. 'And I wouldn't like to give up tutoring those Mill Hill kids. Well, I would like but I couldn't afford it.'

As they walked up Kenilworth Avenue towards the round-about, they were discussing the possible location of the house they intended to buy, whether it should be near here or further out, perhaps Barnet or Totteridge if those areas weren't too expensive. The day was pale grey and still, warmer than it had been. The trees had shed most of their blossom but gardens and window boxes were full of flowers.

'I'd like a garden,' said Rose. 'I've always wanted one but never did because I've always lived in flats.'

'Darling Rose, you shall have your garden whatever else we don't have. Now that Latin is coming back as a GCSE subject I shall get rich.'

They had come to the green and the kissing gate. McPhee was already inside, running free on the grass. Rose and Marius followed him slowly, staring at the far corner where the children's swings were. The whole area was cordoned off with blue-and-white police crime tape.

'Oh, what's happened? Do you think some child has had an accident? Sometimes they swing those swings much higher than they should.'

'The police wouldn't put up crime tape for that,' said Marius. 'I did notice several police cars and a van parked in Kenilworth Avenue.'

'I'll put McPhee on his lead again. They won't like him running about free.'

'I don't think we'd better come in here at all.'

So, much to the little dog's chagrin, they walked back the way they had come. In their absence, two police cars had arrived and were parked outside. The automatic doors opened to receive them.

'Your place or mine?' asked Marius.

It was a joke they had. For the past week they had been spending one day and night in her flat and then one day and night in his. Since that visit of Rose's to Marius's flat, his confession and hers, they had barely been apart.

'It's your turn.' Rose headed for the stairs. To her surprise Marius summoned the lift. 'But you've got a phobia,' she said.

'I *had* a phobia. Or I deceived myself into thinking I had. But since you and I – well, it's gone. You've banished it, darling Rose.'

The large detective sergeant with the moon face and the big belly and his sidekick DC Bashir had found no one at home but Noor who was awakened from a deep sleep after four or five attempts on the doorbell. They asked her some questions but she knew nothing. She hadn't seen Stuart since the party, she had never been to Kenilworth Green. She had been in a club with her boyfriend until the place closed at 4 a.m. Could she please go back to bed now? Detective Sergeant Blakelock thought Olwen's flat was also empty. They went back to Flat 4 and this time they got an answer from Marius Potter. He invited them in and introduced them to his fiancée, a word he hated using because he found it ridiculous in someone of his age – but 'girlfriend' would have been worse.

Neither of them knew much about Stuart Font, both of them aware that, while he had seemed perfectly amiable and pleasant, he wasn't the kind of person they would want to make a friend of, just as he had shown no desire to be friends with them. But he had, along with the rest of the Lichfield House residents, invited them to his party. Marius remembered that party very well, he remembered the irruption into it of that man and the threats he had made. After the police had gone, having learned nothing from them, he said to Rose, 'I phoned the police. Do you remember?'

'Yes, I think so. I suppose so.'

'What was that chap's name?'

'Freddy something.'

'Do you think I should have told them? Should I have told them he threatened to kill Stuart Font?'

'Oh dear,' said Rose, 'I don't know. Someone else who was there will tell them.'

'I would if I knew his name. He never told us his name, did he?'

'I'm sure he didn't,' said Rose.

*

186

Michael Constantine had given up the depression idea and was writing the culminating vitriolic sentence in his denunciation of cranberry juice as a remedy for cystitis, when the police came. His only previous encounters with the law had been when he was stopped for driving his father's car at excessive speed and when, as a long-haired, nose- and lip-pierced teenager, he had been stopped and searched. How pleasant it was to be questioned by them when conscious of his perfect innocence! He and Katie told them they had seen a white shape lying on the grass at nine thirty the previous evening. It might have been poor Stuart Font but on the other hand it might have been a heap of tree blossom.

Someone was in the hallway when they got out of the lift. He looked to Blakelock as if he was trying to make himself scarce by heading for the stairs, but Bashir stopped him with an 'Excuse me!' Bashir had a very loud resonant voice.

Plain-clothes policemen think they look like other members of the public but they don't. Something about the way they dress, their manner, their self-consciously imposed 'ordinariness', makes them immediately recognised by those with a guilty conscience. Wally knew there was no escape for him. He turned round, smiling pleasantly, and said that he was the caretaker, name of Walter Scurlock. No, he knew nothing about Mr Font, he said, no idea what time he went out the day before.

'You want to talk to my wife,' he said, passing the buck. 'She cleaned for Mr Font. That is, until he got the young lady from Flat 5 to do it for free. I'll get my wife to give you a bell, shall I?'

'We'll come back here when your wife's in,' said Bashir, sensing that there was no need to call this fellow 'sir'. 'What time would that be?'

Wally didn't want them in the flat. 'I tell you what. She's over in Ludlow House now. Flat 2. Just ring the bell.'

Before going there, they called on Duncan Yeardon and the people at Springmead. Duncan was very helpful. He invited them in for a coffee, which was accepted, though it was 3.30 p.m. by then. Oh yes, he had known Stuart well, he was 'inexpressibly shocked' to hear he had been murdered.

'It was murder, wasn't it?'

Bashier said they were treating it as an unexplained death. 'I heard someone had stabbed him in the back,' said Duncan.

He decided he owed loyalty to Stuart's memory and said nothing to them about how attracted he had been by Tigerlily or how much he had liked coming over and watching her over the fence. 'He had a party,' he said. 'Kind of house-warming affair. Or flat-warming, maybe I should say. There was this chap burst in, made threats, said he'd kill him for – well, I won't say the word – doing something he shouldn't with his wife.'

'Whose wife?'

'The chap's wife.'

Bashir started writing things down in his notebook. 'Do you know the man's name?'

'I can't say I do,' said Duncan. 'Not to say, know his name. A big burly sort of chap with a reddish face. Mind you, everybody was there, all the people in the flats. One of them could tell you.'

Springmead was next. But here the ugly face of racism poked up in Blakelock's mind. The man who answered the door – or didn't answer the door but came round the side of the house when they rang the bell – was plainly from South-East Asia. China? Malaysia? Singapore? Bashir couldn't tell any more than Blakelock could but Blakelock knew he had to be careful. There was something in the man's wary yet aggressive expression that told him this short, stocky, black-haired, copper-skinned individual would be on the phone complaining if one of them stepped an inch out of line. This was where a 'sir' was definitely required.

'Can I help you?' was all the man said but it was enough to send out a warning signal.

'Just to ask you, sir, if you've heard of the unexplained death last night of Mr Stuart Font from Lichfield House?'

'Never met him,' said the South-East Asian man.

'Don't know him or any of them.' From somewhere he had picked up a useful phrase. 'We keep ourself to ourself in our home.'

'Nothing doing there,' said Blakelock when they were back in the road. 'Now for Mrs Scurlock.'

Richenda had finished work at Flat 2 Ludlow House and moved on to Flat 4. The first thing she did wherever she started work was turn on the radio. Stations were unimportant to her, it could be a game show or a comedian or a play or classical music or an economist talking, it mattered not at all so long as she had background sound. Silence made her uneasy. So when Blakelock and Bashir finally tracked her down, a gardening programme was on, a fluting upper-class voice telling listeners they were wrong if they thought nothing was to be done in the flower beds in May.

In her usual costume of miniskirt, high-heeled sandals and tight low-cut top, Richenda caused some eye-bulging in the detective sergeant and a small recoil in the Muslim constable. She no more got a 'madam' than her husband had a 'sir'.

'I knew him well,' she began. 'I can tell you all about him. His relationship with that blonde woman, for starters. They was having a hot affair. Claudia's her name.'

Blakelock, realising few questions would be needed here, sat down in one of the armchairs and prepared to listen. No,

Richenda didn't know Claudia's surname or what she did for a living, if anything. A man who said she was his wife had burst into Stuart Font's party, attacked him, broken his arm and threatened to kill him. It was much the same as what Duncan had told them but he hadn't mentioned the broken arm.

'Mind you,' said Richenda, 'Stuart was a bit of a sex maniac. He got rid of me so that one of those girls from Flat 5 could come and clean for him. Not that there'd have been much cleaning done.'

With no need to enquire but purely out of fascination, Bashir asked her if Stuart had ever made any advances to her.

'Oh, all the time,' said Richenda.

Police had been searching the Kenilworth Green area for several hours, looking for the weapon, but no knife had been found. The evening was still light but they worked on till nine. Half an hour before that they moved into the churchyard. There, leaning against a gravestone not far from the fence, was a large canvas bag, containing a pair of garden shears, a trowel and a small garden fork. They placed it in a plastic bag and took it to the murder room which had been set up in the Bel Esprit Centre.

There, Darren Blakelock examined the bag and its contents, wearing gloves to handle them gingerly. The tools were fingerprinted. Someone had printed *WS* in felt pen on the outside of the bag. Blakelock couldn't immediately connect those initials with anyone he had yet talked to and soon after looking at them, and looking at them again and again with no result, he went home to bed.

He woke up in the small hours and thought: Walter Scurlock. Visualising the bearer of that name, he saw a medium-sized man with an enlarged belly, balding head, unmemorable features – to himself he called them 'ordinary' – a nervous man. What had he got to be nervous about? And what had he been doing in St Ebba's churchyard?

If it hadn't been three o'clock in the morning but a couple of hours later, Blakelock would have got up, dressed and driven back to Lichfield House to question this Walter Scurlock. As it was he lay sleepless, thinking about it. When he did get up, he went straight to the Bel Esprit Centre and had another look at the bag, hoping it would tell him more. It didn't. He was wondering whether Scurlock had been in trouble before, in which case his fingerprints might be on record, but that hardly mattered. If the bag was Scurlock's the tools most likely would be. Unfortunately, no knife had been in the bag. He was interrupted by the arrival of a woman who looked fourteen in the distance but forty close to.

She introduced herself as Amanda Copeland. 'It was my friend Daphne Jessop who reported to you she'd found a body on Kenilworth Green.'

Blakelock nodded. A woman had phoned them, said she had been exercising her dog and called them on her mobile when she came upon Stuart Font's body.

'There was something she didn't tell you. She said she didn't want to get the man into trouble.'

'What man?'

'I knew who it was all right. She saw him bending over the body but he ran away when he saw her coming.'

And Amanda proceeded to tell him everything she knew about Wally Scurlock and a lot she had imagined.

CHAPTER EIGHTEEN

I t was about seven on the previous evening that Wally
Scurlock realised he had left his bag in St Ebba's churchyard. His first thought was that he must abandon the
bag. No one could identify it as his. Initials were nothing,
thousands of people must have the initials WS. For all that,
he might go up to St Ebba's and check that it was still there.
If it was he could retrieve it. He was eating – or picking at
– the meal Richenda called 'tea', though no tea was served
and the food consisted of a lamb chop with Bisto gravy, rather
hard, once frozen Brussels sprouts and salt-and-vinegar-flavour
potato crisps.

'What's the matter with you?' Richenda said, breaking off
from the account she was giving of her encounter with the
two policemen. 'Something wrong with your tea? You're lucky
not to get one of those ready meals.'

Wally sounded quite dignified. 'I have no appetite,' he said.
'I've been feeling off colour ever since I heard about poor
Stuart.'

'Well, that's funny, considering you couldn't stand the sight
of him when he was alive.'

Wally wasn't going to get into an argument. Later on, saying
he needed some fresh air, he walked up to the roundabout.
Several police had passed him, including a van full of uniformed

officers, but when he reached Kenilworth Green, the last car was moving away.

The place where Stuart's body had lain was still cordoned off with crime tape, but no tape was in the churchyard. He made his way in there just as St Ebba's clock was chiming nine. Where had he left the bag? Up beside a gravestone near the fence, he seemed to remember. But perhaps not, perhaps he had left it on the opposite side, by the grave that over-looked the primary-school playground. There was no sign of it anywhere but Wally began a systematic search of the place, even pushing aside bushes and fumbling about underneath their branches. Then it occurred to him that someone might have found it and put it in the church for safe keeping. Some thoughtful parishioner or sexton, whatever that was. He expected St Ebba's to be locked but it wasn't. The door, black-ened wood, thickly studded, creaked open when he pushed it. It swung shut after him but almost soundlessly.

The church was little and very, very old. Wally thought it was in need of a paint, for one of the walls had pale red and grey patches that looked as if they might once have been drawings. It was still and silent, unlit except by the greenish roof light which filtered through the small windows which Wally had expected to be of stained glass but were not. Standing in the nave, looking up at the beamed roof, he felt as if he was in some country place, not a mere quarter-mile from an arterial road in a city. The silence seemed to him unnatural and when he began to walk up towards the chancel he found himself moving on tiptoe. He was very conscious of the lack of any living thing, but not quite a deadness, for he could feel a kind of ancient strength in the place and – though it was nonsense, it was stupid to think this way – something condemnatory, something that frowned upon him and told him, if not in words, that he should leave. He wasn't welcome.

God it couldn't be, he didn't believe in God and never had. But he did believe in the supernatural, he did believe in ghosts and bad spirits and even demons. It must be one of those. He had seen things on television that lived in old churches or came out of graves or stood, waiting, in dark corners. Don't be a fool, he told himself, and searched around for his bag, pushing aside hassocks, smelling the sweetish dusty smell. It wasn't here, he had been sure enough from the start that it wouldn't be. Time to get out, for it was no longer a frown that pursued him but a stare, invisible eyes boring into him, driving him away.

Someone had taken his bag, that was clear, but not necessarily the police. Still, he had to admit that the police, who had been searching the place, were the most likely. Would it be a wise move on his part to go to them in the morning, say, play the innocent and ask them if they'd found his bag he'd left in the churchyard? He knew he wouldn't dare do that, not while there was a chance they didn't know he was the WS of the initials. They had already talked to him, they knew his name. Would they make the connection? Walking home as the sun was setting, he looked with fear rather than interest at the police van and the police car parked outside the Bel Esprit Centre. The place was in darkness. Had he known his bag was even at that moment inside the murder room at the centre, already labelled with an exhibit number, he might have contemplated breaking in and taking it. But he didn't know and, in any case, he felt his nerves were at snapping point, for now he remembered something watching him inside the church, some silent entity.

'You've been hours,' said Richenda. 'What have you been up to?'

'I've been for a walk,' Wally said.

'You can put the recycling out before you go to bed.'

The bins, one for paper and cardboard, one for cans and bottles, had to be carried upstairs and put by the entrance gate.

'Can't it wait till the morning? They're supposed to come at eight but they never do.'

'Just this once they will, you'll see. So do it now.'

'You could say please.'

'I could,' said Richenda, 'but you're not doing me no favours. That recycling is as much your rubbish as mine. More. It's you reads the *Sun*, not me.'

Once he was sure she was in bed and the light off, Wally went into the bathroom. He unscrewed the nuts on the bath panel and removed the printouts he had made. Ten sheets of A4 paper, printed with delectable pictures which, to look at, made the blood rush to his head and his heart pound. He turned them over so that he could only see the blank sides. Once, and not so long ago, it would have been easy to destroy them but no longer. There were certainly no matches in the flat and no gas hob or room heaters to emit blue flames. Nor did he possess a shredder. He dared not put the sheets down the lavatory pan lest he block the drains. So he tore them into small pieces and put the pieces in the paper recycling bin. That bin would be gone and its contents lost by, if not eight, nine in the morning.

He carried the bins upstairs. There was no one about and it was dark in the street. He had once seen a programme on television where a man went into a church and saw something and the thing, whatever it was, followed him back to where he lived. A movement among the cars made him jump, but it was only that girl Noor getting out of her boyfriend's Lexus. He muttered a goodnight to her.

Richenda was asleep. He got in beside her and slept fitfully, to be awakened at eight in the morning by his doorbell ringing. The only time anyone rang that bell was when it was the postman with a parcel that wouldn't go into a pigeonhole, a rare event. He decided to ignore it but it rang again, more persistently. He got up. Two policemen in plain clothes and two in uniform stood outside. Wally's legs felt the way they had when he had seen Rose Preston-Jones talking to that woman with the two little girls, weak and fragile, scarcely able to hold him up.

They came into his flat, pushed their way in just in case he had tried to stop them. Blakelock and Bashir were the plain clothes and the uniformed ones were called Smith and Leach. For the first few minutes they called him 'sir'.

'Am I right in thinking this is your bag, sir?' This was Blakelock.

Wally nodded. He was nodding rather too enthusiastically when Richenda came into the room in a red satin dressing gown, her hair wound round an ancient set of Carmen rollers. She looked at the bag and then at the policemen. 'It's his all right,' she said. 'Where did you find it?' Without waiting for a reply, she said to her husband, 'You never told me you'd lost that bag.'

Wally didn't answer. He took hold of the bag and tried to stand up straight.

'We'll just hold on to that for the time being, thank you,' said Bashir, and then, 'Did you touch Stuart Font's body? Did you turn him over?'

Less frightened than he would have been by the enquiry he truly feared, Wally admitted it. He hadn't meant any harm, he hadn't done anything.

Then the question came.

'Have you got a computer, sir?'

'Of course he has,' said Richenda.

'We'll have a look at that,' Blakelock said. 'We'll do it while we're searching the place.'

Richenda opened her eyes very wide. 'Searching?'

'If you'll permit it,' said Bashir. 'We can get a warrant if you won't, so it comes to the same thing in the end.'

Wally felt faint. This was real terror and somehow quite different from the fear of the supernatural he had experienced the night before. This was reality. He lowered himself into an armchair and slumped into its depths like a sick man. Richenda said something to him but he didn't hear her. The policemen walked about the flat, opening drawers, looking inside cupboards. When they came to his desk, the one called Bashir switched on his computer and asked him for his password.

With the single spark of defiance that remained to him, Wally said, 'I don't have to tell you that.'

'We shall draw our own conclusions if you don't, Walter.'

It was when they used his first name that Wally knew it was all up. 'Barbie,' he said.

'Pardon me?'

'That's my password, Barbie – well, Barbie 1.'

No comment was made. Wally got up and went into the bedroom. He couldn't bear to stay in the living room any longer. He lay down on the unmade bed and buried his face in the pillows as if he could find oblivion that way. Richenda was talking to Blakelock. Wally heard the word 'recycling' and then he heard her say it had been put out the night before but the council collectors wouldn't be here for hours yet.

The front door opened and closed. Richenda came into the bedroom and pulled at him roughly by the shoulder.

'Get up. I want to make the bed.'

Wally didn't move.

'What are they looking for?'

'Nothing. I don't know.'

'If it's what I think it is, they'll take your computer away

and then they'll take you. When you come back – if you do
– I won't be here. Just so you know.'

An hour later, Rose and Marius were still in bed in Marius's
flat. It was the drip-drip-drip of falling water which awoke
Rose. Could he or she have left a tap running in the bathroom or kitchen the night before? She was always very careful
about things like that and she was sure he would be too. She
got up and the movement woke him. Marius was never drowsy
in the mornings. He was alert as soon as his eyes opened and
he knew immediately what was happening.

'That's water coming through the ceiling.'

They both got up. Marius went first into the living room.
Water was coming in but in a spreading stream trickling
under the door while the dripping went on. It was Rose who
opened the door to the kitchen. A shallow lake covered the
tiled floor, its level slowly increased by the drips which fell
not into Marius's sink but on to the overflowing draining
board and splashed into the lake itself.

'It's coming from Olwen's,' said Rose. 'I know I'm a bit silly
sometimes, Marius. I do know that. I asked Michael at Stuart's
party if women had more ribs than men because of Adam
and Eve and I could see he thought I was an idiot –'

'I'll kill him.'

'Yes, well, I am sometimes. What I was going to say was,
you know what happens to that old man in *Bleak House*, he's
drunk so much he sort of explodes – what's it called?'

'Spontaneous combustion,' said Marius, already laughing.

'And he sort of liquefies – well, you don't think Olwen . . . ?'

'No, darling Rose, I don't. This is water. She's left a tap
running. I'll phone Scurlock and then we'll go up there, try to
get in.'

Richenda answered. She sounded triumphant. 'He's not here. The police have taken him away *and* his computer *and* an envelope full of bits of dirty pictures come out of the re-cycling. You want him, you get on to them. I'll see you later.' She slammed down the phone.

Rose and Marius got dressed and went up to the top floor. They expected to see water coming under the front door but there was nothing. Marius rang Olwen's bell and when there was no answer rang it again. Rose took off one of her shoes and hammered on the door with it.

'We're going to have to break it down.'

'Oh, darling, can you do that? It looks so easy in those detective serials but I'm sure it isn't, in real life.'

'I'm sure it isn't too, but I can try.'

Marius tried. He took a running jump at the door, giving it a kick which did more harm to him than the door. As he retreated, clutching hold of the small of his back, a door slammed on the floor below and Michael Constantine came bounding up the stairs.

'Has something happened to her?'

'God knows,' said Marius. 'All I know is she's flooding my flat and she doesn't answer the door.'

'Let me have a go.'

Marius and Rose both knew (they told each other after-wards) that Michael would succeed at first try and so he did. The door flew open. Olwen was sitting on the sofa. She tried to get up but failed and sank back on to the dirty red cush-ions, staring at them with clouded eyes, her mouth half open. Marius opened the door to the kitchen. He released a flood and quickly closed it again. Taking off his shoes and socks, he rolled up his trousers, plunged once more into the kitchen and turned off the cold tap from which water had been pouring into the already overflowing sink.

'We'll have to bale it out or the lot will come through,' he said, pulling out the sink plug.

The three of them began baling out the water, using whatever utensils came to hand, a fruit bowl, a vase and a small milk saucepan. Olwen was ill-equipped with pans and possessed no buckets. It took a long time and the final inch had to be soaked up with cloths. Michael opened a cupboard and found it full of rags. One of these, something which had once been a skirt, black with coloured flowers, Rose used to complete the drying of the floor.

Marius quoted 'The Rime of the Ancient Mariner' and said that there was water, water everywhere, nor any drop to drink, and when they looked about them they noticed the absence of the expected vodka and gin bottles. Olwen was staring at the window. Afterwards Rose said to Marius that the look on her face reminded her of a character in a television sitcom gazing at something out of shot that the viewer can't see but knows, because of her expression, must be terrible. And then Olwen did speak. She spoke the longest sentence any of them had ever heard from her.

'They're climbing up the window again, a whole gang of them, like they were crawling over the sink when I turned the tap on, more of them now, too many of them to count.'

On the other side of the room Rose said to Michael, 'What does she mean?' They withdrew into the still damp kitchen. 'What is it she sees?'

'God knows. But I know what it is. It's called "delirium tremens". It happens to alcoholics, they have hallucinations of animals or people or anything. I've never seen it before.'

'We shall have to do something,' said Marius.

'I'll call an ambulance.' Michael thought he might write about the DTs for his next article, as a warning to binge-drinking teenagers.

*

Richenda had no notion of the nature of the pornography Wally had been watching and no clear idea of what was legal to watch and what illegal. Whatever it might be, it was enough to drive her to leave him, something she had been contemplating for a long time now. She intended not to go far. Working all day and every day except Sunday, cleaning flats in the four blocks, she was making a good income and had decided to rent one of the flats herself, a studio probably, of which there were two in Ludlow House, one presently vacant.

The estate office wouldn't open for another half-hour. She packed the two largest suitcases, stuffing into them, among her clothes, Wally's camera, her hairdryer and their radio. The television she put back into the box it had come in and loaded it on to a shopping trolley she had filched from the Tesco. She considered leaving her front-door key behind but decided to keep it. You never knew what else she might want to come back for.

Getting all this stuff up the stairs was a struggle but after three journeys she had the lot up in the hallway. Standing there, thinking what her next move was to be, she saw the lift open and two paramedics emerge with Olwen on a stretcher. They carried her out and loaded the stretcher into the back of their ambulance. Richenda left her bags where they were but took the trolley and the television set with her.

The letting manager had just opened the office. He knew Richenda well, could almost have called himself a friend, and was happy to offer her a six-month lease of Flat 6, the vacant studio in Ludlow House. Richenda gave him a cheque for a large deposit and by ten o'clock she had moved in. In half an hour she was due at her first job, cleaning Marius Potter's flat.

'Where's all this water come from, then?'

'The flat above,' said Marius.

Richenda nodded. 'There was bound to be a disaster sooner or later but I never would have thought water'd be involved.'

She mopped the kitchen floor, pronounced on the damage and said that Marius would have to get the builders in before he could show the flat to any prospective buyers. 'You remember that do poor Stuart had?'

'Well, I was there.'

'You called the police, didn't you?'

'I did.'

Richenda said no more but she gave herself up to some serious thinking while plying the vacuum cleaner. Was looking at dirty pictures all they wanted Wally for, or did they have him down as a suspect in Stuart's murder? She would be quite happy never to see Wally again and she intended to divorce him as soon as she could, but murder? That wasn't on. Wally hadn't killed anyone. Hadn't the nerve, Richenda thought spitefully, and she remembered what she had once heard someone say about a timid person: got a serious stomach complaint – no guts. That made her laugh to herself as she dusted Marius's aunt's sideboard.

'Did you call the police because that chap threatened to kill Stuart?'

Marius had just come back from consulting Rose about local handymen. 'Probably.'

'What was his name?'

'I don't remember,' said Marius and shut himself in the bathroom.

Richenda was due to clean the girls' flat next. Well, Noor's. It was she who paid. The place was always a mess, dirty dishes not only in the sink and on the draining board but in the bath as well, clothes on the floor and on every chair, make-up everywhere. Richenda often helped herself to a lipstick or a jar of moisturiser. They had so much they never noticed.

The others were out but Molly was at home. Since Stuart's

death she had dressed herself entirely in black every day. And she was losing weight.

Largely because she knew Molly wouldn't care to be complimented, Richenda said, 'You're looking good.'

'I'm feeling horrendous. My heart is broken. I was totally in love with him – did you know that?' Richenda made no reply. 'He'd given up that Claudia, you know. He was getting to love me, I know he was, and then some monster killed him.'

'Claudia – yes, that was the name. What was her husband called?'

'Freddy something. Some place in Italy. Florence? Positano? I don't know. I don't care. Knowing what he's called won't bring Stuart back.'

'I'd know it if I heard it,' said Richenda.

CHAPTER NINETEEN

The only person in the flats likely to have an atlas (as against looking up everything on a computer) was Marius. He was out, so Richenda let herself in and examined with some pleasure and a lot of interest the water damage. Then she spent a few minutes on the map of Italy, and when she had finished her afternoon's work, walked across to the murder room in the Bel Esprit Centre.

Blakelock was there but not Bashir. He was in Flat 5 questioning Molly. Richenda had led him to believe that Molly was another of Stuart's women (as he put it to himself) and might therefore know what enemies he had. She would have liked the police to believe she was having a love affair with Stuart, that she had been a rival to Claudia or even her successor. But Sophie was in the room while Bashir was talking to her and as soon as the suggestion was made and not denied, she chipped in with, 'Oh, Moll, who are you trying to kid? You never came near having a relationship with him.'

'I never said I had!'

'I mean, come on, after that Claudia? Get real.'

Molly decided to forgive Sophie on the grounds that the poor thing hadn't got a boyfriend while she at least had Carl who had reappeared in her life.

'We were very close,' she said to Bashir, 'but it wasn't a physical relationship.' And she told him about Martin and Jack and Hilary and the people in Chester House, all friends of Stuart's who might equally have been his enemies.

It was strange and perhaps rather unpleasant, Duncan thought, the way a murder in the neighbourhood, a murder of someone everyone knows if only by sight, brings people together. Of course, he had known Jock and Kathy Pember before Stuart's death but not to the extent he knew them now. Moira/Esmeralda and Ken, the woman who wore the patch-work fur or had done in the winter, and the man she lived with – Duncan rather disapproved – had called and asked him if he was going to the funeral and could they go with him. He asked them in for a coffee and Kathy popped in while they were there and it was all very friendly.

The weather had turned warm, quite a heatwave for May. Although his French windows were wide open, as were all the windows in the house, Duncan had to apologise for the place being so hot. He had bought a couple of fans but they made little difference.

'Those things just move the hot air about,' said Kathy. 'Our place is freezing summer and winter.'

Out of politeness Duncan asked Moira and Ken about the temperature in their house, and Moira said she hadn't noticed but then she was 'a cold mortal'. Perhaps Duncan hadn't realised that because the Springmead people cultivated exotic house plants they had to keep the place hot and maybe this also affected Duncan's home.

'Our house is detached, you see,' she said with conscious superiority. 'That's why we don't feel it.'

Stuart's funeral was to be in the middle of the following

week. 'When the forensic people have finished with the body,' said Ken, rather relishing the whole thing, Duncan thought.

He poured more coffee, said that the murder was a tragedy for Stuart's parents. They would be holding a small gathering of Stuart's friends at Flat 1 after the funeral. 'I expect we shall all go, won't we?'

'It's the least we can do to show respect,' said Ken, momentarily closing his lineless eyelids.

'Do you think the Springmead people would like to come?'

'Oh, I don't think so, Duncan. They're not what I would call antisocial but they're not *sociable*. There is a difference, you know.'

'But they're very charming people,' said Moira. 'Those girls have lovely manners and Mr Deng is a real gentleman. And they've all got degrees in horticulture, Mr Deng told me. He's their uncle.'

'I thought he was their father,' said Duncan. 'That's what poor Stuart said.'

'Oh, no. He was wrong there. I don't want to speak ill of the dead, but he was wrong there. He's their uncle and the boy is his son. Do you know what Mr Deng told me himself? That they supply orchids to the royal family.'

She had no interest in Wally's fate. Prison, a huge fine, even the death penalty (if only they'd reintroduce it), any of those would be fine as far as Richenda was concerned. They could do what they liked with him. All she was troubled about was not to be known as the wife or ex-wife of a murderer. Wives of murderers got unpleasant treatment by the press, she had noticed, unless of course they were the murder victims, in which case they became saints.

'His name's Livorno,' she said to the big-bellied moon-faced detective inspector. 'Freddy, I think, but I couldn't swear to it. It was his wife Font was having a fling with. She'd been round the block a few times, you could tell. Livorno came to Font's party and said he'd kill him. You ask anyone who was there, they'll remember. That's not the kind of thing you forget.'

Richenda knew nothing of where Livorno lived or what he did for a living, but DS Blakelock did. In the course of his work he had frequent dealings with solicitors, or the suspects he interviewed did. He remembered that no more than a couple of weeks in the past, a man up for causing actual bodily harm, taking advantage of the legal right to call a lawyer, had phoned solicitors called Crabtree, Livorno, Thwaite. It was surely the same one.

M any people lead virtuous lives not because they resist temptation but because temptation never comes their way. Until now, no one had given Sophie Longwich the chance to be dishonest, or else the chances that came her way were not attractive. At school most of her friends had occasionally shoplifted, taking sweets from Woolworths or Maybelline eyeshadow from Boots. Her pocket money was adequate and the idea of stealing frightened her. She was sure she would be caught.

But now her pocket money, or what her father called her allowance, seemed pitifully small. In Noor's company she understood for the first time that her own parents weren't rich, as she had believed, but, with five children and the recession getting worse, less than comfortably off. Her university loan allowed for no buying of clothes, meals in good restaurants, expensive electronic devices. Now Noor was gone, moved in with the prince, all those treats she and Molly had enjoyed, Mexican lunches with tequila sunrises, drinks in that

Hampstead club, loans whose repayment could be indefinitely postponed, had come to an end. Flat 5 might even be sold, Noor had intimated last time she visited. And where would she find somewhere else as good and convenient as this to share at only £50 a week?

It was when Noor had gone off in the prince's white Lexus that Sophie found the Visa card Olwen had given her. Well, had let her use to get money for Olwen's drink. Olwen was in hospital now or hadn't someone told her that she was out of hospital and living permanently elsewhere? And that she hadn't long to live? Using the card, Sophie thought, wouldn't help with finding somewhere nice to live but it would buy her some good clothes and get her hair cut by a good hairdresser and buy her an iPhone, all purchases which would cheer her up. Perhaps to console her for being the only one of the three girls not to have a boyfriend.

Of course she could have used that card at any cashpoint. Some superstitious feeling, not amenable to reason, sent her back to the Tesco beyond St Ebba's and the green, to use the machine she had used before for Olwen and draw out all the money that had come into Olwen's account at the end of April.

Reading of Stuart's murder in the *Daily Telegraph* had shocked Claudia but not had the effect she might have expected. It hadn't plunged her into misery, it hadn't broken her heart. But for Freddy's behaviour she might have felt almost relieved. 'Behaviour' wasn't quite the word perhaps. Though he must have read about it, must have seen it on London TV news, he hadn't mentioned it to her, had apparently ignored it. This she felt was unnatural and it made her uneasy. She saw him sitting there with the open *Daily Telegraph* on his knees, Stuart's handsome face staring up at him from the page, his own impassive, mildly interested.

'I wouldn't be surprised,' he said, 'if we had a general election in the autumn.'

Her thoughts went back to the party. She hadn't forgotten, would probably never forget, how Freddy had burst in, uttering threats and brandishing a cudgel. Claudia didn't exactly know what a cudgel was but it sounded more fearsome than a stick. He had threatened to kill Stuart but that was nonsense, that meant nothing, it was just the kind of thing an angry man said. It was a pity newspapers and the Internet didn't tell you a bit more about the circumstances of a murder. For instance, though Stuart's body had been found on Thursday, 21 May, it seemed he'd been killed on the evening of the 20th. It seemed. No one had actually said so. Claudia knew exactly what she had been doing on that Wednesday evening. She had been attending a book launch at the Ivy. But first she had phoned Stuart to remind him that he hadn't booked a table for their dinner on the Friday. That was when she still thought their affair was on. What happened at the Ivy changed all that.

The book was a designer's memoirs, as much glossy pictures as text, and for the greater part of the evening she had been enjoying a heavy flirtation with the photographer. Stuart had gone out of her head and what with the photographer inviting her out to dinner, she hadn't thought of him again until she read that he had been killed. But where had Freddy been that evening?

She hadn't got home herself until almost eleven. Freddy had fallen asleep, watching TV. But had he been there all the evening? She didn't know and she couldn't exactly ask. They spoke to each other very little these days and hadn't shared a bedroom since the night of Stuart's party.

The police came on the Sunday. Both she and Freddy happened to be at home. It was seven in the morning, an unbelievable time to call on anyone, as if picking Sunday itself wasn't bad enough. Claudia had never been to church in her life, unless it was to her own christening, but still she thought it positively wrong to disturb people at home on a Sunday. And she said so, when, inadequately clothed in a transparent robe, she answered the door to two police officers, a man with a huge belly and a fat woman. Claudia categorised any woman as fat who took a size bigger than a 14. They were, they said, Detective Sergeant Blakelock and DC Fairbairn. Could they speak to Mr Frederick Livorno, please?

Of course it was a command, not a question. Claudia left them on the doorstep while she went to summon Freddy but, though uninvited, they came in and shut the front door behind them. Freddy put some clothes on before he sauntered down and when Blakelock asked him what he had been doing on the evening of Wednesday, 20 May, he said he had been murdering a shit called Stuart Font.

'That's not funny, sir,' said Blakelock. 'This is a serious matter. Perhaps we may sit down?'

'You can as far as I'm concerned.'

Marilyn Fairbairn asked him about Stuart, if he had struck him, breaking his arm, and if he had threatened to kill him. Freddy nodded in an offhand sort of way, and when she asked him why, he said, 'Because he'd been fucking my wife.' He added, 'I wouldn't use this sort of language to everyone but you police are used to it. I know you'll understand.'

They put up with a good deal of this and then they took Freddy away with them to the police station. There was a bit on the London regional news that evening about a man helping the police with their inquiries. Claudia began to wonder if Freddy really could have killed Stuart. But Stuart had been stabbed and Claudia couldn't imagine Freddy wielding a knife. Knives seemed to her like teenagers' weapons.

Lichfield House was half empty. Stuart was dead, Olwen was in hospital being treated for alcoholic poisoning, Noor had moved in with the prince, and Wally Scurlock, released on bail and finding Richenda gone, had resigned before he could be sacked, and had gone to stay with his sister in Watford. After his sister had seen in the papers that he had appeared in court, charged with possessing indecent photographs of children, she hadn't wanted him, she had wanted never to see him again, and at first she turned him away. She looked out of the window and saw him sitting outside the front door on the wall between her garden and the one next door. Then she hunted out the newspaper cutting she had taken of his court appearance with the picture of her brother being hustled into the court with a blanket over his head while a baying crowd shook their fists and screamed abuse at him.

Her name was also Scurlock, Ms Diane Scurlock, for she had never married. The name was uncommon. Her neighbours must know already or guess. They would soon identify the miserable figure sitting on the wall, his head in his hands. She opened the door, said, 'You'd better come in.'

'You're a good girl, Di. I don't know what I'd do without you.'

The door was closed behind him. 'You can have the spare room,' she said, 'but I'm not feeding you or doing your washing or all that. And I'm not speaking to you. I mean it. These are the last words I'm going to say to you. What you've done, it turns my stomach.' He put out his hand to her but she recoiled. 'I'd rather touch a slug,' she said.

Wally had been convicted of nothing. He had only been charged with an offence and remanded. Officially, legally, he would have done nothing until he appeared in court again in three months' time and a jury decided on his guilt or innocence. But everyone who associated with him, the howling crowd, his sister, her neighbours, those residents of Lichfield, Ludlow, Hereford and Ross Houses he had encountered before he left, all of them took his guilt for granted. In child pornography cases, Wally realised, it was always so. And it was worse than that. From what Diane's next-door neighbour said (before she spat at him) when he emerged fearfully next morning, these people – for why would she be alone? – believed he hadn't just been looking at pictures of men and women doing things to children but had actually been doing the things to them himself.

Stuart's funeral was to be in the middle of the week, but Annabel Font and her husband Christopher had quietly moved into Flat 1 on Monday evening. It was theirs now, or soon would be. The sun didn't set till after nine but it was dark before they came, Christopher parking his car, without thinking much about it, on the single yellow line. In the absence of a porter or caretaker, Rose and Marius let them in.

Once they were back in Rose's flat, Marius said, looking out of the window, 'Springmead is always in total darkness by night. They never put a light on once it gets dark. I suppose they all go to bed early.'

'I suppose they do, darling,' said Rose.

At twenty past eight in the morning, just in time as he said, Duncan came over the road and rang the bell of Flat 1 to introduce himself and tell Christopher Font that if he left his car where it was he would certainly get a parking fine within the next half-hour.

'But help is at hand. Mrs Pember that's at number 1 says you can put it on her drive as they haven't got a vehicle of their own.'

Later in the morning Annabel walked up to St Ebba's Church where the service was to be held on Friday. The melodious clock struck eleven as she entered but after that there was silence, deep and cool. The pews were made of oak, very ancient, black and shiny, and the hassocks were covered in gros point, a yellow fish on a green ground, a red cross on a black ground, a white dove on blue, all worked by the few very old parishioners who still went to church. These same elderly women, the last of the faithful, had filled two vases with white lilac and placed them on the chancel steps. Annabel sat in a pew, thinking about nothing much, until she was sickened by the heavy scent of the lilac. She got up, went out into the sunshine and back to sort out Stuart's clothes and find someone who might like to have them.

C hristopher Font put his car on the Pembers' driveway and Kathy came out to say how sorry she was about Stuart and what a tragedy it was. She and her husband and Duncan Yeardon were inside having a coffee and if he and his wife would care to join them they would be very welcome. Christopher thanked her but said not just now, thank you.

If they had accepted the invitation, Duncan and the Pembers could hardly have continued with their conversation. Its subject, like most conversations in the neighbourhood, was Wally Scurlock. All that varied between what Duncan and his companions said and what Amanda Copeland and Rose Preston-Jones were saying, between what the Constantines and Molly and Sophie were saying, was the tone, the epithets and the level of revulsion. The shocked horror and the anger was much the same. What was remarkable was that the murder of Stuart Font was far less popular as a topic of discussion than Wally Scurlock's not yet proven offence.

Marius commented on this when, at 1 p.m., he dropped in to the Bel Esprit Centre to take Rose to the cafeteria for lunch.

'So does that mean that we think looking at indecent pictures of children is a more heinous crime than killing someone?'

'I'm afraid we just think it's more interesting, darling.'

'You're right, of course. You always are,' said Marius.

Like the other residents of Lichfield House, Rose and Marius thought the least they could do was support Stuart's parents; and this even though, with the exception of Molly Flint, they hadn't much cared for Stuart. Molly was already in the church, dressed in deepest black, a style which rather suited her now she had lost weight, and sitting between her and Sophie Longwich was Carl. Sophie edged away as far as she could from proximity to Carl's long greasy hair and leather jacket. Maybe the jacket wasn't dirty but it looked it. A white hairy knee protruded from the hole in his jeans. Richenda glared but Annabel and Christopher Font gave him vague smiles, glad to see anyone there who might have been a friend of their son's.

Duncan sat in the second row from the front. Unaware of Molly's association with Stuart, he had set himself up as the dead man's closest friend, noting those who attended and those conspicuous by their absence. Michael and Katie

Constantine came in this latter category, for which Duncan awarded them black marks along with the occupants of Springmead. It was all very well Mr Deng saying he and his nieces and son kept themselves to themselves but there was such a thing as neighbourliness and, considering what an interest poor Stuart had shown in Tigerlily, turning up at his funeral was the least they could do. It was only a matter of a short drive. The Pembers were both at work but Moira and Ken had come. In fact, they had very thoughtfully come to fetch him and brought him with them.

Duncan and Molly accompanied the Fonts to the crematorium. Carl, telling everyone he was Molly's fiancé, wanted to go too but Molly stopped him. 'You'd never even spoken to him,' she said, wiping away her tears.

It was a very warm day and all the funeral flowers, swathed in gleaming plastic, began to wilt in the sunshine before the coffin had disappeared. Arrangements to entertain the guests with wine and canapés (Annabel), coffee and biscuits (Duncan) or hot chocolate because Stuart loved it (Molly) came eventually to nothing, and Annabel and Christopher went back to Flat 1 alone with Molly.

Apart from Stuart's clothes which Annabel had packed up, ready to dispose of at some Scope or Oxfam outlet, the contents of the flat were as Stuart had left them. Molly confirmed that. All that had gone, she told Annabel, was a toothbrush, a razor, a change of underwear, a shirt and the clothes he was wearing.

'He had a small suitcase,' Annabel said to Christopher. 'Don't you remember, when he came to us after he'd broken his arm he brought his things in a small suitcase? It was beautiful – very soft blue leather. Well, where is it?' And she began to cry again.

Molly remembered and remembering also reduced her to tears. 'It was blue calfskin. He loved blue. He had it with him when he went out. I'd forgotten.'

'We should tell the police,' said Christopher.

CHAPTER TWENTY

Keeping an eye on Tigerlily was something Duncan thought he owed to Stuart's memory. He hadn't seen her since some days before Stuart's death. The boy and the other girl were often to be seen going into the summer house but Tigerlily was never with them. Duncan had very little to do these days. His home was immaculately tidy, his decorating was done and the two men he had thought of as his friends, Stuart and Wally, had gone. A house that was three storeys high was more than he needed and often he wandered through the rooms, wondering if he could make one of them a study and another an exercise room. But he never studied and apart from walking up to Tesco he never exercised. How did others occupy their time? Those who were retired like him, who never read a book, didn't care for music, didn't possess a computer and found most of television not to their taste? He missed his car, gone for over a year now. His old hobby of people-watching seemed all that was left to him but some of his prime targets had disappeared. Even the alcoholic woman hadn't been seen for weeks. Stuart's parents had left, Richenda the 'busy lady' had apparently moved and no new caretaker had yet arrived. And where was Tigerlily?

The weather had grown very warm, unnaturally warm for early June, Duncan thought. He had always been a person who felt the cold and thought the temperature could never be too high for him, but though he felt comfortable outside in the garden or when walking, the heat indoors was almost too much for him. He had been back to the electrics shop at Brent Cross to try and buy a fan but they had run out, just as, back in the snowy winter when he'd bought his toaster, they had run out of room heaters. He kept all the upstairs windows open night and day but was afraid to leave a downstairs window open overnight. When he came down in the morning the heat was intolerable.

Did they have the same problem at Springmead? He put his head over the fence and called to the boy when he came out of the house, heading for the summer house. But the boy only shook his head and waved his hands about in a gesture Duncan took to mean he didn't understand. Meanwhile, the heat increased. Duncan bought himself a thermometer, just out of curiosity, as he put it to himself. The temperature in his living room one morning at seven was twenty-eight degrees Celsius. One comfort, though, was that just as he was beginning to worry about her, he spotted Tigerlily lying face downwards on the Springmead lawn under the shade of the big ash tree. Her arms and legs were bare and the skin very white apart from what looked like bluish-black stains. Bruises was Duncan's first thought but that must be his imagination running wild again.

The lawyer Freddy summoned to be present while the police questioned him was his own partner, Lucas Crabtree. Lucas constantly had to suppress a desire to laugh while Freddy teased the police with impossible answers to their questions, coolly offering to show them his knife collection and somehow contriving to leave a bloodstained T-shirt among the soiled linen at Aurelia Grove. The blood turned out to be from a joint of beef and Freddy was told that any more of this and he would be charged with attempting to pervert the course of justice. Freddy hadn't much of an alibi for the evening of 20 May but nor had any knife been found to correspond to poor Stuart's fatal wound. No one had seen anyone resembling him in the neighbourhood of Kenilworth Green that evening, whereas someone had seen through the front window of the Aurelia Grove house the head and shoulders of a man who might have been Freddy.

Apart from the joking, Lucas Crabtree was sure that Freddy told DS Blakelock nothing but the truth. He gave meticulous accounts of his visits to Stuart's flat, the attacks he had made and received, and described in detail the small electronic devices by the means of which he had discovered his wife's affair and the identity of her lover. When they asked him to repeat what he had said he did so with absolute accuracy. After hours of this, Lucas constantly interjecting that it was time they let his client go, they released Freddy in exasperation, assuring him that this wasn't the end of it as they would certainly want to talk to him again. Laughing a lot once they were outside the interview room, Freddy and Lucas went off to a club they knew and got drunk.

The four weeks she had spent in the private clinic paid for by her stepchildren was probably the longest time in her entire life Olwen had been without a drink. Hallucinations no longer came to her, but the doctor who ran the clinic told Margaret that the test they had done for end-stage liver disease measured the severity of the cirrhosis on the very high score of six. This figure forecast no more than a ninety-day survival. A nutritious diet was prescribed, plus diuretics, oral antibiotics and beta blockers.

Olwen could go home but not to her own home. Margaret didn't want her and Richard, her brother, refused to have her. He had just remarried and his new wife was expecting their first child. An invalid in the house was out of the question. Margaret clung on to the prediction of Olwen's life extending no more than ninety days, twenty of which had already expired. She could put up with Olwen for seventy days, couldn't she? She and her husband and their teenage children would have to submit.

The prospect of living with Margaret brought her despair and then anger. It was explained to her that she really had no choice. They gave her a room on the ground floor of their small house. It had been a dining room but no one had ever eaten there, so Margaret took away the table and chairs, installed a single bed and a television that was too outdated for the children's taste. For the first two days Olwen stayed in bed. She washed and went to the lavatory in the cubicle known as a cloakroom, though no one had ever hung cloaks in it. After that she dressed herself and sat in the living room with Margaret and her husband. The children she hardly saw. If they weren't at school or out somewhere else, they were in their rooms ostensibly doing homework. Olwen, who understood duplicity, supposed that they were really playing video games.

Her own subterfuge she was planning. She never asked for drink and never talked about it or the lack of it. Margaret and her husband, who probably drank wine and even gin and tonic when alone, behaved abstemiously in her presence. 'Out of consideration for you,' Margaret explained.

'Olwen appreciates that,' said her husband, 'don't you, Olwen?'

'Not really,' said Olwen, and added, 'I don't care.'

She wanted to go home but knew she never would. They

had told her to take daily exercise, take her prescribed medica-
tion and a healthy diet, and she wondered what the point was
when she was going to die anyway. If she was going to die she
wanted it to be soon. She often thought of her intention to
drink herself to death and how she had done her best but her
strong heart had betrayed her. After she had been a week in
that house she started going out for walks. The first time
Margaret insisted on coming with her but she could tell Olwen
was walking quite well, provided she used a stick. Olwen walked
round the block, reflecting that she had probably never in her
life before done this without a purpose, shopping or visiting
someone.

At home (which was a way of putting it, that was all) she
behaved so well, was so quiet and apparently content that
Margaret went out on her own. Her best friend lived next
door and she liked calling on her. Olwen suspected they had
a bottle of wine between them when there was no risk of her
seeing. She could smell it on Margaret's breath. While she
was out Olwen searched the house for drink but she hadn't
far to look. In a cupboard in the living room which didn't look
like a drinks cupboard she found several bottles of wine, an
almost full bottle of gin and an untouched one of brandy. No
doubt they had all been in the cabinet in the room which
was now her bedroom but they had been prudently removed.
Resisting those spirits was probably the hardest thing she had
ever done.

But resist she did. She would not always do so.

June isn't usually a hot month in the British Isles but this
one looked as if it would be. The temperature in Duncan's
house mounted. He left a ground-floor front window open
overnight because he couldn't face coming down into that

furnace in the morning. A silent intruder came in and stole his DVD player, his mobile phone which he had left on the kitchen counter, his food mixer and the two notes and a hundred or so coins amounting to £62 that had been stashed away in an instant-coffee jar.

After that he had no choice but to shut and lock the windows, leaving only those in his bedroom open. The heat, he decided, must be due to something more than the high outside temperature and the excellent insulation. That which had been a source of comfort to him and of pride in his domestic arrangements had now become a curse. And there was no reason to hope that July and August would be cooler. Even when it rained, lowering the outside temperature, indoors it remained the same, thirty degrees Celsius when he had come downstairs that morning after a night of tossing and turning in the heat, sweat pouring off him.

It must be coming from next door. The tropical plants they grew for the royal family must demand the kind of heat experienced in South-East Asia and some of it infiltrated here. That must be why the paper had peeled off his walls. Duncan hated the prospect of complaining to the neighbours. He had once or twice done so in previous homes but mostly it was Eva who handled this, aggressive little firebrand as she could be. It was Eva who rang up about the noise the night before or banged on a front door to complain about footballs coming over the fence and breaking down their flowers. Eva, he thought, would have been into Springmead long before this, demanding they turn down their heating.

But he had to do it now. First he consulted Jock and Kathy Pember, inviting them round for drinks because you couldn't give people coffee at six in the evening. But he got cold feet – how he wished he literally had! – and bought more garden furniture in a Brent Cross sale, two chairs and a table with an umbrella, on condition they came that day. You could make conditions in a recession. Jock and Kathy admired the white-painted ironwork and the pink roses and yellow daisies on the seat cushions and after they had each had two glasses of rosé, ventured into the house to test the temperature.

'You can't live in that.' Jock wiped his forehead.

'I am living in it.'

They all climbed the stairs in the tropical heat, looked out of the top-floor back-bedroom window and down on to the Springmead garden. Tigerlily was just coming out of the summer house.

'Lovely-looking girl, isn't she?' Jock leaned out of the window.

'If you like flat chests and slant eyes,' said his wife.

'Why don't we go down,' said Jock, 'and talk to her over the fence? Tell her you want to speak to Mr Deng?'

Duncan really needed more time to consider it but he agreed. Jock wasn't quite tall enough to get his chin over the fence so Duncan brought a box from the shed, Jock stood on it and called out to Tigerlily who was sitting on the grass. 'Excuse me!'

Duncan thought he had never seen such a look of terror on someone's face, not even when he was called to help a woman whose borrowed car had broken down because she had put diesel in the tank instead of petrol. Tigerlily's pale skin had gone quite white and her eyes had grown huge. She stood up as if poised to flee.

'Excuse me. Sorry to bother you, but can you –'

'No,' said Tigerlily, 'no, no. No English. Sorry.'

She ran into the house.

'You'll have to pluck up your courage,' said Kathy, who was quite aware of Duncan's nervousness. 'Go to the front door and keep ringing the bell till that man Deng answers it.'

They weren't much help to him, Duncan thought unfairly.

He sat out in the garden for a long time as the tree shadows lengthened on the lawn and a pair of bats appeared, swooping through the blue air after insects. The coffee he had made himself, two mugs of it, should hardly have been drunk so late in the evening. Now he wouldn't sleep even if he could have endured the heat in the bedroom.

Upstairs he sat by the open window in the top-floor front bedroom, people-watching once more. Two couples turned into Lichfield House, the ones he called the lovebirds, the plump girl (Duncan used this kinder word) and her skinny boyfriend, holding hands. Molly her name was and Duncan thought they must have quarrelled because she looked as if she would have liked to take her hand away but the boy held on to it tightly. Ah well, the course of true love never did run smooth, there would soon be wedding bells there. They were followed by the older couple. They walked side by side but not touching. A platonic relationship, Duncan thought, just good friends or maybe brother and sister. The lights came on in Flat 2 where Rose Preston-Jones lived soon after they went in. He noticed that Mr Deng's black Audi was parked at the kerb outside Springmead and he wondered which of them would be going out at this hour. It was a quarter past eleven.

He looked down into the Springmead front garden and as he did so, Mr Deng came out of the front door with Tigerlily and the other girl and they got into the car. To Duncan's surprise, the boy came running out, carrying a suitcase and closing the front door behind him. He would never have believed the whole family would go out together but that was what they were doing. The black Audi moved off.

Where could they be going? From Duncan's viewpoint, going anywhere at eleven fifteen was something confined to the young, teenagers perhaps. And if those young people went out to a club, for instance, or a pub or bar they wouldn't go under the supervision of a forty-five-year-old uncle. Some of those supermarkets stayed open all night. Maybe they had gone to one of those. But all of them? The two girls and the boy? It was pleasant by the window. A little breeze had got up and it was as quiet as it ever got. The traffic on the main road was beginning to slacken now. Had they ever gone out all together before? All four of them? And what was that boy doing with the suitcase? Surely it must mean that they had gone away somewhere for the night or even for longer.

The heat was worst of all up here. Of course it would be, for heat rises. Slowly he got up and went downstairs where it was infinitesimally cooler.

He hooked the ring on which his keys hung on to the little finger of his left hand, took a torch from the hall cupboard – Springmead looked to be in total darkness – and left the house by the front door. Now he was in the front garden he could tell the house was empty. Blinds covered all the front windows but they were the slatted kind through which slits of brightness would show if lights were on inside. If there had been a letter box he could have looked through it. Perhaps that was the reason there wasn't one. He walked round the side, turned the handle on the side gate and, somewhat to his surprise, it opened. More blinds at the windows here. He came into the back garden, a place he had often looked at from his rear windows, but he had never seen or noticed what a barren place it was, the lawn unmown but green with the moss which overgrew it, not a flower, only weed shrubs, elders and brambles. The great ash tree overshadowed everything. Duncan went across the grass and on to the steps of the summer house.

But on this mild summer night, the moon gliding out of clouds into clear patches of sky, his torch was barely needed. Feeling very daring, feeling almost sick, he climbed the steps, opened the door of the summer house and stepped inside. It was furnished with floor cushions and pillows, and although no one would have called it cold, it was a good ten degrees cooler than the interior of his house. They came here to get cool, he thought, to escape the heat of Springmead, a heat which must necessarily be much hotter than his own home.

Behind the summer house, opening on to the lane behind, was the garage where Mr Deng must keep his Audi. Duncan went down the steps and into the garage by its rear door. He shone his torch round it but needlessly. There was nothing to see. What he had really come to see, he reminded himself, was the interior of Springmead, as much as he could even if the rear windows were hung with blinds.

They were not. Or if they were the blinds hadn't been pulled down. He could see through the French windows which corresponded to his own or he would have been able to if there was any light. But the whole place was in absolute darkness. He switched on his torch and shone it on to the glass, expecting to see plant pots, those royal orchids he had been told about, maybe twenty or thirty of them. What he saw instead was a thick black curtain hanging some six inches from the window and the half-raised blind. It covered the rear wall and French windows from floor to ceiling.

It was only a curtain but it frightened him. He had to stop himself from actually running home.

CHAPTER TWENTY-ONE

Blakelock knew Freddy Livorno would refuse to let them search his house without a warrant, and he would probably refuse for no more reason than to annoy. He would know that they could easily get one. It was simply a matter of time, of delay. So Blakelock didn't bother to ask Freddy, he got his warrant and, armed with it, went along to Aurelia Grove. Claudia was at home and she made a fuss, but beyond shouting and stamping there was nothing she could do. Bashir told her to calm down and eventually she did. They refused to tell her what they were looking for.

Nor did they tell her, when the search was completed, that they had failed to find Stuart Font's blue leather suitcase.

'I thought,' said Claudia, trying to use police language, 'that you'd eliminated my husband from your inquiries.'

'Did you, madam?'

'You let him go.' She added, keeping in the mode, 'Without a stain on his character.'

'If you say so,' said Blakelock. 'No doubt we shall want to see him again.'

The Scurlocks' flat in the basement of Lichfield House remained much as it had been when Wally and Richenda lived there. Richenda had no interest in any of the old furnishings and had equipped her new place entirely from Ikea. Run to earth while vacuuming a flat in Hereford House, she told DC Bashir that they could search her old home as much as they liked. What were they looking for?

They hadn't told Claudia but they happily told Richenda.

'That little blue suitcase of Stuart's? I'll be very surprised if you find anything like that. I've brought all the luggage we've got with me.'

And again they searched in vain.

The Springmead people's electricity bill would be enormous, Duncan thought. Or perhaps it was gas they used for heating. Their business must be highly lucrative. No wonder they could all afford to go away on holiday. He wondered where they had gone. The Maldives maybe or perhaps, being from South-East Asia themselves, somewhere in Europe. Monte Carlo? Athens?

His time was mostly passed outside and he congratulated himself on the purchase of that swing recliner. Two nights after his adventure in the Springmead garden he slept outdoors. Even in the night-time, even in the small hours, it remained warm. The air swarmed with insects, mostly moths, their big soft wings brushing against his face. Something less pleasant stung him on the cheek, leaving a red swollen lump.

There was no sound or sign from next door. It occurred to Duncan that plants needed looking after. Watering? Feeding? And how long did they plan to leave the heating on? No doubt they had paid someone to come in and do whatever had to be done. Trying to resist scratching his swollen cheek, he put his rubbish and his recycling out in the lane and tried to see into the Springmead garage. An up-and-over door was of course closed but he was able to see through a very narrow crack between its wooden boards. Something was inside the garage.

He was nearly certain he could see Mr Deng's black Audi inside. Perhaps one or some or all of them came back from wherever they were staying to attend to the plants. It must be because they, like him, could barely stand the excessive temperature. If the heat hadn't been such a problem, Duncan thought, this investigation of his – for this was what it was becoming – would be quite exciting. He had found himself an occupation.

He hardly knew why he needed to know what was going on next door. It wasn't just a matter of the excessive heat. He was consumed with curiosity so that he could think of little else. In the evening he went back to the lane, telling himself that this was just to bring back his bins. But he had another look through the crack in the boards of the garage door and this time the car had gone. Or, rather, whatever had obstructed his view of the rear window and door of the garage had been removed. Maybe it hadn't been the Audi but something else stored in the garage and now removed.

He passed the night in the garden and next morning the temperature had dropped a little. A light drizzle was falling. But it seemed too much to hope that the heatwave might be over. The house was still very hot inside but, with all the windows open, not unbearable. The Pembers came in for a coffee and Kathy asked him what he had done to his face.

'An insect bit me.'

'Americans don't say insects, they say bugs,' said Kathy ir-relevantly. 'We saw you sleeping in the garden. If that was because of the heat you must come and stay with us. Our spare room is like a fridge.'

Duncan said, no, thank you very much, he did appreciate their kindness but he intended to have it out with the Springmead people that day. He'd tell them that if they didn't turn their heating down he would have to report them to the council.

Would he actually do that? It was one thing to say so, another thing to carry out this threat. Meanwhile, he would continue his surveillance, and to that end he brought a chair and table into the front garden and sat there reading the paper and watching for the Audi. The lovebirds came out, holding hands quite amicably this time. Rose Preston-Jones emerged, without that teacher chap for once and without her dog. He watched her go into the Bel Esprit Centre – of course they wouldn't allow the dog in there and quite right too – and just as he was thinking he had better go indoors and start thinking about his lunch, the Audi arrived. Duncan hurried indoors and watched from the bay window.

Mr Deng, that he had once called Mr Wu, had come and his son with him. No sign of Tigerlily and the other girl. The two men went into the house and closed the front door behind them. Now was his chance to ring that front door bell and complain about the heat coming from their house through the walls into his house. But what if Mr Deng simply denied it?

What he would really like to do, if he could do so without putting himself in danger, was get into that house and see for himself, even locate the source of the heat – and turn it off. He wondered if he would have the nerve to do that. They would know someone had done it, that it hadn't gone off of its own accord. But at least he would discover if it was hotter in there than here in his own house. He could find the boiler or the various heaters. He would have liked to see their electricity bill but that of course was impossible.

The Audi had gone. That meant nothing. Mr Deng would have put it into the garage. The mist had cleared from the air, the sun was coming out and it was warming up again. Duncan took his sandwiches and glass of orange juice out into the back garden and sat on the recliner. He realised that he had never heard any sounds from next door, but he hadn't ever listened, hadn't put his ear to the dividing wall. When he had finished his lunch, he took the tray to the kitchen and in the hallway pressed his right ear – his good one – to the white-painted wall. Nothing. Silence.

They hadn't gone to Monte Carlo or wherever. They were still here, staying somewhere, perhaps with relatives. Duncan imagined a brother or even an uncle of Mr Deng who ran a Chinese restaurant but whose home was a fine house in Totteridge. It would have air conditioning and maybe a pool in the grounds. Naturally, they wouldn't want to spend more time than they had to down here when they could be in a beautiful garden, perhaps with a Chinese pagoda in it, a smaller version of the one at Kew. Duncan had his mid-afternoon coffee sitting in the front garden. He saw Richenda go out on a bicycle with a big basket on its front for her shopping and marvelled how anyone could dare to ride a bike in heels that high and a skirt that short. A woman he thought might be an estate agent arrived with a couple to look over Rose Preston-Jones's flat. Through her front window he saw them walking about the interior. But he saw no activity at Springmead. Some vandal had thrown an empty crisp packet over the fence into its front garden, which wasn't really a garden but a paved and pebbled area with a few dispirited shrubs. Duncan watched the breeze blow it about until it attached itself to the spiky top of a small cypress tree.

The presence of that crisp packet irritated him and after a while he let himself into the Springmead front garden and removed it. Carrying it into his own house to dispose of it, he realised that he had nothing for his supper. It was cooler than it had been but still too hot to walk all the way to the Tesco. He listened again at the hallway wall and again heard nothing. What he was planning to do later brought his heart into his mouth – it really felt like that, as if he had a blockage in his throat that half stopped him breathing. You haven't got the nerve, he said to himself, you know they'll guess who it was. But yes, maybe you have got the nerve . . . How dare they make it impossible for someone to live next door to them? And wasn't it, anyway, against planning restrictions to use a private house for a commercial purpose, even though they might be renowned orchid growers?

Slowly, he walked up to Mr Ali's, carrying a Tesco bag for the sake of the environment, though he knew that Mr Ali scrutinised the bags his customers brought in and disapproved of any from the big supermarket chains. He seemed to think that those who bought anything from his shop should exclusively shop with him. Duncan bought a chicken breast and some frozen peas and they were slipped into a brand-new plastic bag before he could produce his Tesco one. Mr Ali often seemed to read customers' thoughts.

'Why bother with this environment business,' he asked rhetorically, 'when Chinese are building a new power station each single day?'

Could this be true? Duncan didn't know if it was but the remark reminded him of Springmead and its inhabitants. Those girls would be swimming in their uncle's pool now, Mr Deng smoking a cigar with his brother on a shady patio, or enjoying a sake in the pagoda. He walked up to the end of Kenilworth Parade, crossed Kenilworth Avenue and turned into the lane. If the Audi had been there it was gone now and the up-and-over door was wide open. Because Mr Deng meant to come back? At any rate no one was there now. Duncan looked longingly at Springmead but what he contemplated doing must wait until dark.

*

Margaret was visiting her friend next door. These days she went there more and more and stayed longer and longer. When Olwen remained in her bedroom her step-daughter stayed at home but the moment she appeared in the living room, Margaret was off to see Helen, murmuring that she would 'just pop next door for five minutes'. Olwen didn't mind. She was accustomed to being no one's favourite person, in fact accustomed to being generally disliked and avoided. It was many years now that she had come to terms with the truth that she was first in no one's world or, come to that, second or third.

Now it was simply a matter of choosing her time for what she meant to do. Afternoon would be best and immediately after Margaret had gone to have tea or coffee or something stronger with Helen. It brought Olwen a small amount of grim amusement to listen to Margaret's sanctimonious comments on alcohol consumption stories in the *Evening Standard* while the smell of gin was apparent on her breath.

'Do you know that it says here the British drink more wine than the French and Italians put together?' Or, 'It says here that binge drinking has doubled in the past five years.'

Mostly all this just bored Olwen. However much of a hypocrite Margaret might be, however much drink she consumed on her own or in her conspiracy with Helen, she wasn't and would never be in Olwen's league. Although it was many weeks since anything alcoholic had passed her lips, now that the best of it was past, she felt a strange pride in the consumption she had achieved over what was only a few months. She hadn't been a drinker, she had been a drunk, and as a drunk she meant to die. One afternoon, when Margaret, poor pathetic thing that she was, had gone next door to visit Helen, then it should be done.

In Margaret's absence she once more opened the drinks

cupboard and looked at the bottles. Her throat opened and she gasped, yearning, even placing a hand on the neck of the blue bottle and the brown bottle and clutching their necks, but she went no further than that and she closed the cupboard door again.

At about nine in the evening when it was still quite light, Duncan went out of his gate into the lane. The Springmead garage door was still raised and the Audi was missing. Duncan returned to his recliner, scratching his insect bite, the remains of his chicken, peas and chips supper still on the table. Mr Deng and the boy would be back in Totteridge, possibly sitting by the pool and eating a delicious meal of butterfly-prawn delight and lemon chicken and luxury fried rice. Or they had all gone out in the Bentley to Mr Deng's brother's restaurant – would he also be called Deng or didn't it work that way?

He carried the tray indoors and opened the kitchen drawer where he kept his house keys. There was a different key for every room as well as a spare front-door key and a back-door key. The houses, his and Deng's, were identical. It seemed likely that one of these keys would open Deng's back door or the French windows – well, not *likely* but possible. They all looked alike but for some minute difference in the bit of the key that went into the lock that Duncan didn't know the name of. He put all the keys into his pocket, returned to the recliner and lay there, sleepless but calm. At one point he dozed off and when he awoke he saw that it was almost one thirty in the morning.

He got up and then he did something quite alien to him. It was seldom he drank anything alcoholic. He didn't much like the taste. But now he needed courage and he poured himself a small whisky. Shuddering, he drank it down neat.

Almost immediately it galvanised him, charging him with energy.

The torch might be needed. He put a new battery in it to be on the safe side. Better enter their garden by the gate into the lane. Would it be locked and if it was would one of his keys unlock it? He checked that they were still in his pocket. The night was dark, moonless and overcast. Duncan made his way down the garden, slapping at the insects which homed in on him. The air was heavy with heat and humidity and utterly still. He let himself out into the lane and tried the next-door gate. It was locked. He began trying his keys, one after another. The fourth one turned in the lock and the gate opened. Duncan saw it as a good omen. It surely meant that one of the other keys would open the back door.

As he had expected the house was in absolute darkness. He approached the back door and paused, telling himself that he was about to commit a felony. Not breaking and entering, there would be none of that, not the breaking anyway, but entering was what he intended to do. He found himself almost hoping that none of the keys would work. At first it looked as if none would; none at least unlocked the back door. He moved along to the French windows and started again. This time the last key he tried turned in the lock. He was pleased but angry too. It wasn't right that they would do that, make keys for people which opened neighbours' doors. He didn't ask himself who 'they' were.

With his hand grasping the knob but not turning it, he stood there, assailed now by doubts. That black curtain will be inside, he thought, and I shall have to draw it back. I shall have to find what's on the other side and it may be something dreadful. Don't talk rubbish, he muttered to himself, don't be stupid . . . Why am I doing this? I'm not really going to turn off their heating, am I? Go back, go home, complain to the council . . .

But he didn't go home. He stood there in the warm humid stillness, stood for a minute or two. Then, drawing in his breath, he turned the knob, stepped inside and closed the door behind him. He was between the window and the curtain. It was hot and dark, stuffy and airless, and he could see nothing but thick black cloth. Carefully, in the dark, he felt along the curtain until he came to its left-hand side. Switching on the torch, he held it in his left hand, and with his right drew the curtain aside. It slid easily as on rungs, rattling slightly, an alarming sound in the silence.

Before he lifted up the torch to shine it into the place that was on the other side of the curtain he could feel leaves brushing against him just as the insects' wings had done. He raised the light and heard himself gasp aloud. He was standing in a forest or plantation, filling what had once been a room, the same size and measurements as his living room. The entire space between the French windows and the front window, also black-curtained, had been taken over by these plants, row upon row of them, green, flowerless, as far from orchids as could be imagined. They looked rather like tomatoes but somehow he knew they weren't tomatoes. He knew, without knowing quite how, that they lacked the *innocence* of tomatoes or sunflowers or artichokes or any other of those plants they slightly resembled. And a scent came from them, very faint but one he had smelt before in the street, long ago when he was young, a scent that even then he had been afraid of.

He was afraid now, fearful of walking among them, of damaging them. It was as if, bruised by his passing them, their leaves would emit a stronger substance or gas into the hot air. And now he was aware of how extremely hot it was, hotter than his own house, hotter than it had been even in the noonday sun of the past days. He began to lose his fear of them and as he walked round the outer row to the door into the hallway, or where the door had been, for it had been removed from its hinges, he picked off the top of one of the plants. Then he picked another, about four inches of stem with leaves on it shaped like splayed hands, and put both pieces in his pocket. The hallway too was full of plants, and the dining room. The kitchen was full of plants but for a passage to the fridge and sink. Sweat began spouting from his forehead and cheeks. Now his eyes were becoming accustomed to the darkness and he could see as well as he had in the garden. He stared in wonderment at the hundreds – thousands? – of plants, the long stalks, the green leaves, and passed his hand across his forehead, wiping away sticky moisture.

A cupboard on the wall here, exactly where there was a cupboard on his kitchen wall, would contain the electricity meter. Why hadn't he thought of that before? Never mind. He thought of it now. He opened the door and there was the meter, where it ought to be. But the reading on the gauge was so much less than his own that it was laughable. A low figure preceded by three noughts. How could that be? Duncan remembered reading somewhere that unscrupulous householders who didn't want to pay exorbitant electricity bills somehow bypassed the meter and connected a supply for themselves from a source in the street.

But was that controlled from a temperature gauge and time clock in a cupboard on the landing as his was? Keeping gingerly to the narrow space between the outer row of plants and the wall, he reached the stairs and began to climb them. His progress was necessarily slow because the heat was almost too much for him and sweat actually dripped from his cheeks on to his shirt. That there might be more plants upstairs he hadn't expected but there were: plants along the landing, plants in three of the bedrooms, a motionless sea of dull green. The doors to these rooms had been removed but the one to the fourth, and smallest, bedroom was still there and it was shut.

Duncan didn't know what might be in that room. Not plants, though. He would look inside and then he would find the cupboard where the boiler must be. He opened the door very slowly and cautiously. The floor was covered with quilts and what he thought were called futons. There was also a pair of bunks, again laden with quilts. No black curtain here but only the blind which was pulled down. He retreated, leaving the door open, and began stepping gingerly through the rows of plants to find the source of this overpowering heat.

In the small room, naked but for a thin pair of shorts, Tao woke up when he heard someone downstairs. Not Deng Wei Xiao. *He* would have phoned first and come in by the front door. The girls would never be allowed to come alone. Besides, Deng had beaten Xue so badly when she'd been going to meet that man, that she was afraid to step an inch out of line, afraid to move out of the room she now shared with Li-li in the flat. The boy sat up in his bunk and listened. Whoever it was, that person was coming up the stairs, had reached the top. Tao shivered when he thought how the plants must be getting crushed, bruised, spoilt.

The door moved a little, came open. By then Tao was under the quilt, as still as a stone. But he could just see out. The intruder was the old man next door. Tao had often seen him staring into the Springmead garden and gazing down from a window at the back of his house, when he and Xue had been on their way to the cool plant-free summer house. The old man moved away, leaving the door open. Tao got up very quietly, very stealthily.

For just this eventuality Deng Wei Xiao left whoever might be here a selection of weapons, a hammer, a knife, a baseball bat. No guns. Whatever must be done must be done silently. Tao chose the bat. He squatted down in the doorway and watched the old man go into the boiler cupboard and turn off the heating. If that happened, Deng said, if it happened for more than half an hour, the plants would die and they would lose thousands.

Tao watched the old man begin to descend the stairs. Being so old, he was probably deaf. Tao remembered his grandfather in Chang-Sha who had gone deaf when he was this man's age. The old man lumbered down, clutching hold of the banister rail. He didn't seem to hear someone following him down the stairs as Tao moved softly, waiting for him to reach the bottom. Then, as he waded between the plants, and reached the inner glass door inside the front, Tao struck. He brought the baseball bat down on the old man's head and watched him drop with a long-drawn-out groan to the floor.

He lay on the floor, crushing the plants. Never, never damage a single plant, was the warning that had been instilled into Tao and the girls. But what was worse, sacrificing five or six plants or leaving the old man to call the police? The old man mustn't be here, though. He mustn't be found in here. Tao got both doors open, the inner glass door and the front door. In moving Duncan he saw with horror and some panic how many more of the plants he was crushing and spoiling, but there was no help for it. Deng would understand, wouldn't he? It was three in the morning, still and silent. He dragged Duncan or Duncan's body – was he dead? – out into the street and and laid him on the pavement, close up against the low hedge. Taking his mobile and his money

239

would make it look more like a mugging but Duncan didn't have a mobile or any money on him beyond a few copper coins. His pockets were full of nothing but keys.

Then Tao went upstairs very fast and switched the heat on.

CHAPTER TWENTY-TWO

Marius was having less than his usual luck with the *sortes*. He had opened *Paradise Lost* the evening before at Rose's request. She wanted to know if the man who was buying her flat would sign the contract next day. Marius's saying the *sortes* were only a bit of fun and not to be taken seriously, made no difference. The page at which he opened the volume was halfway through Book X and what he read was: 'But death comes not at call; Justice Divine / Mends not her slowest pace for prayers or cries.'

'Nothing to do with buyers or house agents, I'm afraid, sweetheart.'

'Well, I don't know, Marius. That slowest pace sounds like my solicitor and I've certainly been praying if not crying.'

'The death bit doesn't seem to apply,' said Marius, 'for which we should be thankful.'

But perhaps it did. When he was young Marius had longed to sleep in till ten or even midday. He seldom got the chance. Now there was nothing to stop him sleeping in he invariably woke up at six, and this morning because of the heat, it was just before four thirty. The sky was the colour that has no name, a gauze of grey veiling palest blue. He stood in Rose's open front window, savouring the fresh cool morning that would become milder in two or three hours' time. Kenilworth

Avenue had its dawn look, depopulated, still, crammed with cars on both sides. In the gap between two of the cars, a space about a yard long, he could see something lying up against the hedge. Or someone. Someone or something lay on the pavement.

Marius took his keys and his mobile and ran across the road.

'But death comes not at call,' he murmured to himself. On his knees by the body, he soon knew it wasn't a body but a living, though unconscious, man. Duncan still clutched a single key in his hand. A torch lay beside him. Marius dialled 999 and waited. He took off his sweater, rolled it up and laid it under Duncan's head. He sat there, waiting as the sun came up. Oh, come on, come on, what are you doing? Where are you? 'Justice divine,' he thought, 'mends not her slowest pace for prayers or cries.'

And then the waiting and howling came from far off, grew louder, waking up everyone in Kenilworth Avenue, as the ambulance arrived, parked and two paramedics came running.

'That's four times we've had an ambulance down here since February,' said Molly. 'Two times for poor Stuart, twice for Olwen and now this.'

Carl nodded slowly. 'Somebody like mugged him, is that right?'

The two of them were drinking cappuccinos in the Bel Esprit Centre. 'Hit him on the head with a blunt instrument, poor old thing. That's what they call it, a blunt instrument. His money and his mobile were gone so they must have got those.'

'Is he going to make it?'

'I don't know. Fingers crossed.'

'May as well be dead at his age, though.' Carl yawned.

'I'm getting you a ring as soon as I've like got the dosh. It won't be long. Then other guys'll see you're engaged.'

'Oh, Carl, I don't know,' said Molly.

Today was the day to do it. Olwen had planned it carefully, having nothing else to do. Things would have been easier if she had had any money but she had none and no means of getting any. A look of unmistakable relief had crossed Margaret's face when Olwen told her she had lost her bank card.

'Well, you won't need it, will you?'

'Not really,' said Olwen to be on the safe side.

'You've got to take some exercise. Some gentle walking is all that means. It's not as if you want to go shopping.'

Someone who's going to die soon ought to be able to do everything they want, Olwen thought. There was only one thing she wanted – to drink and die. To drink herself to death, as she had always intended, but do it in her own time. If she had to do that by stealing, well, so be it. She would steal. Others had stolen from her, that girl especially, that girl who had her bank card. It no longer mattered. She no longer cared.

Part of Olwen's plan had involved going out for small walks. Just so that when the time came she could get as far as the taxi. Using a stick helped. It displeased her that she was better able to walk, that she was stronger, because she knew this must be due to having no alcohol for the past weeks. The day was very hot, the whole of this month of June was being one of the hottest Junes ever. Olwen was wearing her black tracksuit bottoms and an old black T-shirt with a faded and no longer identifiable logo on its front. Margaret switched on the fan for Olwen and said she was going next door to see Helen.

'I'll be an hour at the most.'

That meant at least three hours. One hour would have been enough for Olwen's purpose. Once Margaret was out of the way, Olwen found the number of the taxi service the family used in their personal directory and with it the account number. She pressed the requisite keys on the phone, gave Margaret's name and the password she had so often heard her use, and when they asked her where she wanted to go, she said, 'Kenilworth Green.'

'What's the postcode?'

Olwen didn't know. Maybe she had known once but she didn't any longer. They looked it up and it took a long time.

'When would you like it?'

'As soon as possible.'

Olwen found an environmentally friendly shopping bag in a kitchen cupboard and put into it the almost full bottle of gin and the unopened bottle of brandy from Margaret's drinks cupboard. If they had known her better, Olwen thought, her cunning, her need, her unscrupulousness, they wouldn't have left it there. Margaret wouldn't see the taxi come because she and Helen invariably sat in the room at the back.

It came two minutes early. Carrying her bag of drink in her left hand and grasping the stick in her right, Olwen made her way down the path and the driver got out to help her into the taxi. It was quite a long journey from Harrow but when she reached the kissing gate there was, of course, nothing to pay because the cab was on account. The Kenilworth Green turf was no longer a uniform green but bleached in patches to pale straw.

Olwen had intended to find some tree or shrub cover under which to hide herself, and trees there were in plenty but none to sit under and not be seen. She had only once before been in the place and then had hardly been aware of the neighbouring cemetery. That was a place which had plenty of cover – trees with undergrowth, overgrown slabs and tombstones. What better, what more appropriate place to die? The hedge which separated it from Kenilworth Green was low, no more than three or four feet high. Climbing it had been easy for Stuart and Wally and all those others who frequented this place, a mere matter of stepping over. Not for Olwen. Limping up here with the aid of her stick had been almost too much for her. She crawled along the hedge, stopping every few moments to rest, and just before the hedge met the high boundary fence she saw that it had been broken down. Purposely? Perhaps, for it looked as if someone or even some animal had forced a way through. Olwen just managed to step over the broken bit and on the other side found herself up to her knees in grass and nettles, brushwood and brambles.

Children were out in a playground on the other side of the cemetery, running around, shrieking and pushing each other. Olwen had no idea there was a school there. She had noticed very little of the neighbourhood when she lived at Lichfield House. Blundering on, holding on to gravestones for support, she gave up when she found herself a shady spot between a large cuboid tomb, box-shaped and of dark granite, and a dense wall of privet. This wall was perhaps four feet high as if someone had intended to create a hedge across the cemetery but given up after putting in no more than three or four plants.

It reminded her of when she was very young, a child of seven or eight. There had been just such a section of hedge in her parents' garden, with a space between it and the rear fence, and she had spent many hours inside it, first covering the top of the space with branches and calling it her camp. She had had cans of Tizer in there – oh, the innocence of it – and biscuits and had taken her pet dog with her when he would come.

Inside this sanctuary she sat down on the grass, sat down with great difficulty, squatting first, then kneeling, then easing herself to lean against the side of the tomb. It would be impossible for her ever to get up unless aided and she wouldn't be aided. All was silent now, the schoolchildren had gone in, traffic was a distant murmur. The ground was very dry and dusty, the air still and warm. Slowly, because she was savouring this moment, this preliminary, she unscrewed the cap on the gin bottle, lifted it to her lips and drank.

Olwen thought she had never in her entire life experienced such ecstasy. It was the most blissful drink she had ever taken. Briefly she thought of the cruelty of those who had taken it from her and would keep it from her. But she had eluded them, she had triumphed. Closing her eyes, she tilted the bottle and poured gin down her throat. She was happy.

Half a dozen miles away, Duncan had regained consciousness soon after he arrived at the Royal Free Hospital. They gave him a scan and then another scan and it seemed he had no brain damage. A doctor told him he had had a very lucky escape as if what had happened to him was his own fault. Perhaps it had been, Duncan didn't know, because he had no memory of events prior to and immediately after the attack. The hospital wanted to know if there was anyone near to him they should contact and Duncan said Jock and Kathy Pember. He could remember things like that but not what had happened to him just before he was hit on the head. A policeman came to see him and Duncan told him he thought he must have been for a walk somewhere in green fields.

He remembered a lot of leaves. No, he no longer had a mobile and he was sure he hadn't any money or credit cards with him when he went out. The policeman thought his mind was wandering because he had never before encountered anyone without a mobile.

Later in the day the Pembers came. Jock asked if he could describe his attacker but lost interest when Duncan said he could remember nothing about what had happened to him. Then Kathy told a long story she had read somewhere about a woman in the United States picking out her assailant in an identity parade. How could she tell it was him?

'He was the only one wearing handcuffs,' Kathy said.

Duncan said rather crossly that his case couldn't be a parallel because he had no memory of an assailant, wouldn't have believed he had an assailant but for the bang on his head. He told Ken and Moira about the leaves when they came next day. Not a few leaves as it might be on a single plant but fields of them.

'You were dreaming,' Ken said. 'That's what it was. Were you brought up in the countryside?'

'I suppose I was.'

'Well, there you are then. You were reverting to childhood. Sugar beet, those leaves would have been.

Duncan was allowed to go home next day. A wall of heat met him when he got inside the house. The first thing he did was take off his jacket and then he felt in his pocket for his handkerchief to wipe off the sweat which had started all over his face. No handkerchief was there. Perhaps he really was doing what Ken had suggested and reverting to his childhood, for what he brought out was a crumpled tissue and with it two green stems with withered leaves attached. Then he remembered. The memory came back in disjointed fragments but it came back, the green rows, the intense heat, the smell, the stairs, the cupboard with the heating gauge, the movement behind him as he reached the foot of the stairs . . .

He had to sit down for a while because he felt weak. But from the moment he left the hospital in a small new-fangled kind of ambulance, he resolved he would seek out the man who they told him had found him lying on the pavement and had called for help. Marius Potter. Duncan didn't really know him but he remembered seeing him from his window at Stuart's party and the funeral. He took himself carefully across the road, thinking he could do with a stick but not wanting to start that, not that slippery slope to old age, that thin end of the wedge. No caretaker was about, apparently they hadn't yet found a replacement for Wally Scurlock. Duncan rang Marius's bell and then he rang Rose's. Neither was answered. Unbeknown to Duncan, or any other neighbours for that matter, Rose and Marius were in St Ebba's, getting married, their only witnesses Marius's sister Meriel and her husband.

The vicar, who was old and quiet and short-sighted, told them they were the only couple 'of your age' he had ever been called upon to marry who hadn't been married before. He found it a matter for wonderment that each had attained such seniority yet remained single. Marius and Rose smiled but said nothing. Rose wore a very ordinary summer dress and Marius wore the only suit he possessed. The ring he put on her finger had belonged to his mother. After the ceremony they walked across the cemetery to step over the hedge to Kenilworth Green, passing quite close to Olwen in her leafy nest, but not seeing her. They passed through the kissing gate and hurried back to Lichfield House because McPhee fretted if he was left alone for too long.

They were going up the steps and the doors were already opening to receive them when Duncan came across the road for the third time. Neither Marius nor Rose said anything to Duncan about being the first to congratulate them but Marius asked Duncan how he was and how he hoped he was fully recovered.

'I want to thank you for rescuing me. Finding me on the pavement like that and calling an ambulance. Beyond the call of duty it was.'

Marius would have liked to say that he couldn't very well have left Duncan where he lay but he only smiled and said he had rather enjoyed it. It had been a small adventure.

'Well, now I've run you to earth, perhaps you can tell me what this is. Not orchid leaves, is it?'

'It's cannabis,' said Marius. 'We should tell the police.'

Deng, Tao and the two girls were having a conference in the back garden of Springmead when the police came. Or Deng was taking Tao to task, not for attacking Duncan but for not finishing him off. They could have disposed of a body but not of a living man. That Duncan was living they knew for they had seen him in his garden lying on his recliner. The girls took no part in this. They knew better than to intervene.

Deng was telling Tao to take Xue and Li-li back to the flat and leave him at Springmead to watch and wait, when there came from the front the unmistakable sound of a door being broken down.

'To the car. Now,' Deng said and then ran to the garage. They were out in the lane, heading for the Watford Way, when the police burst through the black curtain, got the French windows open and were in the garden. It wasn't Blakelock and Bashir

249

but officers of the drugs squad. Upstairs they went, through the plantations, into the tiny room where the Chinese people had slept. The heat and the ultraviolet lights were almost over-powering.

'There are a good five hundred plants in here,' a woman officer said. 'They'll have bypassed the electric meter. I wonder if they wired it to a street lamp. Could be.'

'Yeah, but where are they?'

The four officers went out into the garden. The open back door into the garage told them how the cannabis farmers had made their escape. They went next door and Ken Lee told them all about Mr Deng and Tao and the girls he knew only as Tigerlily and 'the other one'.

Duncan wanted no further contact with the police. He lay low inside his house, which was rapidly cooling down. He would be happy to talk to all the neighbours and had already invited all those he knew, including Rose and Marius, round for drinks at six. It was a celebration of his recovery, and, now he had learned about it, of Marius and Rose's wedding. Coffee hardly seemed adequate on such a momentous occasion.

He watched for the police to go. Someone had now arrived to put crime tape all round the front of Springmead. The police were in number 7, talking to Ken and Moira. That suited Duncan very well. He could have told them about Tigerlily and Stuart, about how keen Stuart had been on her and, though Duncan didn't really know, he could guess there had been more to it than that. Maybe her uncle Mr Deng had resented their relationship. He wouldn't be surprised if . . . But no, he wasn't telling the police that. Ever since Marius had told him that the leaves he had found came off cannabis plants, he had been afraid the police would find out he had illegally entered Springmead. He hadn't broken in, that was true, but he had – 'effected an entry' was the term. They might prosecute him, they wouldn't just let it slide. He would say nothing more.

The drugs squad, if that was what they were, left as Duncan was eating his lunch. Then the crime-tape men left. It had begun to rain, the first rain for weeks. Duncan lay down on his sofa, pulled a blanket over him because it was starting to feel chilly – quite an enjoyable sensation – and fell asleep.

CHAPTER TWENTY-THREE

Sophie often listened outside Olwen's door but heard nothing. Though she asked everyone at Lichfield House and those she knew in the other blocks, no one could tell her what had become of Olwen. Helping herself from Olwen's bank account had seemed an enormity at first. But when no retribution had come and the source showed no sign of drying up, she had worried less and begun to take it for granted that when she needed money she would help herself to it with Olwen's card and Olwen's pin number. She knew better than to make excessive demands on the account and had learned that money came into it on the 24th of the month. When it was raining and she didn't feel like walking all the way to the Tube station she took a taxi to college; when she saw something to wear that she liked in a shop window she usually went in and bought it, and she had her hair cut and blonde streaks put into it.

She had resented Noor and Molly having boyfriends when she didn't, but now that she had smartened up her appearance and walked with more confidence, standing up straight and wearing one of her new bras, things had changed. The university was up for the summer, she wasn't going home to Purley unless she absolutely had to, she had met a boy in the Kenilworth Arms and was meeting him again this evening.

'You want to come to a party with me? It's an old guy called Duncan but there'll be food and drink and we could go on somewhere afterwards.'

'How old?' said Joshua.

'Oh, come on. We don't have to stay long.'

They encountered Marius and Rose in the lobby. Rose was carrying a bottle of wine in one of Mr Ali's bags.

'Maybe we should have brought one,' said Sophie.

Joshua looked at her as if she had suggested bringing champagne and caviar. 'Give me a break,' he said. 'We don't do that stuff, not like at our age.'

They all went across the road together. The crime tape was still strung over the front of Springmead. Molly, who had followed them up Duncan's front path, said she'd heard the whole house would have to be sprayed with chemicals, if not gutted. Moira and Ken and the Pembers were already out in the garden, drinking wine and eating snacks from Marks & Spencer's. Jock Pember claimed to know all about the raid on what he called the 'pot house', information he said he had got from his friend who was a detective sergeant based at Paddington Green. Mr Deng wasn't the boss, he said, but only the one in charge of the Springmead enterprise and the two girls and the boy no more than slaves.

'That's what my friend says. Slaves, he called them. Illegal immigrants, of course, brought over here to work on cannabis cultivation. Given all sorts of promises of the kind of work they'd have to do and you can bet your life it wasn't growing pot plants. Pot plants, that's funny, isn't it, when you come to think of it?'

Duncan asked him who was the head man, then.

'No one knows. And they won't. It's the underlings who have to carry the can, that's always the way. The police found them all in a flat in Edgware, the two girls, Xue and Li-li, and the boy that's called Tao. He's the one that hit you on the head, Dunc. What did you want to go in there for? – that what's my friend said. He should have called us. He's lucky to be alive, he said, the silly sod.'

Duncan thought it was a bit much, a neighbour coming in here and saying these things about him while drinking his wine and eating his canapés. And he was pondering a crushing remark when Noor arrived with her Indian prince or sultan or whatever he was, a very handsome young man dressed all in white. Carl came next, carrying two cans of lager.

'It got to six thirty,' said Molly, 'and I got fed up of waiting for you. No one's going to drink beer, you know. It's not a middle-class thing.'

His own crushing remark overtaken by Molly's, Duncan fetched another bottle of wine from indoors. 'I'll open that.' Jock proceeded to do so and refilled his own glass first. 'So the thousand-dollar question is,' he went on, 'was it Deng who stabbed poor old Stuart Font?'

'Why would he?' Molly asked.

'Ah, well, that girl Xue, or Sue as I prefer to say, seems to have been going about asking people to get her a passport.'

'What d'you mean, people?' said Noor.

'I know for a fact she asked Ali at the corner shop and the guy who has the paper shop at the roundabout. She asked him while Deng was waiting for her in the car. Ali told me himself. Deng'd have done anything to stop that.'

Noor laughed in a scathing way. 'Stuart couldn't have got anyone a passport. He didn't work for the Home Office or anything like that. He didn't work at all. The fact is Stuart just wasn't very bright. In other words, thick.'

Molly's shout made everyone jump. 'What does that mean? Not very bright? You didn't know him. You only met him once when you went to his party to get a free drink.'

'That was enough,' said Noor, turning her back on Molly. 'Hey, look, Carl's getting over your fence, Duncan.'

'You can't go in there,' Duncan shouted.

But Carl was already in the Springmead garden, raising his glass to the guests he had left behind. He bounded down to the summer house, opened the pink door and jumped inside. Molly stood close up against the fence, hesitating, but only for a moment. She set her glass down on Duncan's lawn and began to climb over. Joshua followed her, ignoring his host's shouts.

'Stop that! You can't go in there. You're trespassing.'

'I don't see why we shouldn't all go in,' said Jock. 'I can make it all right with my pal.' Noor and the prince were already half over the fence, each with a bottle tucked under their arms. As Kathy scrambled over, fell but picked herself up, dusting off leaves and earth, Jock rallied those who remained behind. 'You'll be all right with me, only we'll go in by the back lane, not being quite as agile as these kids and my lady wife.'

Calling to Moira to bring a couple of bottles with her, he led the way out through Duncan's back gate and into the next-door garden. Leaving the summer-house door open, Carl, followed by the whole troop, headed for the French windows. Ken Lee, his head thrown back, was drinking wine out of a bottle from which he had unscrewed the cap. Aghast, watching his party disintegrate, Duncan was begging Marius and Rose not to follow them – something they had no intention of doing – when Michael and Katie turned up. They had brought two bottles of rather good red wine which Michael said was a farewell gift because they were soon moving, and had just stepped out on to Duncan's patio when someone – it was Joshua – smashed a pane in the Springmead French windows with a brick.

Duncan gave a piteous cry. 'Don't have anything to do with it! They're all going to get into terrible trouble. That's breaking and entering, that is.'

He shooed his four remaining guests indoors like someone driving a flock of geese and shut the French windows so that the shrieks of the explorers could no longer be heard. The heatwave had come to an end, anyway, and it was growing chilly. For the first time the house felt cold and a little of that unwanted heat of the past months would have been welcome. They sat talking rather awkwardly and at Michael's news fell silent. He didn't say that the newspaper he worked for had terminated his contract as a result of the latest piece he had written, an article on delirium tremens which got most of the facts about this condition wrong. He said nothing about that but told them he had defaulted on his mortgage and the building society were going to foreclose and repossess number 4.

No one knew what to say. Marius and Rose had intended to make conversation by talking about the house they were buying in Finchley but this was of course impossible now. Duncan was making an effort at sympathy and had just said something about every cloud having a silver lining when the silence from next door was broken by shrieks and yells and roars and pounding feet.

'They've all gone mad,' said Duncan.

For a moment the four visitors sat silent, listening to the tumult, to breaking glass and peals of laughter, eldritch howls and a noise like someone tobogganing down the stairs on a tray. Then, as one, they got to their feet, thanked Duncan for a 'lovely party' and left.

As he drank a fourth glass of wine, Duncan realised that for a half-hearted drinker like himself it was one too many and he would likely feel ill next day. One thing was for certain, he would never have anything more to do with those Pembers.

It may have been Molly's remark about going to Stuart's party only for a free drink, or Joshua's breaking one of the panes in the Springmead French windows in order to get into the house, one or the other, which resulted in Noor's announcement. She, Sophie and Molly with Joshua, Carl and the prince were all out in Kenilworth Avenue and it was ten thirty. Duncan's older guests had gone home and Springmead was once more empty.

'I may as well tell you,' said Noor, 'that my dad's putting Flat 5 on the market. There's no point in keeping it now I've moved in with Nasr. You two'll have to find somewhere else to live.'

'I wouldn't stop there if you paid me,' said Molly.

'And that's not very likely, is it?'

'You can come to my place, sweetheart,' said Carl. 'Don't you waste your time arguing with her.'

Sophie noticed that Joshua didn't follow his example and offer her accommodation. She wouldn't have been surprised if he'd just said he'd see her later – which could mean tomorrow or never – and gone off to the Tube. But he took her hand and reminded her that they had made a tentative arrangement to go up to the disco in the basement of the Kenilworth Arms. Hand in hand, they walked towards the roundabout. The prince's driver had fallen asleep waiting for him at the wheel of the white Lexus but woke up smartly as his employer and Noor appeared. It wasn't too late to go to the Wolseley for supper as Nasr was such a good customer.

Molly didn't want to spend the night in Carl's room in Cricklewood and since Noor's notice of eviction wasn't going to come into effect immediately, she took him back with her to Lichfield House. It looked as if she might be spending the next couple of years in that room of his, if not the rest of her life.

About to enter the Kenilworth Arms, Joshua said that he hadn't any money. With very little experience of male companionship, Sophie had nevertheless thought that a boyfriend – could Joshua yet be called her boyfriend? – ought at least to pay his share of the expenses. But she didn't like to raise the subject so early in their relationship and she said that was all right because she would draw out some cash at the hole in the wall. Her own bank card she only used these days when she had exhausted Olwen's supply. As it happened, Olwen's pension or whatever it was would come in next day, so she felt quite happy about inserting the card and keying in Olwen's pin number to draw out a modest sum. Joshua stood behind her, standing very close, and as she picked up the five ten-pound notes, he kissed the back of her neck.

After that, the first real show of affection, he was quite loving, moving cheek to cheek with her like the people in *Strictly Come Dancing* while everyone else was leaping about and swinging around. They left at two and walked back through Kenilworth Green, passing quite close to the tombstone and the little hedge inside which Olwen lay, but too occupied with each other to notice the leg and the shoe dew-covered in the long grass.

It was the first cold night for weeks. Midsummer was past and the temperature should have held up high if the weather forecast had been accurate. But it dropped down to less than ten degrees. It was a woman walking a dog but not Rose with McPhee, who found Olwen, coming out at seven in the morning. The dog homed in on her, whimpering at the brown leather brogue and the legs in tracksuit bottoms. If you are not prepared for a shock, it is almost impossible to repress some sort of cry. The dog's owner was prepared for nothing but a chilly morning, a decaying churchyard and an ill-tended green space. She let out a scream and clapped her hand over her mouth.

She thought Olwen was dead but the paramedics who came knew better. They wrapped her up and took her to one of the hospitals she had visited before. Olwen had hypothermia and her liver was almost destroyed. There was very little to be done and she died that night.

It was nearly forty-eight hours since Olwen had left her house in a taxi and Margaret had not noticed her absence until twenty-four of those hours had gone by, assuming that Olwen was in her room as she often was for long periods of time. Even then she supposed Olwen would come back of her own accord. She had seemed so much better in the past week. She reported her as a missing person only when her husband said she must.

Was it necessary to arrange a funeral? The undertaker said no, they would see to everything. Presumably, Margaret would want cremation. Margaret would. Now that had been settled she need think no more about it.

Living in Noor's dad's flat, even though sharing with Noor and Sophie, Molly had been spoilt. Two large bedrooms, one cleverly subdivided, a beautiful bathroom and unlimited hot water, a huge fridge, microwave, washing machine and dryer – and all for a nominal, a *tiny*, rent. As a kind of trial run she had spent a night in Carl's room. It had been an eye-opener. Literally, as she had scarcely closed her eyes all night.

The room was up three flights of stairs at the top of a Victorian house in Cricklewood. It measured perhaps fourteen feet by twelve and instead of furniture was full of junk. There were no cupboards. Carl kept all his possessions, including his clothes and trainers, two or three broken radios and a couple of mobile phones, in transparent plastic bags. The floor was covered in carpet of a kind, though threadbare and dirty, and the bed was a double mattress pushed into a corner. The TV stood on the floor and a laptop next to it, hedged in by stacked rubbish bags, stuffed full. Outside the single, uncurtained, window the poles and planks of scaffolding kept out much of the daylight but did little to exclude the glare from street lamps.

From where she lay, under Carl's dirty duvet, she had been able to view the contents of the nearest bag, old magazines, cans of lager, packets of crisps, one of those broken radios, CDs, two DVDs that she could clearly see were of *Saving Private Ryan* and *Death Becomes Her*, several empty cigarette packets and, rather frighteningly, a syringe. The remaining contents of the bag were hidden from her view by a rolled-up blanket and a T-shirt with a skull on it.

Lying awake, she asked herself if she was really going to live here. And if so, when? What about Sophie? When the three of them moved in together, three 'best' friends from school, it looked as if it would last the three years each intended to spend at their colleges. The generosity of Noor's father had seemed at first to be too good to be true. A big flat in a new block on a bus route and near a Tube station! They didn't even have to clean the place because Richenda did all that. The only cleaning she ever did had been for Stuart and that, she thought, had been out of love.

She tossed and turned, Carl snoring softly beside her. Did he ever change the sheets? And if he did where did they get washed? Molly had seen launderettes, had walked past them, but never been inside one. She *couldn't* live here but where else could she go when Noor turned her out?

Now she needed to go to the bathroom. Wrapping herself in the blanket she pulled from the floor, she tiptoed down the long passage only to find a light showing in the glass panel over the bathroom door and the door locked.

The change in the weather was violent. In the last week of June the temperature changed overnight from thirty-two degrees (or ninety as Duncan put it) to seventeen, or sixty-five. The rain began and everyone knew, in spite of the optimistic forecast, that the real summer was over. Duncan, who had come to believe his home would always be warm, sometimes too hot to live in, now found himself shivering when he got up in the morning. Number 3 Kenilworth Avenue was actually *cold*, something he had never known in all the time he had lived there. Brought up in a little house on the Essex marshes where the fire was never lit before November, he was shocked at the idea of starting the central heating in July, even turning it on for a few hours. He went off to Brent Cross where the same man who had sold him a toaster in January and told him they didn't sell room heaters in the summer, told him the same thing again. It was incredible but no matter how cold it might be in June they didn't sell room heaters. Now if he wanted a fan . . .

Duncan shivered, wrapping himself in a blanket as he walked about the house. Heavy rain fell and soaked the recliner. He had never considered what to do with it in the winter, still less this premature autumn. There was no room for it indoors or even in his garden shed, so he covered it with ten of the black plastic bags he kept for putting the rubbish in.

While he was outside a uniformed police officer arrived in the Springmead garden and with him a man to mend the broken window. Duncan thought they would ask him if he knew who was responsible for breaking the glass, but all they said was good morning.

CHAPTER TWENTY-FOUR

E state agents' boards sprouted all over the little garden at the front of Lichfield House. Columba Brown were handling the sale of Marius's flat and Smith Mawusi Green the Constantines'. The late Stuart Font's Flat 1 was in the hands of NW Woodlands, as had been Flat 2. Contracts were signed on Rose's flat but NW Woodlands hadn't yet removed their board. Olwen's Flat 6 had long been empty, but while doubt remained as who it belonged to, it could neither be rented nor sold. In the middle of a cold wet July, on the day Michael and Katie Constantine and a mountain of luggage got into the taxi that would take them to Paddington Station and the train for Cardiff where her parents lived, the classiest agent of all, Wood, Lasalle & Stitch, arrived to put up the board that would offer Flat 5 for sale.

The prince had proposed and his father the nawab and Noor's father the multimillionaire were engaged in arranging the wedding. Noor, with a palace in Kerala and a house in Mayfair in prospect, was in the giving vein and had told Sophie and Molly they could remain in Flat 5 until the end of August.

'Or when Daddy accepts an offer. Whichever is the sooner.'

Sophie had given up. On 24 July Olwen's money should have come into her bank account but, ready to go up the road and draw out the entire sum, she couldn't find Olwen's bank card.

She remembered last taking it from the pocket of her Gap jeans and presumably putting it back there. Not presumably but certainly. And it fitted there snugly because the jeans were very tight and nothing could have been abstracted without her being aware of it. Therefore she must have taken it out and put it somewhere else. She searched Flat 5, searched through her clothes, looked inside all the books she had been reading or ought to have read for her uni course, and all in vain.

She thought back to that evening after the party when she and Joshua and Molly and Carl and Noor and the prince and some of those oldies had all gone into Springmead and rampaged about, running up and down stairs and drinking an awful lot.

Joshua – she hadn't seen him since that night. He had stood behind her when she used Olwen's card for the last time, watched her key in the pin number and kissed her neck. And later she had taken him back to Flat 5, he'd stayed the night and next day he'd disappeared. It had been a short-lived love affair.

By this time she had long got over hoping that she and he might find a place together. There was nothing for it but to go back to her parents' house and live with them, not just until uni started again but until two more years had passed and she got her degree. It meant commuting from Purley, a long and costly journey. She was pondering on this and consoling herself with the thought that her own bank account would be in a better state than it had probably ever been, when Molly walked in.

'What d'you think, Olwen's dead.'

'Olwen?'

'You remember Olwen, don't you? She's dead. Mr Ali told me.'

'How does he know?'

'He always knows everything. And he said we've got a new caretaker coming and it's a woman, how about that?'

'Everyone's a woman these days,' said Sophie. 'Soon there won't be any men about.'

'I can't wait.'

With luck, Sophie thought vindictively, no money would have gone into Olwen's account after 24 June, so that rat Joshua would be disappointed when he tried to use the card. Molly was beginning to see Carl as her fate – and her landlord. She couldn't go home to her parents. After she left school they had moved to Torquay. Living with them was a possibility only until art school started again in October and maybe getting a job in one of the numerous restaurants or cafes. She hated the prospect. Almost better to throw in her lot with Carl. He told everyone she was his fiancée and he had given her a ring which she knew for a fact came from Topshop.

N W Woodlands called the little house in Finchley Marius and Rose were buying a 'Georgian cottage'. Marius said that must be George VI, the Queen's dad, but never mind, it was ideal for them. He still had to sign the contract on the sale of Flat 3 and meanwhile Rose moved in with him while they waited to get possession of number 1 Fortescue Cottages.

One evening when they were coming out of the Almeida Theatre and walking down Upper Street they met Freddy Livorno. Marius thought Freddy wouldn't have known him on his own or Rose on her own but he recognised them together and suggested they all go and have a drink somewhere. On the way to the pub he told them about his coming divorce, the prospect of which made him roar with laughter. After their single foray into champagne, Rose and Marius had sampled no more alcohol but they were happy enough to drink orange juice while Freddy drank whisky.

'The cops have given up on me. I had a cast-iron alibi

I fabricated,' Freddy said, mixing his metaphors, 'and they swallowed it.'

'It wasn't you,' said Marius, 'and it wasn't Wally Scurlock. Possibly the Chinese pot-grower but I don't think so. I suppose they're still looking.'

'They say they never give up but they do. You still living at Lichfield House?'

'We're moving into a little house we're buying,' said Rose, and she added, 'We got married.'

'Well, congratulations.' Freddy sounded genuinely pleased. 'Hope it turns out better than it did for me. I doubt if I'll take the plunge again.'

Duncan was feeling quite excited. His offer to drive the rented van which would carry Rose and Marius's furniture to Finchley had been accepted. It would give him the chance to drive again and cost Rose and Marius only the day's rental instead of what a removal firm would have charged. Marius wanted to keep only his books. All the furniture that had belonged to long-dead aunts and uncles was to be taken away by flat clearers who had offered him £200 for the lot. He said it would be a relief to see the back of it. Rose had pretty painted furniture and delightful ornaments and pleasing watercolours which Duncan and Marius carried out to the van. McPhee sat on Rose's lap in the passenger seat while Marius sat in the back in Rose's pink velvet armchair to watch over the rest of the furniture and the nine large boxes of books.

Sitting high up in the driver's cab, bowling along to Finchley, Duncan felt as if he were going on holiday. He rather wished Rose and Marius were moving to Scotland so that he could have driven all day.

*

Sophie moved out a week later. Her parents pretended they were delighted to have her back in Purley and she pretended she had been homesick and was happy to return. Of all the residents in Lichfield House now only Molly remained. Carl nagged her daily to move in with him but she intended to hold out as long as she could, clinging to the Micawberish hope that something would turn up. She had till the end of August, Noor had said so, and so she was unpleasantly surprised by the arrival of a small fat man in a silver-grey suit and wearing a diamond ring. He let himself in with his own key, announced that he was Noor's father and seemed shocked by Molly's emerging from the shower (decent in a towelling robe) at ten in the morning. She would have to be gone by the next day, he said, as he had decorators coming in to renovate the flat. And he walked about, scrutinizing tiny marks on the woodwork and a scrape on the floor tiles which he seemed to take for granted had been made by Molly alone.

Obliged to make two journeys, she struggled over to Cricklewood on buses, her clothes and books in a suitcase and three Sainsbury's carriers. It rained lightly, then very heavily. Carl was out at his window-cleaning job or it might have been his car-washing job in the car park at Brent Cross. One of the other tenants let her in but didn't help her up the stairs with her bags and her suitcase.

Surrounded by her own property and by Carl's property, all similarly encased, Molly sat down, then lay down, on the bed. She started to cry, she couldn't help herself. And like the rain which had begun as a drizzle and become a tempest, her snivelling turned into a full-blown storm of sobs and floods of tears.

*

L ichfield House was empty. The management had paid Richenda quite generously to clean those vacated flats to which they had access. This didn't include Olwen's. Flat 6 might remain untenanted for years. Olwen had died intestate, her parents and both her husbands were dead and she had had no children. Margaret had started proceedings to claim the flat, though she had been told it was a hopeless attempt. Meanwhile Flat 6 was locked up and inaccessible. Richenda could do no cleaning there, and Flat 5 was awaiting the arrival of decorators, though none had yet appeared. She spent a couple of hours at the Constantines, but it was so clean that there was really nothing to do except scour the place for unconsidered trifles. In somewhere so spick and span she expected nothing and was surprised and rather excited to find a condom still in its pack fallen down a crack in the floorboards where the bed had stood.

All that ugly old furniture was gone from Marius's flat. There was nothing to do. Stuart's place required only a quick once-over with the vacuum-cleaner brush and Rose's not even that. Richenda went off to her jobs in Ludlow House, thinking with some satisfaction about her decree nisi which had come through that morning and Wally's trial scheduled for a date in the middle of September.

A ny housewifery skills Molly had she had learned while Stuart's servant. You pushed the vacuum cleaner about and you wiped down surfaces with a bit of cloth. You scattered scouring powder over the basin and the sink and the bath and rubbed at it and rinsed it. You didn't know what to iron so you ironed everything. This was the extent of Molly's expertise but she had performed these actions from love so they had been pleasurable and she had been rapturous when receiving Stuart's rare thanks. She felt very differently about Carl. While she was living with him – and she meant to live with him for as short a time as possible – she wasn't going to sweep and dust but she must do something about the bed. It had begun to smell. No, he hadn't got any other sheets. When the ones that were on the bed got in too bad a state he took them to the launderette, washed and dried them and then put them back on the bed. Because she wasn't paying any rent to Noor while she was here, or any rent at all come to that, she went down to the British Home Stores and bought two sheets and two pillowcases and remade the bed.

'You're a star, you are,' Carl said. 'Do you know that? You'll make a wonderful wife.'

'Oh, I don't know, Carl.'

'I do. We better fix a date to get ourselves married.'

'I'm not twenty yet,' said Molly. 'I can't get married.'

'My nan was sixteen when she got married.'

'Yeah, well, that was olden times.'

She took the dirty sheets to the launderette and learned how to operate the washing machine and the dryer. It was very different from the arrangements at Flat 5 Lichfield House. On the way back she found a charity shop where they had a pair of green-and-black-striped curtains for sale. If they were hung up and the light excluded she might be able to sleep at night instead of lying there looking at the street lamp and the car headlights flickering across the ceiling. And the workmen who came by day and walked about on the scaffolding wouldn't be able to see in and whistle at her.

Carl said that when he'd finished work next day he meant to go down to the registrar's office at Burnt Oak and find out what you had to do to get married.

'I'm not getting married, Carl,' Molly said, hanging curtains. 'I'm not getting married for years and years. Before I even think of marriage I'm going to be an art historian or maybe the curator of Tate Modern.'

'It won't do any harm finding out how it's done, though, will it?'

Someone with a car parked at Brent Cross offered him £20 a time to clean his car every week for the next six months. On the strength of that Carl bought two gold or gold-plated wedding rings.

'I'll want to have one too, so all the girls know I'm not in the running,' he said.

Molly looked through all the papers for people advertising for a third or fourth tenant to share a flat. She phoned all the ones that looked possible but so far they had been more than she could afford. Could she live in a hostel? Would she be able to bear it? In the evenings Carl brought in doner kebab and chips or pizza and they ate it sitting on the floor watching TV. Then they mostly went down the pub.

With nothing much to do all day but fruitless flat-hunting, Molly started sorting through the bags that furnished Carl's room. She found a lot of *Heat* and *Knave* magazines but no essential bathroom requisites. 'If you take a toilet roll down that bathroom,' Carl had said, 'you have to bring it back with you. But you like don't, you forget. Same applies to soap.'

'Then what do you do?'

'Me, I do without.'

That made Molly shudder. She took the soiled T-shirts and torn jeans down to the launderette with the sheets but when they were washed they fell into rags. In another bag she found a couple of empty vodka bottles, a woman's handbag with a broken strap, about a hundred old copies of the *Star* and a framed photograph of an old woman Carl said was his grandmother, the glass cracked diagonally across her face.

'Is she the one that got married at sixteen?'

'That was the other one,' Carl said uncertainly.

Sometimes she saw herself spending the rest of her life groping through dirty rubbish in plastic sacks. In a gloomy half-dark *dump* with the workmen's Radio 2 playing outside the window. Even though she'd be back at college in five or six weeks, she ought to get a job. In her school holidays she'd worked serving in a greengrocer's and another one cleaning offices. Noor said she'd worked as a croupier but Molly didn't believe it, though she was good-looking enough. But why would she when her dad was rolling in money? She wondered if Mr Ali might need an assistant and one morning she took the bus and then another bus to Kenilworth Avenue and his shop. It was more for the outing, for something to do and somewhere to go that she went, for she had no real hope. Mr Ali would want a Muslim girl who wore a headscarf. But he didn't, or he couldn't get one, and he agreed to take her on, three days a week, the 3 p.m. to 8 shift.

He was obliged to pay the minimum wage. Molly thought that with that coming in she might be able to afford a room of her own. A flat, even a studio flat, to herself she had long realised was hopeless. Elated, she told Carl when he came home from Brent Cross.

'I'm not having you do that.'

'*You're* not? What's that supposed to mean?'

'I'm not having my wife work.'

'Carl, I'm not your wife – remember?'

'You will be and I'm not having you work. No wife of mine works, right? I keep her.'

She had never thought of herself as much of a feminist but then she had never heard a man talk like that before, a skinny weasel-faced man in dirty jeans holding a bag of doner kebab slices in one hand and a greasy package of chips in the other. Standing glaring at her in a dirty room cluttered with bags of junk. She started to laugh; it was so ridiculous, she threw back her head and laughed. He said nothing. He threw down the bags of food and punched her on her uplifted jaw. It was a hard punch because, although puny, he was young, and he followed it up with a slap to the other side of her head and then a harder blow to this side.

Molly fell over, shrieking. But she got up again quickly, holding on to her face with both hands. He muttered, 'No woman of mine works.'

She thought she wouldn't be able to speak but she could. The words came thickly. She had bitten her tongue when he hit her. 'That's it. I'm going. I should never have come to this dump, this *shithole*.' Her suitcase stood where she had left it and she turned. It took courage to turn her back on him and she braced herself for renewed blows but none came.

'Don't go,' he said. Tears had come into his eyes.

Now she was facing him again. 'You think I'd stop here after what you've done? I've nowhere to go but I'm going. I can get on a train and go to Torquay, I can ask Duncan to take me in. He would, I bet he would.'

To her horror and disgust he fell on his knees. He was really crying now. 'Don't go. Say you won't go. We're engaged, we're going to get married. I'll never lay a finger on you again, I promise. I never will.'

'Next time you get angry you will.' But she knew that even in arguing with him, she was halfway to giving in. How much would the train fare to Torquay be? A lot. And Duncan – suppose he wasn't in? Everybody went away on holiday this month. He might be away. 'I'll stay for just tonight,' she said. 'You'll have to sleep on the floor.'

'I don't mind. I'll do anything, Molly. Say you won't leave me.'

She wrinkled her nose like someone smelling something bad. It made him wince. 'Let's have a look at your face. I haven't done much, have I?' He got to his feet. 'It won't scar. I haven't done much. I don't know what came over me.'

'That's what they all say.' She didn't know how she knew that was what they all said. She ate the meat and the chips. There was nothing else. He had brought in cigarettes and she smoked a couple, not because she much liked smoking but because they reminded her of Stuart. Carl said he would go out and buy a bottle of wine.

'Not for me,' she said. 'You won't get round me that way.'

But when the cheap red wine appeared and he had poured it out into cracked cups she drank some of it. There were no mirrors in the room. She went to the bathroom, carrying soap and toilet roll, and actually managing to get in there without having to wait outside the door, looked at her bruised face. She would have a black eye and a swollen jaw. But as she stood contemplating her damaged image she thought, well, she had experienced something. She knew a lot more of what life was about than she had that morning. This was *domestic violence* and she had been the victim of it at the age of nineteen. She could talk about it now, not as something she had come across in a book or a newspaper, but at first hand. That didn't mean she was going to stick around for more of it. Come the morning, let him go off and clean some woman's windows, and she'd be out of there.

CHAPTER TWENTY-FIVE

I t was a bit much, Duncan thought, a bit over the top. He hardly knew the girl. And he knew very well what happened when people asked if you could put them up for one night or maybe two. They stayed for ten years. His imagination got to work. She would move in with all her stuff, cases and cases of it no doubt and boxes and bags, and take over the largest of his spare rooms, the nice one on the first floor with the view of the summer house next door and the lane and the magnolia tree in the garden beyond. Her clothes would be left all over the floor and she would of course want to use Eva's hairdryer. The noise of the dryer would roar through the house early every morning. The bathroom she would fill with cosmetics and bath essence and body lotion. She would have baths and leave a sticky rim of bath oil round the tub. She would be always washing her clothes and would commandeer his washing machine and dryer.

Moira next-door-but-one had suggested this last when he told her about Molly's phone call. 'You wait till you get your electric bill, Duncan. That'll be an eye-opener.'

Especially now he wasn't getting that marvellous heat from next door.

Would he have to feed her? Cook? He couldn't quite place

her in his memory. Was she the one whose male companion had broken the glass in the French window or the one whose boyfriend had brought the beer? And how long, oh, how long, would she stay?

She had said she had a job working for Mr Ali. He went down to Mr Ali's shop to stock up with supplies. Bottled water – all the young drank that – crispbread, apples.

'A very nice young lady,' said Mr Ali. 'I'm happy for her she'll be living in a nice house while she works for me.'

'She won't be staying for more than a day or two.'

'She'll be company for you, you'll see. And with Ramadan coming on apace, only a few days away now, I shall be glad of her assistance. In the late afternoons I get quite faint from fasting, you know.'

On the way back he met Richenda. She dismounted from her bicycle to chat to him about the emptiness of Lichfield House. 'It gives you a weird feeling. Kind of creepy, all them vacant rooms.'

He told her about the imminent arrival of Molly. 'That little madam lost me my job with poor Stuart. She was after him but she never got nowhere. You want to watch out, Duncan. She's got her eye on you.'

Duncan made up the bed in the spare room and put clean towels in the bathroom, a bath towel, a hand towel and a face-cloth. It didn't look right so he took them away, folded them again and laid them on the bed the way Eva used to when they had a guest. Since her death no one had come to stay.

Molly hadn't stayed many nights in Carl's room but still she had accumulated more stuff. There had been things she had had to buy because he hadn't got them: the ever-needed soap and toilet paper, tea bags because he only drank beer and wine, apples and bananas so that she didn't get bowel cancer from living on doner kebab.

Her face ached and she could feel a lump on her left cheek which started to throb as she packed her suitcase and bags. She couldn't get it all in. Another carrier would be needed, preferably one of those bags with pictures of fruit and vegetables on them that were supposed to last a lifetime. In her searches through the bags which cluttered the room she hadn't come across any but several remained that she hadn't sorted through.

Carl had gone to Brent Cross. At five to four the builders – they never seemed to build anything – had turned off their radio and knocked off. Apart from the throb of traffic in Walm Lane, it was strangely silent. She ought to go before Carl came back but she needed another bag. She sat on the floor, tugged one of the bags over and began pulling out its contents. Not a hoarder herself, Molly wondered why anyone would want to keep all this stuff, most of it broken. Boxes that had once held mail-order purchases, ripped open, a calculator that didn't work, a broken torch, lots of carriers but all of them the flimsy sort, a much-thumbed copy of a book called *The Story of O*. She left the contents of the bag where they lay and started on the next one. It had been buried under several of the others.

Newspapers on top, mostly the *Sun* but a few copies of the *Daily Mail*. A bag of metal bits that looked like the inside of a computer. Another of DVD cases with no DVDs inside them. A cardboard box full of broken china wrapped up in cling film. A small suitcase. She was actually thinking that this would do, this could be used to contain her extra stuff, when she did a double take and saw what it was. She let out a sound, something halfway between a cry and a gasp.

What she had found was Stuart's blue leather case and if there was any doubt there were his initials – *SF* – on its lid.

*

Molly's first reaction was not anger or sorrow or even wonder. It was terror. Sweat broke out on her upper lip, yet she was shaking. Her hands were shaking so much that they had become almost useless. What you were supposed to do in this situation was take deep breaths. She took deep breaths. She clenched her hands and released them. There was something else in the bag, something wrapped in rags, but she was afraid to unwrap it. Taking it in her now steadying hands, she felt through the cloth the outlines of a large knife.

She knew exactly what all this meant but still she remained sitting there, holding the small blue suitcase in her hands. Without putting it down she struggled awkwardly to her feet. Carl would soon be back. She knew what she must do before he came, call the police, find her mobile and call the police. She could see it on the dusty cluttered mantelpiece. Standing now, taking a tentative step, then another, she reached for it and found it – dead. It had been all right when she'd phoned Duncan but that had been the last of the battery before it needed recharging.

The suitcase was still in her arms when she heard Carl's feet on the stairs. She kicked one bag after another in front of her and took refuge between them and the window. He walked in, said, 'Give me that, bitch.'

Afterwards she thought how amazing it was that strength and energy came to you when you needed them, when it was a matter of life and death. She bent down, grabbed the box of china and hurled it at him. It struck him on the head, making him duck. She flung up the window sash, threw the suitcase out and leapt after it.

He was half out of the window when she pulled the sash down, trapping him, his head and arms held like a man in the stocks.

Down on the pavement she could see Stuart's suitcase, saw

a woman come out of a house, pick it up and look up at her. 'Call the police,' she shouted. 'Call them now.'

A crowd began to gather. A crowd always does. When he saw them Carl retreated back into the room, letting the window fall shut. Molly went slowly down the ladder, crying now, making little moaning sounds. At the bottom, another woman, big, blonde, motherly, stepped forward and took her in her arms.

'You poor dear, you poor lamb, and look at your poor face.'

D uncan had dreaded this happening but when it did and he got used to it he liked it. Molly came for one night, then for two, sleeping in the big spare room with the view and putting her bath essence and body lotion in the bathroom. But there his imagined scenario ended and when she started cooking for him and making real coffee for visitors he said he didn't see why she shouldn't stay on and be his lodger while her course lasted.

Carl Rossini and Walter Scurlock came up in court at much the same time, but Carl's appearance in the magistrates' court on a charge of murder was only a preliminary hearing which would lead eventually to his trial at the Central Criminal Court. Wally, who was charged on several counts in connection with indecent images of children, went to prison for a year and had his name put on the sex offenders' register.

Richenda took no special interest in the trial and its outcome beyond reading about it in the *Daily Mail* where there was a triple-column picture of Wally being led between two policemen past a baying crowd, a bag over his head.

'Hope they tie a string round it and pull it tight,' said Richenda to one of the ladies she cleaned for in Hereford House.

Later that same day she was standing on the opposite pavement chatting to Duncan about the empty flats in Lichfield

House, all those For Sale notices on poles sprouting like *trees* in the front garden, when a taxi drew up outside and a woman got out. The taxi driver followed her, making two journeys to drop large suitcases on the doorstep. She was a large woman. Someone less dignified or with less perfect posture would have been called obese. About forty-five years old, she wore garments which could be taken for a uniform, though they were not, a small black hat that might have had a peak but did not, a black suit with epaulettes and brass buttons, a mid-calf-length skirt and sensible lace-up shoes. The taxi driver was tipped – not generously if his expression was anything to go by – and the woman lifted the cases one by one into the hallway. When the automatic doors had closed behind her, Richenda said, 'That will be Mrs Charteris.'

'And who's she when she's at home?' Duncan asked in his facetious way.

'She's at home now. She's the new caretaker, that bastard's replacement. And she wants to be called Mrs, not whatever her first name is. We'll see how long that lasts.'

'Caretaker, is she?' said Duncan. 'She's got no one to take care of.' And he went indoors to where Molly was making a cassoulet for their dinner from a Nigella Lawson recipe.

But gradually the new occupants came, a married couple, an unmarried couple, two girls sharing, a single woman, a single man and a single mother with a small girl. Duncan watched them from his front windows, imagining lives and dramas for them that bore no relation to reality.